The Root of the Matter

The American Puritans Book One

Lynne Basham Tagawa

for my family

Chapter 1

A Failed Test

"I ask the way to lost Zion; I witness what I believe..."

— Roger Williams, letter to John Winthrop, 1636

I WAS WORRIED about Dr. Howard, but I forced my concerns away and thought instead of the luscious chocolate croissant I'd had for breakfast.

And the precious discovery before me.

Conscious of the CarbonFilm gloves encasing my hands, I slid the yellowed paper onto the Archive's reading stand. The document had been restored and treated to resist further damage, but the protection was only a dozen molecules thick, so I took every precaution.

I inhaled slowly and purposefully, but my pulse thrummed in my ears. Most of our collections were in the Cloud for researchers, but some things weren't. Certainly not new finds. This discovery was huge. At least for me.

Water damage blurred the salutation, but I could make out the recipient—*Williams*. Roger Williams. The beleaguered founder of Rhode Island.

A tingle shot up my spine.

John Winthrop and Roger Williams had corresponded until Winthrop's death, so this wasn't a total surprise. Still, it was an amazing discovery. And just in time. I needed everything I could get my hands on if I was to come up with a truly meaningful thesis on Winthrop. What motivated the governor of the Massachusetts Bay Colony? Even now Dr. Howard was preparing for a research Trip focused on those two men.

I scowled, knowing how he'd approach the issue.

The document reclaimed my attention. The content was similar to another of his letters. Practical advice plus theological questions. Between the lines, I imagined Winthrop pleading—

Did you really have to do this?

There was nothing new here. I would have to keep looking for the bombshell I needed.

My gaze fell upon his signature.

John Winthrop.

Such well-formed letters. Controlled, perfect lines. Beautiful script.

My job was to compile facts here in the Archives, helping Travelers to make sense of their destinations. What I wanted to do was figure out what these people were like as individuals. It was hard to believe Winthrop was a rigid, autocratic zealot as some seemed to think. Everything I'd read—his letters, his diary—spoke of a tender-hearted man.

I'd read a book on handwriting analysis once. What did his handwriting reveal? The careful discipline of the familiar signature was broken by a tiny flourish.

The book would say he was self-possessed. Confident, but not egotistical. And the curlicue?

Winthrop's personality slipping through the control. Did he have a sense of humor?

"Good morning, Dr. Howard." My assistant Lucy's strained voice filtered through the door to her office. "I will let her know—"

The door pushed open, none too gently. Dr. Howard, the senior Traveler, strode into the room, his facial hair trimmed into a goatee. His jerkin and breeches announced his destination as he always wore period clothing close to a Trip. He tossed a Pad at me, and I lunged to catch it lest it damage the ancient paper. "Geneva Fielding!" He spat my name like a curse word, dark eyes blazing. "It's your fault!"

Dr. Howard was preparing to Travel to 1631 Massachusetts. What I wouldn't give to be a bug on his shoulder. John Winthrop, Roger Williams. The conflict, the trial. But traveling through time? No.

"What's wrong?" The Pad revealed Dr. Howard's test score. Not a good one.

He glared at me. "They told me *you* wrote the theology test."

"It was s—" Simple. No, rephrase that. "Theology can be difficult."

His face glowed cherry red above his stocky shoulders. "The drop date can't be changed." He paced a circle. "Peter said so."

"When do you leave?" It was soon, I knew. The rules were strict on preparation to go to another time. Language, customs—including theology, in this case—medical, costume. He'd have run the gamut already.

"Three days."

"Oh." My worst fears were realized. He'd have to pass it by tomorrow. I scrolled through the results of his test on his Pad. He'd missed antinomianism by a mile. And his answers regarding schism and separation were simplistic. Separation was the core of what Roger Williams was all about, the source of the initial conflict. He maintained the churches in New England should completely separate from the Church of England.

Of course, Dr. Howard didn't have to *believe* the theology. Who did? But he couldn't ignore it. And it wasn't just a theological dispute.

There were political implications. Dr. Howard was totally unprepared for his destination.

My shoulders slumped. It was my fault. I should have made sure he took the test two months ago.

"Look," he said. "Theology wasn't everything. The Charter was a business document!"

"The dean needs to know," I said to his back.

The Archives door swung wildly behind him.

There must be a way to salvage this mission. I'd find a way. I needed whatever information Dr. Howard could muster from this Trip for my thesis, even if his prejudices corrupted his observations.

I pulled my hair from its elastic and smoothed it before finagling it into a new bun.

Peter. I'd talk to Peter.

I reached for the pump bottle on my desk and squirted lotion on my hands. But for once, the scent of chocolate and mint failed to comfort me. I left the Archives and crossed to the Launch Room.

No Peter.

I skipped the elevator and made for the stairs, wanting to stir my circulation. I crossed the first-floor atrium and scanned the carrels.

No dark, curly head.

I finally spotted Peter in the cafeteria, filling a CarbonFoam cup with coffee from the dispenser.

More like sludge than coffee, but it was warm, and the Archives were cold, taking up half of the subbasement. The sensitive Travel apparatus filled the other half. Peter, head of the techies, was wearing a thick blue turtleneck, sensible clothing for both summer and winter in our work environment.

I joined him at the dispenser and filled a cup. "Peter, we need to talk."

He lifted his brows and motioned toward a booth. "Is it Dr. Howard?"

I blew on my coffee, still dark after a good dollop of fake cream. "How did you know?"

"Saw him in the hall, looking red in the face. Is it the theology test?"

I slumped in my seat. "Yes. It wasn't a near miss, either. He botched it."

"You know his preconceived notions about New England in general."

Peter's dark eyes were calm in his youthful face. He was a physicist, not a historian. And not a Traveler.

"I didn't realize you knew that much about it."

He gave me a wry smile. "Because I run the techie side of things?"

"Yeah, I'm guilty of false preconceptions about physicists. And yes, I'm aware of his notions. He should stick to the nineteenth century."

"He's not the only one. It's hard for folks today to understand why people left England and settled these cold, rocky shores."

Peter surprised me sometimes. But he was a friend, one of the few in this place. Okay, granted, I was an introvert and loved paper and old relics better than socializing. Peter was just plain easy to be around. I didn't feel exhausted after talking to him.

The dean would need to know about Dr. Howard, and when he did, there'd be a meeting, I was sure. "Join me for an early lunch?"

He nodded, and we joined the line. Burgers—probably lab-grown meat—and chicken. At the end of the row, slabs of meatloaf lay like dominoes in a tray. Peter chose the meatloaf.

I gave him a pointed glance.

"You can put ketchup on it," he said.

Ketchup could also doctor burgers. I slid one onto my tray.

We returned to our seats and the conversation.

"Dr. Howard said the drop date can't be changed."

Peter didn't respond at first, his mouth occupied with meatloaf. He swallowed. "Not exactly true. But the math shows a good window in a limited number of places. There's this one in the winter of 1630 with extraction in the summer of the next year. We've nailed it down well. But the way the math works on this end, it has to be either three days from now or two years from now."

"Two years?" No wonder Dr. Howard was mad. "But Peter, we are traveling a discrete number of years in the past. That doesn't change. So how—"

He raised his hand while he swallowed another bite. "It's a complex calculation involving space as well as time. You see, the solar system travels through the galaxy at a certain rate. Our Earth describes a spiral motion as we travel forward in time. Think of two trains on separate tracks. To jump from one to the other, the tracks need to be close together. And the motion of the two trains needs to align."

I stared at the limp lettuce inside the burger. "In three days, the motion will be similar."

He shrugged. "Kind of. The math works."

I shivered at the thought of trusting math for Traveling. But we'd never lost a Traveler. Not yet. It was dangerous in a multitude of ways, but careful preparation reduced some hazards.

"Peter, I don't want to miss this window."

He set down his fork. "What are you suggesting?"

"Hey, Gen!" Lucy's round face appeared at the entrance, strands of hair escaping from the perfect shell of her blonde bob. "Dean Hutchinson has called a meeting."

I stuffed the last bite of my burger into my mouth. At least I wouldn't face this on an empty stomach.

On the way to the meeting, I passed the dean's office. The brass plate on the closed door proclaimed *Dean of Applied History* in nearly unreadable, fancy script. Nearby, the doors to the conference room were open. I entered to see Houghton Library through the large multi-paned windows. An underground tunnel connected it to the Archives.

I waited for everyone to arrive. It was chilly in the library too, but at least only in winter, when the cold found its way through every crack and windowsill. I tugged at my cardigan, thankful for the leggings beneath my skirt.

Dean Hutchinson plopped down at the head of the polished table, and I found a place next to Peter. The Chairs—a ridiculous title for the heads of various offices—trickled in.

Dressed in an eighteenth-century bodice and skirt, Candy Jeffries from Costumes found a seat near me. Ancient clothing usually looked warm. Maybe that's why she wore it all the time. The doctor from Medical came in and sat next to her, looking put upon. He often dozed during these meetings.

The dean glanced up. In the doorway stood Dr. Howard, still in costume. All he lacked was a cutlass to be a pirate.

"Come in." The dean's voice was curt. "Madeline?"

His secretary scurried to his side, tottering on pink stilettos. I wriggled my toes inside my comfortable slip-ons, in pain just watching her move.

Madeline produced what seemed like reams of paper from a satchel and placed them on the table before her boss. Rather old-fashioned, but the dean insisted on hard copies of everything, one of the few things I liked about him.

"Mr. Rice, have a seat." The dean waved the prop master inside.

Wearing a heavy blacksmith's apron over his jeans and tee, Scott Rice was the craftsman who headed up the section of Candy's department that dealt with tools and other supplies. He was not a Chair, but he often attended these meetings as he had to have a heads-up on Traveling news. He chose a seat and his long legs vanished under the mahogany tabletop.

The dean shoveled copies down the table. "We have a decision to make. Dr. Howard will not be ready for the Trip. Our first concern is safety, but we have an obligation to donors and researchers. The Department of Applied History is not an entity with its own goals."

That sounded ominous.

He scanned the group, his beady brown eyes lingering on Dr. Howard, then sliding to me.

I avoided his gaze and reached for my copy of whatever it was—minutes of their last meeting? The current proposals? Each Trip was scheduled as a result of someone's research. Competing proposals were examined and the most promising selected. The whole preparation for the Trip in question had been months in the making. No wonder Dr. Howard was slumping in his seat.

John Winthrop's Commercial Motives in Moving the Charter to New England—the title of the grant revealed what kind of details Dr. Howard would have been looking for. It was right up his ideological alley. But why were we seeing this now? We'd already approved this. Well, my consent was under protest. As was my vote for the second grant, which I found on the second page.

Roger Williams's Suffering: The Danger of Organized Religion. I sighed. Religion was ubiquitous in those days. Folks who should have known better judged these people by modern sensibilities. Almost everyone I knew in colonial history took Williams's part in the conflict —and demonized Winthrop.

These were the two proposals Dr. Howard was supposed to Travel to investigate. I snuck a glance at the dean. He wasn't going to cancel the Trip.

"A lot of money hinges on this. And next year's budget. Some whisper this department doesn't pull its weight. We're more or less secret, after all."

My stomach sank. He'd never spoken like this. I loved what I did, Dr. Howard notwithstanding. Defunding the department would throw me out of a job.

I looked at Candy. She was provisionally qualified to Travel.

Several of us had gone through training. And Candy would gather data without layering on a gloss of prejudice. Dr. Howard wouldn't like it, but she could go.

Candy even looked the part, her glossy chestnut hair partially covered by a mobcap.

The dean was talking. "... can't wait two years. How many of you have been provisionally certified?"

I made myself small in my seat.

Candy lifted her hand. Reluctantly, I raised mine, and to my surprise, Peter followed suit.

But Scott was shaking his head no, his black ponytail swinging. He'd failed the medical screening, I remembered now. Certain conditions, such as those requiring medication, were problematic for Travel. For some reason, Scott's seizure disorder could not be corrected by nanosurgical techniques or viral gene splicing.

The dean had fixed his eye on me. "Miss Fielding, you have the historical expertise. But I cannot send you alone."

What? I glanced at Candy, who merely shrugged.

"Dr. Donatelli, can you pass a theology test?" the dean asked.

"Give me a day to prepare."

I turned to Peter in astonishment. Even if he did pass, how could we be ready in just seventy-two hours?

And that wasn't all.

I swallowed and took a slow, deep breath. I couldn't have a panic attack now.

Chapter 2

Tollers

"We must bear one another's burthens. We must not look only on our own things, but also on the things of our brethren."

— John Winthrop, *A Modell of Christian Charity*

I SLUMPED in the vintage plastic chair and glared at Tollers. Tollers wasn't its real name, of course. Tutor for Language Acquisition and Mastery (TLAM) was the official designation of the vaguely android AI.

Someone had adorned the fuselage of the robot with a shaggy wig and a diamond-pattern vest. A briarwood pipe was taped to its "hand."

I smirked at the comical attempt to fashion the clunky droid into the likeness of J.R.R. Tolkien, the famous linguistics professor and writer.

"Repeat," droned the robot. "At a court holden in Boston."

Word for word from Winthrop's journal. Supposedly this was an AI. But that did not guarantee creativity, apparently.

"At a court holden—" *Aht a court hohden.*

"Holden," I repeated reluctantly.

"HOHden."

I squelched a huff. Vowels were important. Without a good accent, I would be screaming *foreigner* every time I opened my mouth. And foreigners were dangerous. The French were pressing in from the north.

Not croissant-eating French. Evil Papist French. *I've got to think like them.*

"Miss Fielding."

Huh?

"Pay attention." The robot's eye ports flashed an ominous red that I associated with the evil computer Hal in 2001: *A Space Odyssey.*

"What?"

"Repeat. That whereas Mr. Williams had refused to join."

I mimicked the singsong dialect obediently. "... had refused to join."

"Repeat. To join."

"To JO-een."

"This concludes part one," intoned Tollers. Someone had programmed the robot with a formal RP accent with a hint of the Midlands, much like Tolkien's own. "Thirty minutes of passive immersion will conclude today's session."

The plastic chair pinched the back of my legs. A few feet away brooded an ancient armchair losing its stuffing like a molting chicken. I changed my seat and laid my head back. I'd stayed up late in the Archives, refreshing the details of the time period. Not theology, but personal details, cultural details—did these people use forks?

Tollers began his program, and whiny vowels surrounded me. I closed my eyes.

"What cheer?... Fare thee well..." *Wot cheer? Fah thee well.*

The armchair cushioned my limbs. My neck muscles relaxed.

How many hosses came ovah?

Not too hard. Just drop the r's and whine the vowels.

My mind drifted.

Pahk your cah in Hahvahd yahd.

No, that can't be right. There are no cars—

I opened my eyes to silence. A blurred figure resolved into a man. It was Peter.

I croaked out his name, and a line appeared between his brows.

"Time for Medical."

I sat up straight and tried to blink the stickiness out of my eyes. "Was I sleeping? For how long?"

Tollers sat resigned and inert against the wall, eye ports no longer red.

"I don't know. We have an appointment." Peter's dark gaze was patient as always, but there was an urgency in the set of his mouth.

"Okay, I'm coming."

I followed Peter down the hall, having been to Medical only once, in the beginning, when they'd screened everyone. My license to Travel was only provisional, the paperwork filled out as a mere precaution.

"We never know," the dean had mumbled then.

No kidding.

"Peter!" A familiar female voice called from behind us.

No one called Peter "Dr. Donatelli" or even just "Donatelli." Except for the dean, who was uber-particular about degrees.

We turned.

Candy waved to us outside a doorway, wearing a gown from the Revolutionary War time period. Was it silk? Damask? It flattered her figure, unlike the lace-up bodice and skirt ensemble she often wore.

"Come in, I need to get you fixed up."

"What about Medical?" I asked Peter.

He blinked. "Well—"

Candy gestured to an open door. Costumes, presumably. "It won't take long."

The room was like Wonderland. I'd seen Candy many times in the cafeteria and even had lunch with her once or twice, but I'd never dreamed of the plethora of *stuff* that was packed in her domain. Millinery, belts, cloaks, corsets—*corsets?*—and a large object I finally identified as a plow cluttered the walls. Like an old-fashioned thrift store's assortment, clothing of every type dangled from racks in a seemingly unorganized fashion. Shirts, skirts, bodices, and gowns made of linen, leather, and wool of every color and description.

The musty aroma of old clothes and the oily smell of worn leather filled the room. I bumped into a dresser with stockings poking out of a drawer. I sucked in my gut to squeeze past. There was no extra space.

"This way." Candy waved a hand high so we could see her. She marched to the back of the room, where a British officer's red coat hung on the wall. I followed, becoming baffled only once, tangling with a leather hunting jacket, size XL.

Peter seemed nonplused by the jumble. "We're going to Massachusetts circa 1630," he said once we'd joined her.

"About that." Candy pushed a bodice stuffed with pins off a support, which turned out to be a computer. "This is where we log you in. The important work. We choose your clothing based on your Traveling personas." Her fingers sped over a keyboard. Rather old-fashioned, but I approved. Better than talking to the thing.

Talking to a computer gave it power somehow.

While she typed, I examined the area. The red of the officer's coat seemed to flash a warning.

"Here you are... Peter Donatelli and Geneva Fielding." She looked at me closely for the first time and followed my gaze.

"See that uniform coat? The perfect weight wool, dyed in cochineal. Top-notch reproduction. Donated from an estate sale. The britches that went with it were polyester." She rolled her eyes. "Polyester!"

I lifted my brows to encourage her. Candy came alive in here.

"I thanked the donor profusely. We are almost totally dependent on donations, there is no way I would even mention it. Polyester goes to the recycle bin, but I didn't say so."

Peter cleared his throat. "So—"

Candy's eyes fell to the screen. "First insertion December 1630 on the docks in Bristol, England."

"Peter! Bristol? Not Boston?" I inhaled sharply. Then I forced myself to take a slow calming breath. I couldn't panic now.

He shrugged, but his face lit with interest.

Candy glanced at me. "You'll join Roger Williams on board the *Lyon,* the ship that brought him to Boston."

Massachusetts in 1631 was a place where everyone knew everyone. I could imagine the question: *What ship did you take over?* Joining the colony from England made better sense. And meeting Williams on board the ship would help us get to know the man before the conflict started.

I wanted to ask Peter about his knowledge of Williams, but it would have to wait.

Candy squinted at the readout. "You'll return, give your reports, and check in again for the second insertion. Fall of 1635."

I'd forgotten that Dr. Howard's Trip had three parts, a long one focusing on the clash between the leaders in 1631, a second to observe Roger Williams's trial in the fall of 1635, and a brief insertion in 1636 to gather data on his exile, if possible.

I simply couldn't handle it three times. Maybe Candy could go for the brief insertions—or even Dr. Howard. The trial was an afterthought, really.

"You're going as a married couple, of course. We'll outfit you as homesteaders, and you'll get Dr. Howard's goods and tools." Candy frowned. "We'll need more salted beef and cheese to take aboard the *Lyon.* And simples. I'll ask Scott about herbs."

Two months on the North Atlantic. The walls began to close in.

"Your names are Peter and Jane Tuttle. That's *Mr.* Peter Tuttle, the mister meant something back then. You'll be Puritans of moderate substance, much like the others coming over. Former landowners, sold their property to finance their relocation." Candy stabbed a button on the keyboard and a chatter started up somewhere. She pushed her way past a rack of shirts and pulled out several small pieces of paper from a vibrating machine.

She shoved them in our hands. They were stiff like shuttle boarding passes. "Your identities. Memorize all the data, place of birth, everything. Now follow me."

We clutched our new lives and followed in her wake to claim our new clothing.

I woke the next day to the sudden realization that we'd never made it to Medical. I bathed, pulled my styling blowbrush out of its charger, and started yanking it through my hair.

"Slow down," chimed the brush. I had fine, thick hair, and the brush could do wonders with it if I obeyed its commands.

But today the voice irritated me. I ran a few more heated strokes—slowly—through my hair, then slapped the implement back into its cradle.

"Not complete," it whined.

I grabbed an elastic and maneuvered my still-damp hair into a ponytail. Then I stopped and stared at my reflection in the mirror.

Sleepy gray eyes stared back at me. Wisps of light brown hair framed my face, the rest tamed and invisible. It was okay for work.

How would I fix my hair in the seventeenth century? Pins? Braids? My brain skimmed the archives of my mind. Winthrop's papers and journal. Anne Bradstreet's poetry.

I ran peach lip gloss over my lips. Up until now, such issues were dry, academic. The possible subject for an essay.

Not anymore.

Candy had given me a linen cap, so that answered one question. It would cover up a bad hair day, at least partially.

I left for the Archives, counting down the time we had left to prepare. One more full day—today—then tomorrow morning I'd dress for the Trip.

One more appointment with Tollers. The robot had to sign off on my accent, apparently. And Peter had to pass the theology test.

How much theology did he know?

I drew a total blank. He hadn't had much time to prepare. What would happen if he failed it too?

I stepped into the Archives and paused, breathing in the comforting scent of old paper and history. My assistant was bent over her desk, a pencil stuck behind her ear, hair once again perfect.

"Hello, Lucy. Any meltdowns while I've been occupied?"

She swiveled toward me and blinked. "Dr. Howard asked for Stonewall Jackson's journal."

For his next Trip, undoubtedly. "Check loans. We may have something from Duke. If not, we'll have to request it."

Leave it to Dr. Howard to ask for stuff we didn't have. Probably in retaliation.

Lucy ran her fingers over the computer interface in her hand. "Loans. Zilch. Nada. Not on Jackson, at any rate."

"I'll be in Medical. Or with Tollers. Not sure—"

She waved a broad hand. "Go. Never mind Dr. Howard. He always wants things yesterday. It'll do him good to wait."

"Don't forget, everything important is filed in the Cloud some—"

"I know, get going now." She turned.

Lucy was capable, but I'd be gone for months—no wait, it wouldn't be that long. Travelers always popped in again much sooner than I expected. I'd have to ask Peter about that. Something about math and trains, I was sure.

Dreading Tollers, I stepped into the elevator and wandered the second-floor halls looking for Medical.

At the end of one corridor, a fat red cross signaled the location. The door was open, and Dr. Howard was sitting in a plastic chair with his sleeve rolled up. Prepping for the Civil War if his request was any indication. And doing it early, like he should.

He squinted at me. A nurse—I presumed—thrust a needle in his arm. Blood rushed into a clear tube.

I glanced away. "Hello, Dr. Howard."

He scowled. "A bit late for medical prep, don't you think? You're leaving tomorrow."

"I'll be right with you, miss," the nurse said. "Sir, just one shot for today. Then come back in a week."

I retreated, but not before hearing the word "cholera." Dr. Howard was being vaccinated for cholera.

New England. I hadn't had time to think about it. What diseases were endemic to New England in 1631?

Smallpox. Scurvy. Random fevers. Had they ever decided on the germ that killed Squanto's village? Add that to the list.

"Miss?"

Dr. Howard sidled past me, and I faced the woman. She was pleasant featured and dressed in layers, a smock over blue scrubs.

"Name?"

"Geneva Fielding."

Her face cleared. "I've seen you in the cafeteria. I didn't know you were a Traveler."

There was no way to explain. Not in this cubicle.

She indicated the chair and I sat. The small space was filled with refrigerators, boxes, and racks of tubes. Strange symbols, warnings, and lists of instructions littered the flat surfaces. An eyewash station perched over a sink.

"I'm going to New England," I said stupidly. I was *in* New England.

The nurse grabbed her pad and moved her fingers over it. "I see the order. Fielding... 1631 New England... tomorrow." Her forehead wrinkled. "No time to establish any immunity."

"What does that mean?"

"Normally we have time to vaccinate you for the worst things. Smallpox, for example." She frowned at the Pad. "You're authorized for immunoglobulins against smallpox." She looked at me. "Do you know the exact risk?"

Her expression alarmed me. "Before 1633, the outbreaks were worst in Native American villages. At least, we think it was smallpox. Sometimes measles can hit susceptible populations hard."

She turned and reached into one of the refrigerators. "You'll need to quarantine either way when you come back. Antibiotics first. It's a special formula developed to protect indigenous populations from our germs. I can give it orally or—"

"Oral." I gulped the liquid and fought the urge to gag.

In another minute she was filling an old-fashioned hypodermic needle with solution. "Sorry," she said. "I have to give this intramuscularly. Into your butt."

I stood, turned, and tried to find a discreet way of uncovering my rear. Protection from smallpox was worth the pain.

"It'll pinch. Just stand very still."

"Ouch!"

A shadow fell. Peter was standing in the doorway.

"Bad?" he asked.

Frowning, I tidied my clothing and rubbed my rear. It didn't just "pinch."

"I see. I came for mine. And for the implant."

Oh, yes. The implant that would signal our return. There was so much to think about.

The theology test. "Did you take the test? Did you pass?" No sense in getting stabbed if he failed it.

The nurse tapped her screen.

He didn't bother sitting down. "Took it this morning. Passed."

The nurse gave him the oral antibiotics. He tossed back the solution and grimaced.

I breathed a thankful prayer. I wouldn't be going alone.

We kept a day of thanksgiving... Winthrop's journal entry popped into my mind. But how had Peter done it? Theology was not common knowledge.

"You passed?"

The nurse got busy, and I looked away while she gave him the shot.

"Did I tell you my maternal grandmother's ancestors lived in Salem?" Peter asked.

That might explain his interest in Applied History. But not much else.

"Ouch!"

I awaited the appearance of the implants. Any pain was secondary. Dr. Howard said they were itchy sometimes. Couldn't be that bad.

What I feared was the journey.

Chapter 3

The Launch Room

"Nevertheless, to keep a good conscience, and walk in such a way as God has prescribed in his word, is a thing which I must prefer before you all, and above life itself."

— William Bradford

THE NEXT DAY, I woke, showered, and dressed. It took a long time to figure out the seventeenth-century garb. First, I pulled the loose linen chemise over my head. The stockings rolled up over my knees and were secured by garters. Roomy pockets were next, tied on with string. The brownish maroon skirt and bodice were sewn together into a dress, but I managed to wriggle into it and laced up the bodice. I took a few exploratory twists and bends but discovered that the stiffened bodice was not uncomfortable.

A garment called the partlet went over the bodice and hid the lacings, but it was frustrating. I was supposed to pin it on, but the procedure reminded me of a wedding where I had to thrust a huge pin through the stem of a young man's boutonniere. I poked him several times and nearly destroyed the poor flower. Finally, the partlet was secure.

I sped through the rest. I combed my hair, arranged it into a loose bun, and secured it with seventeenth-century pins, which looked clumsy but actually worked. Then I tugged on the cap and tied on an apron that wasn't quite white, more like an ecru color, probably an early cotton blend. At last, I was on my way to the cluster of brick buildings that ruled Cambridge, curious whether the stout leather shoes would pinch my feet.

My stomach sent up a complaint as I strode along the sidewalk. I hadn't had time for breakfast. I comforted myself by thinking of the *pain au chocolat* stuffed inside my bag. Last night, I'd stopped at the bakery near my apartment for comfort food. It styled itself a French café and almost succeeded. Some of their offerings were quite good. I'd purchased several items, saving this glorious chocolate croissant for today.

A solar trolley glided past me. The ubiquitous vehicles were small and narrow, perfect for students getting to campus. But I refused to rest my feet.

I wanted a little extra time to think. The costume made me feel strange as if another entity had possessed my body. Tollers had approved my speaking and comprehension, and of course, I knew theology. I also knew now that the only fork in Massachusetts was owned by John Winthrop, who kept it in a special case. I wouldn't ask for a fork.

But I was sure I'd commit an important faux pas somewhere. I knew Winthrop's journal practically by heart, but I knew less about Roger Williams and even less about their day-to-day life.

I had a general grasp of what they ate, and I thought of my bag again. We wouldn't suffer as the colonists did in the winter of 1631, slowly running out of food and hoping for relief from the sea—relief the *Lyon*, the ship we were to board, would bring.

But there would certainly be no *pain au chocolat*.

Red brick buildings loomed in the near distance, and I slowed my pace. I needed to think about my fake identity. I was a "gentlewoman," neither nobility nor working class. My fictional father was a merchant in textiles, the family trade reflected in the finely woven wool of my clothing that swaddled me against the cool September morning. I would have known some luxuries.

Like chocolate.

But we were fugitives, fleeing the oppression of men like William Laud, Bishop of London, later archbishop of Canterbury. And I did not know much about Laud. Not enough.

And what about Peter? He'd passed the tests, like me, but was he ready?

The shoes were starting to pinch by the time I arrived.

"G'morning, Lucy." I weaved my way between the stacks and tables inside the Archives. "I'll be gone for months. Can you cope?"

Lucy popped out her head from her office. "Hey, Gen. I thought they could bring you back sooner." Her gaze traveled over me. "You look like Candy all dressed like that."

I was already overheating, even without the heavy cloak I'd get in the Launch Room. "It's okay. At least I don't have to wear a nineteenth-century corset."

"Do you know your return date?" Lucy asked.

My brain began to turn somersaults. I knew when we'd return local time—late June of 1631—but not how long it would take here. Dr. Howard typically showed up after two weeks when his Trip was supposedly three months long. I'm sure Peter would explain it in terms of trains, but my brain was too full to take in physics.

"Maybe three weeks, possibly four."

Lucy gave me a firm hug. "I'd give you snacks, but—"

"I know." We were limited in what we could bring. It all had to be appropriate for the time period.

"What time do you leave?"

"This afternoon. Three."

"Make sure you eat a good lunch. And don't worry about Dr. Howard."

"Thanks, Lucy. Let Madeleine know if you have problems. Disregard the pink heels."

Lucy winked. "Oh, I know. She rules that office. Go on, now."

I pulled out my croissant and went to look for Peter. I found him in the Launch Room, head bent over the console, consulting with Chamar, a tech. Peter was wearing a thick red jerkin, the seventeenth-century version of a waistcoat. A modest white collar encircled his neck, and he wore neither wig nor hat. Thick curly hair on a man was the *ne plus ultra* in those days. He was lucky.

As I observed the men, I sank my teeth into the pastry. I ignored my gleaming surroundings, imagining myself at a sidewalk table in Paris. The taste of melted chocolate splashed into my mouth and suffused my brain. It calmed me.

I barely noticed the tech walk past me and out the door.

"Gen?" Peter's voice jolted me back to the Launch Room—and Peter.

He was dashing in that outfit. He approached and I noticed his forehead was shiny with sweat, even in here. I shoved the rest of the croissant into my mouth. I refused to chew quickly. This croissant had to last me for months.

I raised a hand until I swallowed. "We need to talk."

He nodded. "In Quarantine."

We passed the launchpad, strewn with boxes and casks. Sometimes Candy or Scott asked me for input on the clothing or household goods of various periods. Sometimes I could find documentation in the Archives, and sometimes Lucy discovered it in Houghton Library. I wondered what was inside the crates we'd be bringing. Tools and foodstuffs, most likely.

Peter opened a door and we went inside. I'd never been to this area, the place where Travelers spend a certain amount of time—between three and seven days—in quarantine after their return. Smallpox had a long incubation period. You could get it and not even know it for days. Weeks, even, but blood tests could rule it out sooner. Otherwise, the isolation period would be a month.

Quarantine turned out to be a little apartment, fitted with a neat kitchenette and decent bathroom. The bedrooms were intimidating. Hospital equipment and limp hazmat suits hung on the walls.

I envisioned a sick Traveler being treated by a doctor entering a separate room and stepping into the CarbonFlex suit. Like being treated by an astronaut. Shivers went up my spine.

This would be my fate if I got smallpox.

Peter sat on the bed. "I had some questions."

"Yes, normally I brief Travelers—they don't just get a test."

None of my briefings had sunk into Dr. Howard's brain, obviously.

"I read bios of both Winthrop and Williams. *Short* bios."

I sat. "Okay, that's a start. They knew each other in England. Williams was in on some of those early conversations about the plan to go to New England. The formation of the Company."

"I didn't realize that."

Peter was so pleasant to be around. At least that aspect of this Trip would be positive.

"Winthrop describes Roger Williams as a 'godly minister' in his journal when the *Lyon* arrives with him on board. He had personal knowledge of the man."

A line appeared between Peter's brows. "Did Winthrop know of Williams's desire to separate from the Church of England?"

"Doubtful. We think Roger Williams was wrestling with these things over a period of time. There might not have been a difference of opinion before."

"We might discover something important. You might get a thesis topic."

I smiled grimly. Yes, my heart's desire. I just wished it didn't involve the dual horrors of time travel and crossing the North Atlantic in winter.

~

I didn't get another chance to talk to Peter before one o'clock, the time we had to come back to the Launch Room. My undigested lunch sat like a rock in my gut as I stared at the flotsam covering the launchpad.

More casks. And two chests, almost buried in blankets.

Candy entered the room.

I pointed. "We take all of this?"

"No worries, honey. We had to add to Dr, Howard's supplies since now two are going."

I poked a crate with a toe. "What's this?" I needed to know everything. I was about to land in a strange place and a strange time with strange stuff.

Peter appeared and wandered over. He seemed calm, although the line between his brows was new.

Candy circled the pad like a bustling hen. "Over there, next to your feet, are your carpentry tools and other dry goods you'll need. This cask of cheese goes to the quartermaster, for the cook's use during the voyage. This smaller cask is some cheese for you when you make landfall, as are these others—pork, flour, and cider."

I kneeled in front of one of the sea chests and set the blankets aside.

"Go ahead and open it," Candy said. "The chests contain your personal belongings, including extra food for the journey."

I managed the latch—it wasn't locked—and looked inside. A linen chemise, a petticoat, stockings, and gloves lay atop a gown. Several candles, dried meat, and apples were tucked along the sides.

"By washing your shift frequently, you can stay reasonably clean. Hence the extra chemise."

I filed that away. "The gown?" It looked nice.

"That's your Sabbath gown. Inside Peter's chest, there's a bag of lemons."

I remembered Winthrop's mention of the juice of lemons being effective for scurvy. Historically appropriate. "Thank you."

"Squeeze some juice in your ale onboard ship."

Motion near the door caught my eye. Scott entered with a small cask on his shoulder, looking like a frontiersman in his plaid shirt. I couldn't tell if he was dressing in costume, as Candy often did, or if the shirt was just comfortable. Probably the latter. I'd never seen him in Native garb.

Easily handling the weight, he placed the cask on top of the rough-hewn lid of a firkin of salt pork. "Cinnamon," he explained laconically.

"For trade." Candy's concerned gaze was on me. "We are limited in what we can acquire. But cinnamon is no problem, and highly valued back then."

I knew all this. I did. I knew each settler brought with them most of what they needed for the first year. They weren't cast naked upon the shore.

Scott reached into a satchel, drew out a small book, and handed it to Peter. "A journal." He slid his hand back into the bag and withdrew a large feather. "If you use this, it will create a vanishing trace that will be recorded permanently."

Peter studied the pen and so did I. It looked like a quill, the nib white like a feather's end. Secret communication. Or rather, a record we could return with.

If we returned.

I took a deep breath and let it out slowly.

I caught Peter's eyes on me.

"Tell me more about where we are going." I directed my request to the room in general. Peter would have programmed in our exact destination, but Candy had to know the particulars too.

"Bristol," Peter said. "The docks. We will get there very early in the morning of the day the *Lyon* is scheduled to depart."

"What if the captain won't take us?"

Candy fumbled in her pockets and drew out a leather bag. She placed it in Peter's hands. "Your fare. All in gold. Ten guineas for the captain. The large cask of cheese for the quartermaster. He'll take you. If he doesn't, you can signal with your implants."

The trip to Medical had resulted in craftily concealed implants in our wrists. They were sensitive to pressure, and three compressions signaled a return. There was no way to test them, but none of the previous Travelers had encountered a problem.

I darted a glance at the chronometer on the wall. There were several sections. Cambridge time, destination time, and Trip time. Cambridge time was 14:32. Trip time was all zeroes. But another section showed a countdown.

57:32... 57:31... 57:30.

Candy surveyed me, then turned her gaze to Peter. "Take a bathroom break, get a drink, then I'll return with your outerwear."

She left, and he looked at me. "The math works."

"I'll be fine."

"Come."

I followed him into the Quarantine apartment behind the launchpad, and we entered the kitchenette. He opened a cabinet and retrieved a dark object.

Chocolate.

The dark chunk covered his palm. Possibly food service variety, probably not Parisian grade, but more than a pound, certainly.

He shrugged and smiled. "Wrapped in seventeenth-century materials, it's perfectly legit."

I nibbled on a corner of the offering. "It's passable." Better than I expected.

"Keep it in your pocket. It won't melt where we're going."

Thankfully, my pockets were big.

The chronometer ticked steadily down from 12:54, and my palms were damp. Candy hadn't returned. Peter and I stepped on the launchpad, and the head tech stood at the control console. He frowned once, poked the screen, then stood back, apparently satisfied.

Candy burst into the room and dropped a pile of clothing at our feet. "Gen, here." She thrust a bag into my hands. "Simples. Herbs. And a contemporary source of instructions."

I knew what she meant. A reproduction of something they had back then. Rose water for this. Chamomile for that. Purging was popular. I hoped I wouldn't fall into the hands of a physician. I felt the bag and something crinkled. Paper—the instructions.

Chocolate was probably better than chamomile in any case. I knew how to deal with anxiety. It wouldn't be a problem. I didn't have a medical condition. I would be fine.

Candy lifted a cape and slung it around my shoulders. It was made of beautiful, soft leather, but too short for winter. And it was surprisingly heavy.

She fingered the hem. "Shillings. Don't lose this cape, it has several pounds sewn in the hem. For emergencies."

Then she distributed the rest. Both Peter and I received heavy outer cloaks. She left and closed the clear CarbonShield door behind her.

We were alone on the launchpad, the chronometer on the wall ticking down. 3:45… 3:44… 3:43.

The tech, Chamar, bent over the console on the other side of the CarbonShield barrier. The wool made me sweat, and my stomach curled into a ball. To distract myself, I reviewed everything I needed to know. My name. Jane Tuttle. The ship. The *Lyon*, Captain Peirce at the helm. The Bristol docks. Cinnamon for trade. Cheese for the quartermaster.

Don't ask for a fork.

0:12... 0:11... 0:10...

Chocolate.

Peter grabbed my hand.

Then all the lights went out.

Chapter 4

The Bristol Docks

"Truly it was as bitter as death to me, when Bishop Laud pursued me out of this land, and my conscience was persuaded against the national church, ceremonies, and bishops..."

— Roger Williams

GASPING, I squeezed Peter's hand. Did we lose power?

Cold brushed my cheek. It was a damp cold, not unusual for New England, but there were no windows in the Launch Room.

Then I smelled the sea. Salty, mucky, even oily. Familiar. When the wind blew from the east, I could smell this from my apartment window. The briny estuary odor of the Mystic River.

A strange creaking sound startled me. I couldn't see, and I gulped for air. Peter's warm presence slipped around me, and he laid his hands gently on my upper arms.

It was night. We'd come before dawn. That's why I was blind.

"We're here," he murmured, his tone half calm, half nervous, half —excited?

My heart beat a nervous tattoo, and I took a slow, deep breath. The Bristol docks. I'd seen the location on a map of the western part of Britain. I forced myself to focus, to think. Bristol was a major port. Easy to get lost in the shuffle here.

But I also knew some Puritans fled more discreetly. Going to out-of-the-way docks or beaches. Some were even disguised. Because at some point, the king's policies had shifted. From inconsistent harassment to hauling-folks-before-the-Star-Chamber persecution.

William Laud had something to do with this, but I hadn't studied him. My ignorance closed in on me like the cold, damp air around me.

My eyes adjusted, and the black seemed less absolute. "Where are we—precisely?"

Peter's grip loosened. "I tried to dial us onto the docks themselves. I knew we could not travel any distance with all these supplies."

I didn't know how long it would be until daylight. But I could just make out the eerie fingers of masts in the middle distance. The moon slid into view from behind a cloud, large and full and about to set. The tops of the ripples in the harbor gleamed silver, and water gently lapped at the pilings underneath the invisible planking of the docks.

"Halloo!"

I jumped. Peter's bellow startled me.

"Halloo, harbormaster! Hail, sentry for the *Lyon!*"

A scuffing of shoes on wood came from my left. I smelled old sweat and onions before I detected a vague shape.

"And who might ye be?" The voice was a surprising tenor.

"Passengers for the *Lyon,*" Peter replied. "We've supplies and a gift for the captain."

The tenor snorted. "The *Lyon* finished boarding yesterday. Just waiting for the tide."

The accent wasn't quite like the dialect I'd learned from Tollers. But I could understand the man.

"High tide isn't till noon," Peter said.

I was surprised—but then, he was a physicist. Probably part astronomer, too.

"Who are ye, landsman, to tell me my business?"

I huddled inside my cloak, listening to the give and take, absorbing the speech of the man.

"A man with gold and cinnamon."

Silence for a beat. "Why have you not said? I will find the *Lyon's* watchman."

Two metallic clangs sounded from the nearest boat. Half a minute later more ringing sounded from somewhere else.

Ship's bells. Another thing I hadn't studied. But would Jane Tuttle know anything about ship's bells, navigation, or the price of a fare?

Unlikely. She'd trust her husband for the fare and not need to know more.

I took a deep breath and settled myself to wait. Was I imagining it, or was the blackness becoming less thick? The ships began to appear in a gray mist of light.

My panic subsided. I was going to be okay.

A shape approached. "Hail, I'm the quartermaster of the *Lyon.* We are carrying provisions, not passengers."

That wasn't true. The historical record counted at least twenty passengers, including Roger Williams and his wife.

"I've a cask of fine cheese for the cook's use," Peter responded.

I could sense the man's reluctance melting when Peter offered him the cinnamon as a personal gift.

"Captain Peirce will make the determination," he said, but I knew by his tone that we'd passed muster.

Peter slipped his hand under my elbow, more appropriate than holding hands and almost as comforting. But his grip was a little tighter than it needed to be.

I realized then that he wasn't fearless, just brave.

The ship was both bigger and smaller than I imagined. A huge mast, the top lit by the rising sun like a candle, climbed several stories from the middle of an area no bigger than my apartment. Another mast rose beyond it near something called the forecastle.

A wood structure loomed behind the mainmast as well. An opening in the middle led to cabins, presumably.

The *Lyon* smelled of wood and tar and unwashed men. Everything seemed tidy, everything put away properly.

Shipshape.

The sailors were wiry rather than muscular and paid little heed to us as they went about their duties. Then a tall man approached, well dressed in leather and wool. He introduced himself as Captain Peirce.

Peter paid him, counting out the gold. Behind us, several men brought our supplies on board. They seemed to know what to do with just a few words from the quartermaster. On the other side of the mainmast, a grate in the deck was removed, and the largest of our supplies was lowered by ropes.

Captain Peirce tugged at his neat beard. "We're full up with supplies for the Company. Ye might find space to make bunks on the gun deck."

Peter nodded.

The captain signaled to a half-grown boy. "Way, would you assist these passengers?"

"Captain," a new voice broke in behind us. "They can lodge with us."

I turned to see who was speaking. A young man was bundled against the chill. It was light enough to make out blue eyes and a face that was almost handsome. Certainly friendly.

"Most kind of you, Mr. Williams."

Williams?

My stomach bunched up. I suspected Peter's did too, for he took a moment to react.

"I thank you, Mister—"

"Williams. Roger Williams."

"Mis—Mister Peter Tuttle, and my wife, Jane."

The seamen had placed our chests at our feet. Way and another man picked them up and helped us aft. There were several compartments on each side. I followed Roger Williams and Peter into one not much bigger than a broom closet.

There was a woman inside.

"Mr. Tuttle, Mistress Tuttle, this is my wife, Mary."

Mary Williams. No one knew anything about her.

Fresh-faced, she looked like an undergraduate in the Yard, but instead of a backpack, she clutched the handle of a valise.

"Hello." I pulled out the chocolate from my pocket and broke off a few pieces. "Might I offer you a sweetmeat?"

The *Lyon* got underway before noon. Sailors' shouts accompanied a bustle of activity as the captain gave orders. Once things settled, Peter accompanied Williams to the rail where they could observe the ship's progress with a few of the other passengers.

I sat next to Mary on a bunk. Across the cabin, about five feet away, was another bunk, a small wooden platform that held little semblance to a bed. It was more like a large shelf. Over our heads, a small window with tiny triangular panes let in light.

I was grateful. In Plymouth Harbor, in my day, the reproduction of the Mayflower had no windows except for the ones in the stern for the captain's cabin. I had no idea as to the tonnage or exact size of this ship; the *Arbella,* Winthrop's flagship, was about twice the size of the Mayflower. So the *Lyon* might be larger, too, but it did not look spacious at all.

The ship rolled slightly and my stomach lurched. The comfort from a small piece of chocolate was gone. Mary had eaten her piece very slowly.

"What is this?" Mary had asked.

"Chocolate. It's Spanish, from their plantations. A bean, ground and sweetened."

"Spanish, you say?"

I scrambled for an explanation. The Spaniards were the reason this ship would take the horrific northerly route instead of a southerly one that might take us within reach of their ships—and their guns. "It was a gift. My father is a textile merchant and sometimes buys from the privateers." I was making it up as I went.

"Ah, heroes like Sir Francis Drake."

He was long dead, but letters of marque—legal piracy—was still a thing. "Indeed."

Peter ducked his head in. "We're midchannel."

I followed him out and walked to the rail. The docks had receded, and I could see greenish shores to either side. The air was brackish.

A cold breeze blew in our faces, and the shadow of the masts over the water pointed out our way. Over our heads, sails hung limp instead of billowing out.

Peter noticed my gaze. "The wind is against us. The receding tide will propel us out of the estuary and into the Atlantic."

"That won't take us far." The mass of rigging seemed an impossible tangle. Memory pressed me. "Tacking. I remember something about that."

Peter sketched a summary of what sounded like a sorry method of propulsion. Navigation was another thing. Mariners of this day steered by the angle of the sun and the stars, and the direction of a lodestone in the ship's compass. Hand-drawn charts, maps, and the captain's seat-of-his-pants sense of the sea would get us to New England.

Braced by the cold, fresh air, I returned to the cabin. I was struck by a cheerful thought—I knew from the historical record that this ship would make it to Massachusetts.

Then I remembered something else. There had been a storm. And someone had been washed overboard, I couldn't remember who.

Chapter 5

The Lyon

O Lord my God in all distresse
My hope is all on thee:
Then let no shame my soule oppresse,
Nor one take hold on mee.

— *The Whole Book of Psalms,*
1621

I WAS SICK. I pawed through my bag of simples, desperate.

Comfrey... hyssop...

There. Ginger!

The packet labeled *ginger* opened to reveal an unfamiliar bulbous root. My granny had told me ginger was good for nausea, but I'd never seen ginger in this form.

I smiled despite it all. This was the real McCoy, not some fake concoction, its raw materials spindled and mutilated beyond recognition.

I showed it to Mary Williams. There was no privacy in this tight compartment, and though we'd all turned green once the *Lyon* left the sheltered waters of the Bristol Channel and entered the open ocean, I was the only one who hadn't gotten her "sea legs" quickly.

"Will ye make an infusion?" she asked.

I had no idea what an infusion was. "Can we make a tea?"

Mary produced a pocketknife. It looked like a museum piece, a small but stout knife I knew they used for eating—and everything else. I had something similar from Scott's workshop nestled in my pocket.

"How much?" she asked.

I indicated an inch, having no idea. She cut off the piece and headed for the forecastle, where the cook ruled, as I soon determined after departure.

The fo'c's'le was how the crew pronounced it.

I lay back on the bunk and closed my eyes. The nausea rose in my throat, and I fought it by thinking about linguistics. Forecastle. Lighten up on the "r" as I had done with Tollers.

Foh-castle. But then the next consonant is a hard "c." Therefore—

In my imagination, Tollers's eyes were an ominous red. Did I have a fever?

Mary was back. "Cook has the ginger, says he knows just what to do. Way will bring it when 'tis done."

Way, short for Wayland, was Captain Peirce's scrappy son. He couldn't be much older than twelve but already possessed an adolescent's rangy height, his twiglike limbs amazingly strong. He carried buckets hither and yon all over the ship, brought food to the passengers in the stern, and occasionally I spotted him, like a monkey, in the rigging.

I sat up. Mary grasped my hand.

"Come outside. It helps."

This I doubted, but I followed. Soon I was at the rail, staring at the waves, the cold wind in my face. The waves weren't that bad. But the sight of the horizon flummoxed me. It was so far away, and this ship was so small. My knuckles whitened.

I took a deep breath and let it go slowly. I *knew* the ship would make it safely there.

And as far as the horizon was concerned, I'd seen it before, from 80,000 feet. Not that I enjoyed the experience. Unlike most people, on a shuttle flight I closed my window and worked on a Pad until the ordeal was over.

But shuttle flights were short. You could go anywhere on the planet in four hours or less, the slow descent half the trip.

I tried to imagine the shuttle. A safe way to travel.

It didn't help.

The vision of the curvature of the earth, misty blue over the variegated continents, fused with the lighter shade of sea and sky before me.

My gut heaved, and I threw up. Thankfully, there was next to nothing in my stomach because much of what I expelled flew right back in my face, driven by the wind.

Shame covered my face under the drips. At least I'd not succumbed to a panic attack. Perhaps I was too sick.

I regained the cabin without conscious thought of my steps. I knelt on the floor and wiped my face clean using water from a bucket.

"Gen?" Peter asked softly.

"Jane," I corrected. My pretend name was Jane, we had to remember that. "I'm okay. Mrs. Williams gave the cook some ginger to make me tea with. Hopefully that will help."

I did my best to tidy myself. I was rarely sick, but I knew that you always felt better if you were clean and dressed and neat.

Peter left the cabin. He'd been spending time with Roger Williams, and I felt only a little jealous. It was more appropriate for a man to get to know the "man with windmills in his head," as Cotton Mather disapprovingly wrote.

Or would disapprovingly write.

I clutched my stomach.

"Ma'am." Way's face appeared in the cabin doorway. "I've your tea." Seeing me, his face looked troubled. "Cook made it special."

He ladled out soup into a wooden bowl. Apparently "tea" could be beef consommé. The smell of pumpkins and hayfields rose in the steam. *Ginger.*

I used the bowl as a cup and sipped slowly. It was heavenly.

Surely things would be better now.

The next day I did feel better. And good thing, because not long after a standard ship's breakfast of salt pork and fresh bread—I assumed the hardtack came later—we were all summoned to gather outside on deck.

What day of the week was it? I had a suspicion.

And if my suspicion was correct, I might get the chance to meet the Perkins family who lodged opposite us in the cabins. Several complete families were traveling with us, as well as a handful of single men. Most lodged on the gun deck below us. Peter had met almost everyone, but my seasickness had kept me isolated.

I put the linen cap on my head and wrapped a scarf around my ears and neck. Then I shrugged on my cloak. Peter was waiting for me at the door. The Williamses had already left.

"It's the Lord's Day," Peter said, confirming what I had guessed. Or as many called it, the Sabbath.

I wasn't wearing my Sabbath gown, but I suspected it didn't matter.

The Perkinses emerged in various states, smiling or grumpy. One child began to whine. The father, a silent man wearing headgear I could only think of as a Pilgrim hat, picked up the noisy child and laid him over his shoulder.

The child ceased his fussing.

The rest of the children filed out of the two cabins they were using. The two oldest were about Mary Williams's age, a young man and a young woman. But as I scrutinized the ages of the others, I wondered. Had Mrs. Perkins lost some?

I knew the historical documents. Many New England women bore eight or more children. But I counted only six. The apparent ages of the children were kind of random—the ones who had survived the diseases of the seventeenth century.

Mrs. Perkins herself seemed healthy, but the crow's feet about her eyes spoke of both age and toil. I was sure the little guy on her husband's shoulder had been a surprise.

Captain Peirce was speaking. "We are blessed to have a godly minister in our midst. Mr. Williams will lead us in our worship this Sabbath."

I looked for Williams in the crowd. Before I knew what was happening, the entire ship was singing.

"All people that on earth do dwell..."

The sound swelled and grew.

"Sing to the Lord with cheerful voice..."

I spotted Way's face, joyfully singing. All except the very youngest formed an a cappella choir, spontaneous and surprisingly in tune.

Peter was mesmerized. I wished I knew the words by heart. I'd never given much attention to the Psalter, the metered paraphrase of the Psalms the Puritans used for worship.

The final *Amen* resonated like the grand final chord of an organ. I stood marveling until I heard a voice—Roger Williams's voice.

"Reading from the prophet Isaiah..." He read something about a vine and a hedge.

I maneuvered until I was standing next to Peter and I could also see Roger Williams's face. He was holding open a large Bible which I had seen in the cabin. He finished the reading and flipped several pages.

"Psalm 107 speaks of the merciful providence of God governing all things for His good pleasure. It speaks of men in various states, those in open rebellion, or those simply going about their lawful business."

His voice was melodious. I wouldn't call him a great speaker by modern standards, but his face was earnest, and he had everyone's attention.

"'When they wandered in the desert and wilderness out of the way and found no city to dwell in...'"

He spoke of God leading them to a city, a place of habitation. It certainly applied to these people.

"'We read of those that go down to the sea in ships, and occupy by the great waters...'"

Peter's gaze was fixed on Williams, his lips slightly parted. Glancing at the crowd, I wondered if Peter stood out in his fake costume, which was probably sewn together in modern CarbonFiber thread. He might smell better, but that would not last much longer. We were going to really blend in soon.

Williams's voice snatched my attention back. He was speaking of a ship in a storm.

"'They are tossed to and fro, and stagger like a drunken man, and all their cunning is gone. Then they cry unto the Lord in their trouble, and he bringeth them out of their distress.'"

Reality came crashing down. We were on the ocean. Far from the help of any man. We would only lose one, but the rest of these men and women didn't know that.

"'Let them confess before the Lord his lovingkindness, and his wonderful works before the sons of men.' The meaning is clear to all mariners and travelers, but let us consider the lovingkindness of the Lord.

"This Hebrew word translated lovingkindness has a great depth of meaning. It goes far beyond our puny idea of kindness. The translators attached the term 'loving' because the great love of God is here. And not our puny love, not the poor affection we bestow on our children."

Peter's eyes were suspiciously shiny.

"God's lovingkindness is a covenant-keeping love, a steadfast, unbreakable bond. 'He hath sworn by himself' we read in Hebrews, as God can swear by none greater. 'Behold what love the Father hath given to us.' A steadfast love. A forever love. Let us honor God in thanksgiving."

Roger Williams prayed briefly, then his gaze swept over the crowd. "Is there any man here who wishes to prophesy?"

I was startled, but a passage in Winthrop's journal mentioned "prophesying." From the context, I guessed it wasn't any sort of prediction of the future.

"Mr. Perkins."

The man's son still slept on his shoulder. He gave the little boy to his wife before he began to speak. "The Lord has blessed me with a wife, children, and goods. And persecutions also." His face twisted a little at this. "But my greatest joy is that discovery years ago, of the kingdom of heaven. Like the man who discovered a treasure in a field, I have sold all to gain what I cannot lose."

His wife smiled and nodded slightly.

"Captain Peirce." Roger Williams stepped aside. The captain prayed.

As soon as the prayer ended, I snatched a glance at Peter. He was staring into space. He stirred himself and gave me a little smile.

As the passengers began to mill about, the way people did when dismissed, I aimed for Mrs. Perkins, wishing to finally meet my neighbor. The youngest child had a fistful of her apron.

"Hello, my name is Jane... Tuttle."

She shaded her eyes against the sun. "I am glad to see you walking about."

I tried to match her accent. "Still queasy. But much better."

"Is your husband also a minister?"

"Oh, no. But he has... studied." I swallowed.

She nodded sagely. "That explains much. I have seen him

speaking with Mr. Williams." Her glance took in her child, who was rubbing his eyes. "I must see him to bed. Fare thee well."

Her *fare thee well* was informal, almost slurred. *Fare th' well.*

Farewell. Maybe I could do a paper on linguistics if all else failed.

~

That night was a challenge. Peter and I shared a bunk—a very narrow bunk—and while previously I was too sick to care, now I felt hesitant. We were fully clothed, but still.

Roger and Mary Williams murmured to each other five feet away on their bunk. The compartment was pitch dark as the use of fire and lanterns was restricted on board. As a result, after supper Mr. Williams read the scriptures, prayed, and we went promptly to bed.

Each morning we woke before dawn, aching from the hard bed.

Peter lay with his back against the wall, and I lay parallel against him. Lying on our sides was the only way we fit comfortably. It was awkward but warm—nice because the ship had no central heating. Sometimes one of us rose to use the piss pot. When Peter did, he'd just lie down on the floor for the rest of the night. We could stretch out that way.

I tried to tell myself it was just like camping out.

Nah, not really.

Tonight, I wanted to talk. I shifted onto my back, and my right arm flopped off the ledge. At least the bunk was low. Falling out would not hurt me.

"So, what have you learned?" I kept my voice low.

At first, I thought Peter had fallen asleep. Or maybe my voice was too quiet for him to hear.

Then he spoke. "I'm still processing it all. I'm not sure what I expected."

I waited. Roger Williams was regarded by some Puritans—and

some historians—as a troublemaker. Even those who liked him thought him unstable.

I tried to remember William Bradford's exact words, quoted in the footnotes of my edition of Winthrop's journal. Bradford liked him, but said he was "unsettled in judgment."

"Mr. Williams had to leave his former situation," Peter whispered into my hair. "Chaplain to some family. A disagreement, a matter of conscience for him. In the telling of it, he wept. It was hard for him."

I must have read this somewhere and forgotten. But it fit. Roger Williams's whole life was unsettled—not finishing his master's at Cambridge. Then some kind of unsuccessful courtship followed by marriage to Mary on the rebound.

The murmuring across the way had stopped. Mary seemed happy. She adored her husband, you could see it on her face. But she didn't have his intense personality. She was calm, steady, a good match for him.

"You like him, " I whispered.

"Yes. Yes, I do." He shifted a little. "Shall I sleep on the floor?"

"Okay." I heaved a private sigh of relief. I liked Peter, I liked Peter a lot.

But sleeping together was just too weird.

Chapter 6

Roger Williams

"Having bought truth dear, we must not sell it cheap, not the least grain of it for the whole world."

— Roger Williams, *The Bloudy Tenent*, 1644

A WEEK LATER, I woke in the middle of the night. The temperature, already low, had dropped drastically. The little cabin was freezing despite the warmth of four bodies and a lot of wool.

I began to shiver. Peter was on the floor, breathing noisily.

"Peter?" My voice was a croak. "Peter?"

"Hmm?"

"It's freezing." There was no sound from the other bunk, only the background vibrations, creaks, and swish of a large wooden boat plowing through the ocean.

Peter's hand connected with my shoulder and found its way to my head. "You're not cold—you're burning up."

He clambered onto the bunk and shared his cloak, covering us both with it. I snuggled up to his warm back, clutching the fabric of his thick jerkin.

My mind drifted. My body ached everywhere. I wished I were anywhere but here, on this ship.

It was a long night, full of half-remembered dreams.

The first thing I saw in the gray light of morning was Peter's dark curly head. He was on his knees, digging in my sea chest. I rubbed my sticky eyes. My joints ached and my mouth tasted foul.

"Where are your simples?"

Mary answered him. "Here they be. In her bag."

Peter resumed the search, and Mary looked me over.

"Mr. Tuttle," she said, "Have you anything for ague?"

A muscle worked in Peter's cheek.

"Fever," I clarified. Why was I sick? The nurse in Medical had given us some sort of concoction.

No, that was to prevent *us* from infecting *them*.

I let them handle it. I just wanted to sleep.

Some indeterminate time later, Peter touched my shoulder.

"Here. Sit up." He held some kind of cup. I had visions of my mother giving me soup as a child. I sipped from the cup and almost spat it out.

This wasn't chicken soup.

"Gentian and wormwood," Peter explained.

Wormwood. Gross.

"Thank you."

I don't know if the wormwood had anything to do with it, but my fever broke the next day. I felt suddenly too warm instead of cold and shrugged off the extra blanket that had appeared at some point. I lay on the bunk and stared at the small window, thankful. I was weak but very much alive.

The late afternoon light was fading, but it would linger. Twilight was long in these latitudes.

Peter was sitting next to Roger on the Williamses' bunk, talking, while Mary dozed, sitting with her head against the bulkhead. I remembered her kind face and gentle hands as she lay cool cloths on my head. She must be tired.

I closed my eyes and listened to the conversation.

"Mr. Tuttle, why did you flee the north country?"

"I wish to worship God. And hear biblical preaching. I heard none where I lived."

I heard Roger Williams sigh. "Why is this so impossible? Such a plain thing? That a man might worship according to his conscience, and not according to the king's dictates?"

Peter was silent. It was as if they'd covered some of this ground before.

"Be careful what you say outside this cabin," Williams warned. "Who knows what our papist queen whispers in Charles's ear at night. Not that he needs much excuse to harry God's people."

"Have Englishmen no liberties?"

Was Peter being rhetorical? I still did not know what he knew of English history.

"The king believes he has all rights—obviously. Now he rules without Parliament, with the Star Chamber as his sword of mercy. We have no rights in his mind. And what are rights, but the God-given right to obey Him?"

It was 1630. The only document of English rights was the Magna Carta, restraining the power of King John and guaranteeing the authority of the nobility. From my reading, I knew the rights given to ordinary freemen were easily trampled.

The king's Privy Council—the Star Chamber—tried cases this entire decade as they saw fit. And the king was at this moment beginning to regret he'd ever given Winthrop and the Company a legal charter. At the time, it had been a way to get rid of Puritan troublemakers.

"Have you met Mr. Winthrop?" Peter asked.

"Oh, yes. He is a good and godly man. And cunning, too, for he took the Charter across the sea, effectively moving the government of the Company to Massachusetts."

"You fear the king may renege on the Charter?"

"I will not speculate. I only know that Bishop Laud summoned me, and I had to flee. Christ said to go from village to village, preaching the kingdom of heaven. I will serve where He sends."

"I thank you for your wife's labors."

"My Mary is a jewel among women, never complaining. Your wife seems to be resting quietly now."

"I believe the crisis has passed. I could only pray."

Pray? Surely Peter had not been praying for real.

I drifted, then woke to hear them still speaking.

"What are your plans once we land?" Peter asked.

For a while Williams was silent. "What do you believe regarding the Church of England? Is she a true church, or Babylon?"

A beat. "I believe the Lord knows who are His."

"A wise answer. But would you join a false church?"

"No, of course not."

"Nor would I."

There it was. Roger Williams's decision.

It was a fantastic historical discovery, but instead of gladness I only felt dread.

Dread for the conflict to come.

The next morning, I rolled off the bunk eager to splash water on my face and wash out my mouth. I dried my face with linen toweling and reached for a cup, not caring that the bucket was our communal wash water. I'd often drunk it, even though it was a tad off-tasting.

I grabbed a cup and dipped it in.

"Gen!" Peter's voice. We were alone in the cabin. "Don't drink the water. Have you been drinking it all along?"

I poured out the water and dried the cup. "Yes. Here and there. Not much."

"That's what made you sick, I suspect."

"Don't drink the water when traveling?"

"Amoebic dysentery..."

Well, I hadn't had that. Only fever.

Peter continued his litany of water-borne illnesses. "It might have been a touch of salmonella or typhoid."

"Okay, okay, you convinced me. Only ale. I promise."

A line persisted between Peter's brows. "Tea from a kettle is fine."

I nodded and waved him away. "Yes, yes. I know. Is it time for a lemon?"

We'd started adding lemon juice to our ale a week ago. Peter worked it out to one every three days. We were sharing with the Williamses and the Perkins family across the way.

When I'd offered it to Mrs. Perkins, she'd lifted a brow.

"John Winthrop values lemon juice for the scurvy."

With that, she was agreeable.

As we prepped the lemon, I fought to maintain my balance. The ship's motions were different. I left the cabin to share some of the doctored ale with the Perkins family. Then I made my way to the rail.

The day was fresh and bright, the wind gusty and confused, as if it could not make up its mind about direction. On the ship's left side—to port—large swells approached, not terribly high but far apart and regular.

I thought of a bathtub, with an object dropped in, waves moving out from the disturbance.

There was a disturbance to the south.

Peter joined me at the rail. He turned and looked at the captain, who scanned the sea from his roundhouse perch, one hand on the whipstaff. If this was anything like the Mayflower's reproduction I'd clambered over, the whipstaff connected to the rudder far below. The captain lifted a small telescope to his eye.

I was probably imagining the concern on his face.

No, I wasn't.

There had been a storm on this trip. I pushed the thought aside, pushed away the anxiety that threatened. I'd survived germs in the water. I'd get through this.

"Peter," I said instead. "I heard you talking to Roger Williams." I wasn't sure how to put this. "You sounded so natural when you answered him."

Peter's gaze was on the horizon. A swell pushed us up and then down again, a bit like a rollercoaster ride. I was going to get seasick again.

"I just said what came to mind. I haven't had enough time to prepare."

Way dashed past us and scrambled up the mainmast. Another sailor was perched in the foremast rigging, busy with the ropes.

"Maybe that's a good thing in a way."

He cut a glance my way. "I stay silent most of the time. I learn a lot by listening."

"But you engage him. The things you say... they don't sound like you're pretending."

He was silent for a moment. "I have read the scriptures. I know what the Bible says."

I digested this. I'd read the Bible too, the version authorized by King James. Most Puritans still used the Geneva, the version translated on the continent during the time of heavy persecution in the 1500s and now outlawed because of the Reformers' commentary in it. But the actual text was very similar to the authorized version.

Peter sounded comfortable with the ideas in the Bible. I knew the theology. I could pass a test on the symbolism of Babylon, for example. The prostitute, the fake church.

I couldn't put my finger on what Peter had that I didn't. I only knew that there was an undercurrent, a meeting of the minds, in the conversation I couldn't enter into.

Peter was an enigma.

I woke in the night feeling seasick. Before we all retired, we'd tidied the cabin and tied down anything that could move. Peter had exchanged a few words with Roger, and the men got busy. The sea chests were moved next to the bunks so that sudden movements of the ship would not throw us to the deck.

By sunset, the sky was gloomy, thick with gray clouds. It was only a question of how bad it would be. A polite squall, or a heavy storm.

I stared uneasily into the darkness, wondering what time it was. The rolling waves deepened and tossed the ship. It would have been bearable had they stayed predictable, but as the winds picked up, the waves grew confused. Lying on the bunk next to Peter, I clutched a small wooden bowl. I was determined not to vomit but wanted to be ready, just in case.

I tried to shut my mind to the knowledge that we would lose someone but failed. Not the captain, I knew that. Not the Williamses. But who?

Thunder cracked in the distance, and the waves beat against the ship. It would have been a comfortable sound had I been inside, safe, with a cup of hot chocolate. But in the middle of it, the power of wind and waves made it seem preposterous that men like Captain Peirce would take this awful chance against the powers of the ocean. The thousands of passengers who had crossed to Massachusetts in a single decade were braver than I knew.

The thunder grew closer, and the motions of the ship more erratic. The timbers of the ship creaked, a low, ominous thumping that set my heart racing.

In the cabin, the darkness was profound. I tried to imagine myself outside on the deck, balancing on the balls of my feet, instead of locked in this small space, breathing in the woolly smell of Peter's jerkin.

Then I heard a whistling. In between the splash and groan of the ship, an eerie high-pitched sound mingled with the wind.

Then a creak like a sound from a horror vid.

I never watched horror vids.

I took a deep breath and focused on the smell of the wool.

Then I heard something else. Words.

"We are your servants..." Roger Williams's baritone floated in and out of the other sounds.

I fought to hear him above the cacophony.

"Bring us into our haven. Into Thy haven."

Then we fell, and for a moment, I was weightless. The ship hit the bottom of the trough, and I threw up.

I do not know how long the ship tossed and plunged like a carnival ride. My mind became fuzzy, my whole attention focused on occasional shouts from outside—the sailors—and Roger Williams's prayers.

He did not sound desperate. But he didn't know the end of the story; he didn't know he would survive.

And yet, he did not sound panicked. Urgent, perhaps, but never panicked.

"Hear us, O Thou Most High, Creator of heavens and earth, and of the seas. Have mercy on each life aboard..."

His words calmed me. No, I was not calm, but I did not panic.

The ship leaped and bucked, but after a time, it seemed that the gyrations grew less. The wind still howled, but there were breaks in the sound.

Voices sounded on deck. The captain's. Then the sailors. Some of the voices came from below, where I suspected the men fought to keep the rudder steady.

Slowly, the *Lyon* was coming alive, the normal sounds restored. Gray light filtered in through the small window above. It was morning.

It was morning, and we had not lost anyone. Could the records be wrong?

The stuffy cabin was a little smelly. Peter rose and cracked open the door. Cold, fresh air swirled in. I heard Captain Peirce bark a command.

Peter turned to us. "They're hoisting the mainsails."

I joined him and peered outside, desperate to see the sky. Sailors walked carefully about—the deck was covered in ice. And the ship still yawed and plunged at unpredictable moments.

But at least the storm had ceased, and the wind, while gusty, was not turbulent.

Peter stank of vomit. There were marks on the back of his red jerkin. I looked for the vomit bowl—upended halfway across the room.

Did Mary have soap? Lye soap might neutralize the acid—

A shriek sounded from the bow. Then shouts.

"Man overboard!"

Chapter 7

Lost at Sea

"Give sorrow words; the grief that does not speak knits up the o-er wrought heart and bids it break."

— William Shakespeare

"COME ABOUT!" The captain barked several more orders, followed by the first mate's gruff voice. I didn't understand a word, but it must have involved the rigging, for the sailors jumped to the ratlines. Others ran to the rail.

The *Lyon* heaved suddenly in the rough sea, and one of the crew on the deck slipped and slid to the bulwarks opposite. The quartermaster vanished into the forecastle and returned with a large sack. He dribbled sand all over the deck.

My stomach coiled. Who had fallen overboard?

"Furl the topsails! Right full rudder!"

Slowly, the ship tilted and turned into the wind. A man with an apron tied about his waist—the cook, presumably—scurried to the rail and peered out. A sailor heaved an object over the side, and another man belayed the rope attached to it.

"Have they no lifeboat?" I whispered to Peter.

He shook his head, his frame stiff in the doorway. "The pinnace is packed below... by the time they fetch it..."

I ducked under Peter's arm and stepped outside to see better. Mr. Perkins hovered at the doorway opposite like I did. Some were praying audibly.

Peter murmured behind me. Was he praying too?

The mood was electric, yet the crew said little. It was as if every thought, every sinew strained after the one who had fallen.

"Who is it?" I asked Peter.

He glanced back at Roger Williams, whose expression struck me with dismay.

The young minister knew.

The captain exploded from the roundhouse ladder and brushed past us to the main deck, his face gray. He continued shouting commands.

Wet streaks marked the quartermaster's face as he joined the others at the rail.

The North Atlantic heaved, each rolling crest adorned in ugly gray lace. If the deck was frozen the water would be frigid. I cut a glance at Peter, but aside from his moving lips, his expression was still, as if in shock. He would surely know how long a man could survive in such a temperature.

"I see him!" someone shouted, and there was a rush to the side.

No... let it not be...

The captain's son? I had not seen Way amidst the scramble.

Mary Williams gave a small whimper.

The pale faces of the other passengers peeked out from the hatch leading to the gun deck. Murmurs rose, a swell of prayers. No one was leading them. Once or twice, I discerned words, but otherwise, they were quiet, like the whisper of an urgent request in the ear of a friend.

"Peter, how long has it been?" How long could a person survive in the ocean?

The waters of the North Atlantic had to be as ice-cold as the surface of the deck.

We spent an hour circling that spot, gusts of wind keening in the halyards. Then Captain Peirce gave the orders to hoist sails. As he moved toward the stern, the passengers slowly converged on him as if drawn by cords. Their murmured prayers—and cries—rose.

A woman wailed. Another sobbed, joined by a man's lower tones, tight with distress.

Hats in hand, the quartermaster and other members of the crew stepped closer, and soon the captain was in the middle of a weeping throng.

I could not see the captain's face, but Roger Williams's dark head and steady shoulders joined the mourners. The passengers made way for him—even seemed to propel him—to the captain's side.

"O God, why hast thou turned thy face against us?" I almost didn't recognize the young minister's voice, tight as it was with anguish.

Keening and sobbing swelled, drowning him out. Then the crying subsided and a desperate quiet fell.

I wiped my eyes. Beside me, Peter drew his sleeve across his face.

"The Lord hath given, and the Lord hath taken away," croaked the captain.

Blessed be the name of the Lord was the rest of the verse, the rest of Job's response to the loss of his children, but I did not blame the captain that those words would stick in his throat.

Roger Williams began to speak. But his words were nothing like I had ever heard at a funeral or given to comfort mourners. He expressed a deep sorrow, even a complaint.

His words slid into a holy acquiescence, then a soft command to his listeners. "Weep with those who weep…"

Mr. Perkins blew his nose loudly.

Peter drew me back inside the cabin. One by one, the other passengers did the same, and the crew dispersed as well.

But the ship itself seemed to be in mourning as she cleaved the cold, restless sea.

Three days later, Roger Williams led us in a somber Sunday service. He preached from the book of Job. The singing was brave, the voices quavering.

Afterward, my bunk was attractive. I lay there and stared out the window. I ate my meals mechanically, thinking. Death was real, even in my time.

But Way was so *young*. I clenched my jaw.

I glanced at my satchel, where I had stashed the last chunk of chocolate. But chocolate had no power over this.

Roger Williams did not mope. Instead, he spent hours sitting on the opposite bunk with Peter.

"Recite any passage, and I will take it down," he said to Peter.

"'The quality of mercy is not strained…'"

I recognized Portia's famous speech from *The Merchant of Venice*. Good. Shakespeare's plays had already been written. Peter was being mindful of the date.

"A beautiful passage. Who is the author?"

"William Shakespeare."

"You attend plays?" A disapproving tone.

"Nay, but I have read several."

Roger Williams repeated the passage, reading from his notes.

Peter examined the writing. "Shorthand."

"I suppose one could call it that. Let me teach you."

The days were gray and gloomy, often overcast, the seas forbidding. But at least the lessons distracted me a little.

After several days of instruction, Peter was coming along. But I was cold. I fantasized about a hot shower. Or an old-fashioned bubble bath. Steam rising in my nostrils. A long soak.

A Jacuzzi.

And clean clothes. I was glad in a way for the temperature, for it must be cutting down the stench. Peter's waistcoat was clean—Mary's soap had been effective—but he was becoming disgustingly ripe, and I'm sure I smelled the same.

One morning, Mary Williams approached me. We were alone in the cabin, the men out on deck, talking as they often did.

"I have spoken to Cook about some hot water," she began. "So we might wash."

"Wash clothes?"

"Certainly, but first"—she grinned—"ourselves."

I found myself smiling for the first time in what seemed like forever.

She barricaded the cabin and hung a piece of fabric for even more privacy. Then she drew a crock of soap and a lumpy object from her sea chest. The lumpy object was something I'd only seen in photos in the library.

A sponge. Not a piece of artificial CarbonSponge—nanotechnology was hundreds of years in the future—but real sponge, the skeleton of a living sponge from the bottom of the ocean.

Mary must have noticed my confusion, for she handed it to me.

"My... my husband will want to see this. He is a student of natural philosophy."

"They are not used where you live?"

England seemed a small place in my day, but for these folks, twenty miles was a significant distance. Mary Williams had probably never been to Manchester, where I was supposedly from.

"No. At least, not in my household."

Even with the addition of steaming water to the wash bucket, the water was cold, and the bathing—a true "sponge" bath, I smirked to myself—was done in haste.

Then we repeated the preparations for Mr. Williams and Peter, and we strolled the deck, eventually finding a spot on the rail.

My mood had lifted with the bath. But Mary had something on her mind.

"You... you have no children?" she asked.

I guessed what she was thinking about. "Not yet..." I stopped, feeling embarrassed.

"You have not been married long?"

"No."

"I think... I think..." Her face glowed.

"A child?"

"There has been no quickening. But my courses have not come."

I knew the Williamses would have children, I just did not know how many. What would a Puritan say? "'Tis the blessing of God."

She smiled.

It was a simple, ordinary conversation. But other conversations would not be. Other actions would not be. We really couldn't change history, could we?

The official dogma of the Applied History Department was that it was impossible.

But I was part of history now. The official dogma did not comfort me.

I hoped it was impossible. But I would ask Peter.

I got my chance the next day. For the first time in weeks, the sun was out, and we went to the rail. I lifted my face to the tepid rays. Could we change history?

I opened my mouth, but Peter spoke first.

"I need to ask you something. About Williams. About what happens next."

I studied the waves, large swells from the southwest with smaller waves dashing against them. A complex dance I doubted even mathematics could solve. "He will reject a call to preach."

"They offer him a position? I seem to remember that."

Yes, Peter had skimmed the surface of the biographies of these men. "A minister will return to England this spring. They will need a replacement."

Peter's gaze was on the waves, but I knew his mind was elsewhere. "That's a serious charge he's about to make."

"You know what he will say?"

"I can guess. Something about Babylon, that the Church of England is a false church, and to be part of it is to partake in its adulteries."

The sun made the cold bearable, at least for a while. I still had that question, but Peter beat me to it again.

"I also need to know more about John Winthrop. The governor."

Where to start?

"I remember something about a city on a hill," he said.

"Yes, the sermon he gave in 1630. Winthrop was not a minister, but this sermon is famous in our time, which is interesting because it wasn't in his own."

Peter lifted a brow.

"It was almost totally forgotten. Only one guy copied it into his journal, it's all we have extant. And it wasn't political."

Both brows rose.

"The title is, 'A Modell of Christian Charity.'" As I spoke the words, I saw the double *L*. "It's about how Christians should love one another. How they should behave in this situation."

"The situation of escaping to a new land?"

"Yes."

"How much do you remember?"

My gaze was still on the waves, random traces of contrary ripples sketched on the deeper swells. "He starts with basic stuff. That everyone is different. Some are rich, some poor. These differences are not a problem. Instead, they are an opportunity to bless others. He's saying that we are all in this together, both rich and poor, and we need to share and love one another in practical ways."

"Like the book of Acts."

I paused, trying to retrieve what knowledge I had of the scriptures. Again, Peter surprised me. He always seemed to know a little more than me, and it was my *job* to know. "Hmm. Yes. Let me think. He was saying that God purposed some men to have more, and some to have less, so that all must help one another, and be knit together in 'bonds of brotherly affection.'"

Peter's gaze was intense.

I continued. "'Love is the bond of perfection,' he said. He compared it to the ligaments of the body. He quotes from both the Old and New Testaments, admonishing his hearers against breaking the covenant with God, and to 'keep the unity of the spirit in the bond of peace.' The 'city on a hill' reference is a kind of afterthought. I think he means that in the context of the impurities of the Church of England, their community and churches ought to be a good example. Really, it's just a flourish, not the emphasis."

Peter was quiet a moment. "Christian love. That's what the title is referring to. Yes, I see it now."

"It was ordinary to their ears. So most forgot it."

I was caught up in the implications of that for a moment. Peter stirred as if to go, but I stopped him.

"Peter, I know what the dean would say... but Peter, can we change history?"

Chapter 8

Land at Last

"If there be any endued with grace and furnished with means to feed themselves and theirs for 18 months, and to build and plant, let them come over into our Macedonia and help us..."

— Thomas Dudley to the Countess of Lincoln, 1631

I WAS COLD, but I needed to hear what Peter had to say.

"Change history?" A line appeared between his brows. "By our being here?"

"We do things, speak things." I thought of my conversation with Mary. "We affect these people."

Behind us, the crew scrambled amidships and began the process of turning the mainmast yards. The zigzag pattern of our travel as we tacked against the wind was familiar. But our favorite place on the rail was out of the sailors' way, safely near the stern.

"Yes, we do." He placed both hands on the rail and looked out. "But have you ever wondered why we cannot Travel to Plymouth? Not in 1620 or 21. Not when the passengers of the Mayflower land, not that first winter while they are dying."

"We can't?"

"No, not till 1623. Not until the Pilgrims are settled, more or less."

I had not realized this. "The math doesn't work?"

He smiled, and a tiny dimple appeared in his cheek. I had not noticed it before. "That's right. It's as if the universe—the Puritans would say God—won't allow us to go back to certain times or certain places."

"The universe. Or God." But we could accompany Roger Williams. "I suspect we would not be able to change much here on the *Lyon*. We were allowed to come."

Peter shook his head. "We are lost in the shuffle. Look at the waves."

The swells were constant but ripples over their surface ebbed and flowed. Sometimes several smaller waves clashed and fought, then disappeared.

"See the small waves?" Peter asked. "We are like the whitecaps induced by the wind. We are nothing compared to those swells."

Even the *Lyon* was one ship among many. There was a great swell of migration—the Puritan migration—heading west, and the issues surrounding it could not be stopped by any one person.

Even King Charles could not stop it.

And apparently, no one could change Roger Williams's mind.

Apparently, the universe—or God—knew that too.

Journal

Jan 1630 / 1631 (Gregorian)

Hey Scott! This works! As soon as I wrote the date, the word "Journal" began to fade, just as you said it would. Much better than using invisible ink. I can't imagine writing without at least seeing what I'm writing. And this little "commonplace" book is perfect for my interaction with Roger Williams. I've been learning a form of shorthand (using contemporary ink), which is so helpful, as I am worried about the fact that I have zero skills that would be useful in this century. Especially in the wilderness.

Geneva is fine. She was seasick, then drank the water (not a good idea) but recovered swiftly. I have had helpful conversations with Mr. Williams and some of the other passengers. I am absorbing the sense of how these people think—getting my sea legs, as it were, in this world.

A man named Mr. Onge has asked me about Williams, what his views are concerning the Company and Winthrop in particular. I get the feeling the politics of this settlement are fraught. I wish I had had more time to prepare. Williams tells me Bishop Laud is the Crown's bear-bait dog. Geneva tells me a popular sport was tying up a bear and sending vicious dogs to maul it. Not a pretty picture.

You would love the singing! I can't wait to get to Massachusetts. Peter.

~

I was the last to finish breakfast, lingering over my drink. We had ale—beer they called it—at every meal, and it was thin and bitter. Across the cabin, Mary Williams was tying her cap strings.

A shout sounded on deck. The Williamses looked up with interest. I tossed back the rest of my drink and settled my cap over my mussed hair.

Peter crossed to the door and peeked out. I stood.

I was beginning to get stir-crazy. We'd been on this ship for six weeks. Any distraction was welcome, and when Peter went outside, I followed.

"Fifty-two fathoms!" a sailor shouted.

Perched high before the roundhouse, Captain Peirce leaned over the rail and signaled to the sailor. He lifted his spyglass and scanned the western horizon.

I saw only haze above the blue. But then motion caught my eye.

A bird?

I stepped closer to the mainmast, where I could get a better view. I looked in all directions. Several minutes later, another blur of white wings caught my eye.

A pelican? Albatross? Seagull? "Peter! Birds!"

Behind me, the quartermaster chuckled. The crew swarmed to the stern rail lugging equipment I had not seen before.

Peter came to my elbow. "Fishing gear. Let's hope they have luck. I'd love fresh fish for supper."

"Where are we?"

"Quite possibly the Grand Banks. A fishing area off Newfoundland."

"North of Massachusetts."

"We're almost there."

I could not help myself. I hugged him for sheer joy.

What I did not expect was the ice. I had glimpsed an iceberg once during the voyage, giving me horrible thoughts about the *Titanic,* but I did not expect to see ice clogging the Massachusetts coastline.

I should have expected it. Winthrop's journal mentioned Boston harbor being so littered with "frost" that the *Lyon* had to wait several days for it to break up enough to enter the harbor.

So, we weren't in Boston yet. I knew from the journal that Winthrop didn't wait, traveling north to greet the ship. And I did not blame him.

Boston was hungry.

I had new questions. Despite my fears, I couldn't wait to meet Winthrop, to observe the settlement, to see the interactions between these very real people. But the threat of defunding hung over us. We had to bring back something significant. What could that be?

The morning mist was lifting from the shore. Beyond the ice, tall pines reached toward the gray sky. Not just individual trees. A forest blanketed the land, sending shoots to the torn, uneven coast. It was unrecognizable as Massachusetts. A wilderness.

There were no farms, no buildings, only a cluster of people visible on the rocky beach. At the edge of the water floated a shallop, a little ship not much bigger than a rowboat.

More passengers gathered near me at the rail, watching the activity on shore. The shallop pushed off with several men inside in addition to the men at the oars.

"Does the governor indeed approach?" asked a voice. I identified the speaker as a Mr. Onge, whom I hadn't spoken to. The Onge family slept below us on the gun deck.

Another passenger answered him. "I know not."

The boat took a long time to get close enough to see the faces of the men inside. My pulse began to race. The conversations around me faded.

Winthrop. The real man. I had spent hours wondering. What was he like? Had his biographers done him justice? I slipped my hand inside the pocket tied under my skirt and touched the piece of choco-late there. Chocolate from my time. But I was in 1631. I felt dizzy and removed my hand. I clutched the cold, hard rail instead.

"What think you of the man?" Mr. Onge's question mirrored my own.

"Of Winthrop? They say he is a honest man, but I have not met him."

"I have." Roger Williams's baritone. "'Tis true. He is a godly man."

"There are whispers in England," Mr. Onge said. "That he is courting sedition."

"Say not so," Mr. Williams said. "He is a magistrate, a student of the law. Listen not to whispers, but judge with right judgment."

I confess I liked him in that moment. Whatever Bradford or Cotton Mather would say of him later, I admired him now.

The boat slowly drew near, and I recognized Winthrop's face. He was wearing a thick cloak and a hat. As I watched, he removed the hat and waved it toward us. His cheeks were pink with the cold, but his face was the one in his portrait, narrow and finely drawn, with a long nose and dark, expressive eyes.

The murmurs of conversation fell away as the men boarded. Winthrop was hale enough to climb a rope ladder to the deck easily. He was forty-two years old, his hair and beard still dark, his frame slender. But as he drew near, the memory of his portrait began to clash with the sight of the real man.

This man was haggard and thin, with dark circles under his eyes. The skin of his face was slightly weather-beaten, a detail the portrait omitted. This man did not spend his days inside, as I imagined him doing.

His journal's sparse entries for 1630 told a story of hardship and woe, and now I was reading it on his face. Some things were only hinted at in letters to his wife. Or recorded by others, like how he'd joined in the physical labor of building shelters and clearing land.

The anguish of losing a grown son to drowning during that terrible year he expressed only to Margaret.

But now Winthrop was smiling, joy on his face. "Well met, Captain Peirce." His voice was melodious, his handclasp quick and warm. "How was the voyage?"

Silence fell, the only noise a squawk from an angry gull.

Winthrop's gaze scanned the passengers. "Losses?"

The captain merely nodded and looked away.

The quartermaster spoke. "The captain's son was lost in rough weather."

As before, the passengers drew nearer, as if to buttress the captain against the grief.

Captain Peirce finally found his voice. "Two hundred tons of provisions in the hold."

A muscle twitched in Winthrop's cheek. "You have saved many lives, Captain. You have quite possibly... saved the plantation."

I did not meet Winthrop in person until several days later when the ship finally nudged into Boston harbor and began unloading.

The gangway was wide and sturdy, but I still felt insecure disembarking, the marshy scent of the harbor in my nose. Peter was right behind me, occasionally touching my elbow.

Rough, careless boards in the mud served as a dock. Boston would eventually boast of several wharves, but at this point in history, none of that had been built.

Crude structures populated the ground nearby like mushrooms. One reminded me of an old engraving—of a wigwam. Beyond were areas of cleared land, houses, and stumps. I saw no fences. The heights circling the harbor were thick with trees, evergreens lending a green wash to the mass of naked boughs lifted to the sky. It was February, after all.

I felt shipwrecked. Where were we going to end up? We had tools, but no skills and no plans. Maybe Peter had things worked out in his head. I hoped so.

The other passengers milled about, waiting as we did for our belongings. Above us, the crew was busy. Shouts—and a single curse—sailed over the sounds of creaking ropes. One by one, the crew hefted chests and small barrels to their shoulders and carried them down the gangway. After a time, our chests arrived.

"Peter, how are we going to carry our things?" I sat on my sea chest, feeling like a shuttle passenger after a flight, waiting for the luggage carousel. "And where will we go?" I was conscious of my heart fluttering in my chest, but I felt only mildly panicked. After that horrible storm, nothing could move me now.

Roger Williams stood at our side, his attention fixed on a small group of men making their way toward us.

John Winthrop led the way. Two men flanked him.

I stood, and Peter took my elbow. Were we going to meet the great man?

"Mr. Williams," Winthrop said. "May I introduce Mr. Wilson and Mr. Dudley."

Thomas Dudley was tall, with craggy features. His temples were marked with gray, but his stride was firm. He looked Roger Williams over with the air of a man evaluating a colt for sale. "You are welcome to our fair plantation."

Mr. Wilson's face was rounder, his eyes kind. "A minister? Is that correct?"

Williams nodded. "I am a servant of King Jesus."

"I must leave for England soon," Mr. Wilson said. "I can leave with greater peace knowing the sheep will be fed."

"He leaves on the *Lyon*," Winthrop explained. "Once Mr. Peirce finishes trading along the coast."

I didn't remember the date the *Lyon* left. But it wouldn't be around long.

Roger Williams would be called to replace the departing minister, and everything would come crashing down.

Chapter 9

Mr. Winthrop's Assistant

"The ship *Lyon*, Mr. William Peirce, master, arrived at Nantasket. She brought Mr. Williams, (a godly minister,) with his wife... about twenty passengers, and about two hundred tons of goods."

— John Winthrop, *Journal*

John Winthrop's gaze settled on Peter and me. My stomach cramped with nerves.

"Mr. and Mrs. Peter Tuttle." Roger Williams made the introductions.

Winthrop welcomed us and began asking questions. To my relief, Dudley and Wilson were welcoming the other passengers.

The governor wore only a simple collar, not a fancy ruff or falling band. The finely woven fabric of his clothes was the only sign of rank.

"Mathematics is my field of study," Peter was saying. "And the natural—that is, natural philosophy."

What would the governor think of that?

Winthrop's brows rose with interest, and I started to relax.

"I am a servant of the Most High and wish to serve in any way possible, whether that involves my knowledge or not," Peter said.

That sounded like a Puritan. Peter would fit right in.

Winthrop glanced at Peter's hands.

Roger Williams cleared his throat. "He possesses the skills of a secretary."

My grandma would say, *Bless his heart.*

Winthrop tilted his head. "Mathematics. Would that include land surveying?"

Peter hesitated just a second. "I am not familiar with the trade, but I understand the mathematics employed. Does someone possess the apparatus we would use?"

Winthrop nodded and finally looked at me. I took a deep breath and held it lest I faint.

"Can you cook?"

Peter smiled and answered for me. "I am sure her knowledge exceeds her experience in this area, but we are happy to serve."

Peter! I couldn't make out if that was a criticism or not. I tried to catch his eye but failed. I rarely cooked, that was true. But I esteemed old-fashioned food. I favored continental cooking, replete with bacon, but rarely had the time to dig out my pots and pans.

We were hired.

My lips parted. I was going to cook for *John Winthrop.* On a wood fire. I thrust my hand into my pocket and touched my chunk of chocolate.

Peter's gaze slid to me. He gave a slight nod as if to say, *It will be fine.*

I took a deep breath and let it out slowly. Yes, it would be fine.

It had to be.

The two-story house stood alone on the right side of the lane, buttressed by stone chimneys, a humble template of the ancient New England homes I'd seen with a Historical Building plaque in my time. The nicest house in Boston at this time was unimpressive.

Across the lane, an even humbler home perched alone in the middle of perhaps an acre, a thatched cabin with a single chimney and less interior space than my apartment. But even this was nice and solid-looking compared to the sheds and wigwams I'd already seen. They didn't even have privies but dumped their waste into small pits out back. The smell of woodsmoke did not quite conceal the "eau de chamber pot" that permeated the settlement.

It was hard to imagine how Boston would eventually look as I stood here, the cold smelly breeze in my ears. A huge bank building would claim this spot one day.

The door flew open, and a child emerged, followed by another.

"Adam, wait," said the older of the two.

The younger might have been ten years of age, the older possibly twelve. Both eyed us as we approached the door.

"My sons," Winthrop said. "Stephen and Adam." He introduced us.

Stephen seemed like a miniature adult in his reactions, but Adam goggled at us, and I gave him a warm smile. Their mother was not here.

Children. How was their father managing? How were *they* managing? I knew Margaret and the younger children were still in Britain. I had not pictured Winthrop with children about.

The governor motioned us toward the door, and the kids scooted inside as well, promptly disappearing.

We entered a large foyer smelling of smoke and fresh-cut pine. To the right was a space with a hearth and primitive kitchen. A single shelf was stacked with dishes, and on the floor beneath, barrels and crates probably served as his pantry. I tried not to think about my job as cook in these conditions. Surely it was possible.

The other side of the house was a keeping room or parlor. Another modest fire, more smoke. A desk and chair were nestled up close to a window, and on one wall books crowded modest shelves. Against the front wall was a simple bed, covered with a thick wool bed rug. The parlor was austere, with several stools and an additional chair, simple in design. Windsor chairs with their curved backs were far in the future, and besides, Winthrop was still waiting for his wife and younger children to join him. I suspected more household goods would arrive with them.

Candy would love this. And Scott, of course.

There was no door between the two spaces, which cheered me. I knew I'd be travailing in the kitchen and I didn't want to be shut off from all the fun.

Winthrop spoke to Peter, pointing at the desk. "I shall prepare a place for you here. I have a traveling desk."

A portable writing desk, he meant. Scott probably had such a lap-sized desk in his domain.

The governor directed us to a room behind the kitchen. It was small and furnished with a bed much like the one in the parlor.

"This is the largest spare room. Or you may sleep upstairs."

Largest?

Peter answered him. "I thank you, governor. This is perfectly adequate."

I was glad he said adequate. It was horrible. Even for an English gentleman of the 1600s, it was a humbling situation.

Winthrop looked at Peter and held his gaze for a moment. Then he gave a tiny nod and led the way upstairs.

The door to the master bedroom stood open, and I caught only a cursory glance—a heavy-looking tester bed with ecru bed curtains, a red cape hanging from a peg, and a peculiar chair with a pot underneath.

Across the way were more bedrooms, small and cramped.

I spotted the boys in one of the rooms.

Their father poked his head in. "Have you finished your lessons?"

"Nay, Father. We have two more pages of Latin."

Latin? New England education was divided into roughly three stages—the primer stage, for little kids learning to read and write English as well as memorizing their catechism, the "grammar" stage, for Latin and Greek, and college. Children of educated or wealthy men went to Latin school and sometimes college.

Winthrop motioned to another bedroom. "My man Dixon sleeps here."

I was now the housekeeper, and I tried to look at things from that perspective. I glanced inside Dixon's room.

He was a slob. Good thing he had few belongings. The bed was unmade, and undoubtedly the coverlet needed washing. The whole room needed airing, but that would not happen until spring.

The other bedrooms were empty. I turned and looked at Winthrop. The historical records indicated that he'd lost several servants to disease. Dixon was the lone survivor.

On top of weightier griefs, Winthrop's adult son Henry had perished last year by drowning. Another adult son had died in England.

"I am sorry for your losses," I said.

Peter touched my elbow.

Winthrop hesitated, gave me a nod, and then turned and went down the stairs.

My foot was on the last step when a knock sounded at the door.

Winthrop opened it, and the February chill bit at my ankles. "What cheer?"

I glimpsed a man before the door. "One of thy neighbors doth filch from thy wood pile."

"Indeed? Fetch him here, and I'll cure him of stealing!"

Feeling intrusive, I turned to the kitchen. Peter hoisted our chest and took it into our tiny room. Was a poor man about to be punished? It was the first time I'd heard the governor speak so firmly.

I examined the contents of the crude pantry as I waited for developments. Some flour, pork, and turnips. A few onions, a sack of beans, and one of peas. Our small casks of provisions stood hopefully at one side. Any meals would be painfully simple. How long should I soak and cook beans?

Another knock sounded, and Winthrop opened the door before Peter could.

"Governor, sir..." A new man stood in the doorway, his face thin and chapped. His mouth opened and closed, his power of speech drained before his judge.

"Enter." The governor motioned both men inside. "I said I would cure this man of stealing, and so I shall."

The thief wore literal rags. His clothing was too thin for the weather, and he had wrapped strips of cloth around his arms and legs in a futile effort to stay warm.

Winthrop's face softened. "Have ye a wife? Children?"

The man nodded and relayed the ages of his children. The youngest was three.

"Friend, it is a severe winter, and I doubt but you are meanly supplied with wood. Supply yourself at my wood pile until this cold season be over."

The thief gaped for a moment, and the tattletale looked confused.

"Mr. Tuttle, wilt thou assist this man?" Winthrop asked. "Carry an armload to his dwelling and see to his family."

My heart warmed despite the cold. I had glimpsed the man behind the signature.

The first week was horrible. Wood fires were not easy to start. A few times, Dixon the slob helped, and his simple cheerfulness eased my abject embarrassment. Even the children had chores, and much of the heavy work—hauling water from the spring, bringing in wood each morning, and cleaning out the ashes, was done by their willing hands.

Once the fire was going, that by no means guaranteed mealtime success. Dinner was by turns scorched or underdone. But in the meantime, at least I was warm. And I snatched close-up glimpses of the man, John Winthrop, as he went about his daily life.

The Sabbath was strictly enforced, and it began Saturday evening with devotions and the catechism. On Sunday proper we ate leftovers, and despite a lengthy sermon at church, and another devotion at home, I enjoyed the relief from frustration.

On a Tuesday three weeks in, I managed to start the kitchen fire in just a few minutes. I filled my pot with ingredients, gave the concoction a vigorous stir, and stepped back. I wiped the sweat from my forehead and sat on a stool to rest.

"I have no housekeeper, and my wife is not yet here," Winthrop had explained that first day.

Simple words, but there was grief behind his eyes, and not just because of the loss of his sons. He missed his wife severely, writing her frequently. I'd seen him hunched over his desk, quill in hand.

I was hired to cook and clean only. A neighbor did the wash, coming for a huge smelly pile of linens each week. Another neighbor, Mrs. Alcock, showed up from time to time with bread. I was glad, as there was no way I could manage it all. Washing before sonic cleansers was a forbidding prospect, especially in cold weather.

Peter was hired as a personal secretary and land surveyor. According to the governor, we would also be able to secure a parcel of ground eventually. All the settlers were offered land to improve as they would.

Away from the fire, I cooled off. In another ten minutes, I would be cold.

Two well-fed fireplaces were insufficient to keep the entire dwelling heated, and at night we let the flames die down. The governor took a warming pan upstairs to his bed every night. Every evening I grabbed the parlor's brazier and placed it in our room, but one night our wash water froze despite it.

Sleeping presented a challenge, sharing, as we did, a single narrow bed. We settled on a system of layers. First, we each wrapped a scratchy wool blanket around ourselves; then we lay together with a counterpane over the top, to all appearances man and wife. It resembled the ancient New England practice of "bundling," whereby a courting couple could spend a cozy night innocently.

Thankfully, each night we were so tired we had little time to feel awkward. Well, I didn't think Peter felt too awkward. His breathing became regular well before my thoughts stopped spinning round and round as they so often did.

Can we change history?

Will the devices work to bring us back?

Lying in bed after dark was the time when every possible problem loomed large. When I woke, sunlight chased away the shadows, replacing them with the belief that everything would work out.

I pried myself off the stool and returned to the welcome warmth of the hearth. My concoction was congealing into a fragrant succotash. Given the range of ingredients at my disposal, I sought to use my limited experience to the fullest. Mrs. Alcock had supplied me with "sweet herbs," which upon investigation turned out to be a mix of basil and parsley. Some of that went into my mixture, as well as salt, pepper, and a bit of vinegar.

A clunk, thud, and a blast of cold air jerked my attention away from the pot. Peter was coming in the door, his arms filled with a mass of iron rods. He closed the door, dumped them clattering on the floor, and claimed the stool I'd just abandoned.

"I'm exhausted," he said unnecessarily. Winthrop was using him less as a secretary than as an all-purpose dogsbody. Turned out the Company already had an engineer with surveying equipment. Peter was merely a rodman, and Mr. Graves, the engineer, didn't yet require Peter's mathematics.

I stared at the equipment cluttering up the floor. "Working with Mr. Graves?"

"Yes. We've finished with the Perkinses' and the Pollards' plots. Next week we'll take a break and help Mr. Perkins put up a house. It's been three weeks. We've done nothing since we got here."

Peter's voice had taken a new tone, a plaintive complaint. I understood.

"I disagree."

Peter stood and approached the fire. He was dirty and needed a bath. We both did. "Mr. Winthrop works as hard as anyone."

I stirred the pot and stood off to the side so Peter could get warm. "Precisely my point. He's not some blue blood who came here to get rich. I think that first thesis is easily disproved."

"I want to spend more time with Williams. I don't see that happening."

A timid but familiar knock sounded at the door.

I opened it. "Welcome, Mrs. Alcock." I swiped my hand across my forehead. My hair was hopeless. At least most of it was covered under the cap.

The smiling woman on the doorstep was Thomas Hooker's sister, I'd just discovered yesterday. *The* Thomas Hooker, founder of Connecticut. But Connecticut was still in the future.

"I've baked, and I heard the governor was hosting the new minister for dinner."

This was news to me. "How kind. I thank you."

She thrust a large basket in my direction, full of lumpy bread and a few smaller items that might be meant for dessert. "How fare ye?" She eyed the surveyor's chains on the floor.

Peter was smiling. "We fare well, and in no small part because of your labors."

Mrs. Alcock gave her farewells, and I shut the door. "We'd better clean house, Dr. Donatelli."

"The minister. Roger Williams?"

Who else could it be?

Chapter 10

The New Minister

"...the King is God's immediate lieutenant upon earth; and therefore one and the same action is God's by ordinance, and the King's by execution."

— Bishop William Laud, *Sermon*, 1625

I WATCHED SURREPTITIOUSLY as everyone ate. "Breaking bread" was a literal thing here. Nothing was pre-sliced or even soft. But the toothy loaves were delicious.

Roger Williams had the habit of squinting carefully at the modest piece of bread in his hand and carefully dipping it into his stew. Winthrop was more careless, eating a bite of stew, then following it with a bite of bread, never taking his eyes from Williams's face.

Peter was quiet, but his hands gave him away. He managed to eat, but his area was littered with crumbs. Mary was likewise quiet, but her face glowed with health, something I was glad to see. Pregnancy was fraught in a place like this.

She would be fine—I knew that. But I couldn't stop thinking that way.

Surprisingly, I was hungry, and I put away a decent portion of everything. The strange pastries Mrs. Alcock had baked were not very sweet, but they were surprisingly good. The children must have agreed, for everything they were given—in the kitchen—vanished straightway.

The men spoke of prosaic concerns while they ate. Cattle, land, someone's illness.

"Captain Peirce's provisions have brought health and good cheer to all," the governor said.

It was true. The settlers were still thin, but happy and energized to work the land. Clearing and plowing had started, though the seed would not be planted for several weeks yet.

The conversation was casual, but there was a tension present that I could not put my finger on. When I rose and refilled the men's cups of cider, something shifted.

Roger looked at Mary and she rose and went to the kitchen. I followed her. As I plopped dirty bowls into a pail of soapy water, my attention remained on the conversation behind me.

"Why, Mr. Williams?" Winthrop asked.

"You must think me a fool."

"All know you for a godly man."

I couldn't help myself. I turned to watch, drying my hands on my apron.

Something had happened that Peter and I were not privy to. We'd heard Williams preach in the large meetinghouse, called the "great house." The first, and so far, the only church in Boston. I knew the history. He was offered a post since Mr. Wilson was leaving, and he refused it. No one in my time knew more than that.

Williams cradled his cup in his hands. "I simply cannot take the position, Governor. The Boston church has not separated herself from the errors of the Church of England. If I take this post offered me, if I even assent to membership, I partake of her error and curse."

Winthrop's shoulders sagged. He lifted his gaze to me. "More ale?" His voice was so soft I could barely hear him. I filled his cup and topped off the others'. I set the flagon on the table and copied Mary—she'd found a stool in the corner and focused on her sewing.

It was one way to become invisible as a woman. I grabbed my sewing basket and studied a hole in one of Peter's shirts while I listened. I had managed to figure out how to thread a needle last week. Mending couldn't be rocket science.

"David, when he was anointed, did not presume to think highly of himself," Winthrop said. "When King Saul persecuted him, he did not dare harm the Lord's anointed."

"I would not raise my hand against the supposed head of the church," Roger Williams said peaceably.

I sensed the argument was known to them both. I studied their faces. All who read history knew of Williams's zeal. But Winthrop's calm face was deceiving. His writings revealed a great depth of feeling.

Reasoned passion met youthful zeal over this table. I surprised myself by feeling sorry for Roger Williams. And for Mary. Her life would not be easy.

"'Tis a fair question," Winthrop continued. "What constitutes a true church?"

"Surely you cannot include the likes of Bishop Laud as part of the Bride of Christ."

Winthrop hesitated. "This side of eternity there will be tares among the wheat. Shall we condemn all for the tares?"

"You assume the tares are distinguishable from the wheat. Not the point of the parable."

As I thrust a needle into the fabric in my hands, I poked myself and stifled an exclamation. I sucked my finger and decided to ask Peter about the wheat and tares. This was getting over my head.

At the table, Peter was tracking the conversation carefully and quietly. So far, he hadn't made a comment. As Winthrop's secretary, he had a privileged position, a position of trust. He hadn't been asked to leave.

"To separate is tantamount to the error of the Anabaptists, who fling all restraint to the wind."

I straightened and looked up. The Anabaptists' view of baptism was not the only issue that stuck in the craw of most Puritans like Winthrop. Not only were they viewed as lawless, but some had defective soteriology, a defective view of salvation itself. This was a serious charge.

"Perhaps they desire the restraint of Christ Himself. He is the only King of the church. Our true Head."

"That may be." Winthrop admitted. "But we live in this world. To separate is to put the Charter at risk."

The governor was trying a new tack. Or was his real reason political? Was he secretly sympathetic to Williams's position?

Peter cleared his throat. "On the *Lyon* one of the passengers asked about you, Governor. He had heard some rumors that you were inciting sedition."

Winthrop sighed. "You see, Mr. Williams, what we deal with. I left a clear statement of loyalty to the Crown when I sailed last year. I wanted there to be no doubt as to myself or the Company, or the plantation."

Williams seemed to consider this. "I grant it puts you in a difficult place. But Christ asks us to follow Him, not the whim of the Crown."

"What did the Hebrew midwives do? They obeyed God but misled Pharaoh. They were in a difficult place, as you say. They did what they had to do. I have the well-being of hundreds of people to consider. Women and children. More are on the way. I will not separate from the Church of England because of the conscience of one man."

"Must not every man obey his own conscience?"

Winthrop picked up his cup, stared at it, then set it down. "Perhaps. But my conscience is governed by the love I have for God's people. I must care for the sheep in this place."

Williams looked at the faces of both men. "I understand your position. I accept it. I hope you accept mine."

"I understand it, Mr. Williams. But it grieves me. I hope you will change your mind."

I crumpled the fabric in my lap. Between the lines, Winthrop was saying Williams had no place with them. But where would he go? How would he support his pregnant wife? Eventually, he'd end up in Rhode Island, but that was several years from now.

I cut a glance at Mary, whose placid expression was marred by a line between her brows. She got it.

Where would they live?

The next morning, I struggled to wake up after the late night. Peter had wanted to record the details of the meeting before he forgot anything.

He took out the special quill and crouched over the journal on the bed. We had no desk in our room, only a crude table with our wash water—and that, I knew, was more than many had. For light, I held a flickering tallow candle above his head.

He wrote several lines, then paused. "How dangerous is this sedition thing, exactly?"

I was glad Peter knew theology and the Bible. He fit right in. But in the historical particulars, he was deficient. We both were, with so little time to prepare.

"King Charles hated Puritans and persecuted them. Their ideas challenged the divine right of kings. It was a miracle Winthrop got the charter approved in the first place. The king was probably thinking 'good riddance.' But at that same time, he had other issues. He dissolved Parliament—"

"Could he do that?"

"Charles believed God appointed him, therefore whatever he did was right."

Peter motioned me on, definitely wanting the short version.

"During the 1630s, he ruled alone with his Privy Council, otherwise known as the Star Chamber."

He grunted.

"It sounds nefarious, and it was. These men tried cases as they saw fit. Another arm of the king was the Church of England. Bishop Laud hated Puritans and denied them livings, harassed them, and worse. An influential Puritan, John Cotton, will arrive soon—Laud was on his trail. He was—is—in danger of his life."

A line appeared between Peter's brows. "Massachusetts is in a tenuous position, legally."

"Oh, yes. Absolutely. Winthrop has every right to be concerned. He's still under the jurisdiction of the king, after all."

"So, if Roger wants to publicly separate from the Church of England, how would the king react to that?"

"The king is the head of the church, Peter. It is a slap in his face, a rejection of his authority. Quite frankly, even if the Puritans maintain allegiance, their theology chips away at divine right. They keep insisting the scriptures are the only valid rule of faith and practice."

"Even if Winthrop says he acknowledges the Church of England— and by implication Charles's right as head—he is here, on these shores."

"He has separated himself in that sense."

"As David fled from Saul."

Peter had jumped ahead of me, knowing the Bible as he did.

"Saul was king, right?"

"Yes and came after David to kill him."

Last night's remarks coalesced in my mind. It made sense now. "Well, go ahead. Tell Scott before we use up this candle."

I splashed water on my sleepy face, the previous night's discussion still churning in my mind. I began the day's work, chopping turnips, onions, and a little pork on the rickety kitchen worktable. I threw them into the pot with seasoning and adjusted the position of the pot on the fire so it would—hopefully—simmer and not burn.

Next, I tidied the house, aired the bedding, and swept the floors. Then I sliced the last loaves from yesterday and created sandwiches. I checked the fire where my soup simmered on the hearth and gave our supper a final stir.

One day I would force a fire to obey me perfectly, but for now, I did the best I could. I had a lot of respect for a seventeenth-century housewife.

I hauled my basket of food and a flagon of cider out to the Perkinses' land, where the governor was helping them build a house. It was almost time for lunch.

The sound of hammering drew me to the location. I spotted Peter's dark curls under his wool cap. He was bent over a log, saw in hand. The Perkinses' younger children milled about, giggling, while the older ones helped their father. Roger Williams was there too, minus his coat, the sun catching the pewter buttons of his brown waistcoat. He helped a young man I did not recognize lift a log into place. I did not see the governor.

Peter spotted me and straightened, putting a hand on the small of his back. A sheen of sweat shone on his forehead, despite the cool March weather. "Lunch?"

I nodded. "The governor?"

"He's long gone. Mr. Dudley came. Took him away."

Some minor crisis. Dudley was the deputy governor at this point. I tried to remember Winthrop's entries for this period, but they were sparse. Not much happened the governor thought noteworthy. Some-one's house caught fire, some Indians came for dinner, then nothing until April twelfth, when an important letter was written regarding Roger Williams.

Salem. I remembered now. Roger Williams went to Salem. Or would go.

I studied the sharp angles of the minister's face. He would go, but he wouldn't stay there.

"Come," Peter said. "Let's take a walk."

He relieved me of the heavy cider, and I followed. Beyond the house was an open spot sprinkled with stumps. A couple of scrawny reddish-brown cows hunted for spring shoots, flicking their ears toward us as we passed. We came to a large fieldstone, and I eagerly sat on it. Bumpy, but an adequate bench. Nearby, a large tree lifted bare branches to the sky. Judging by the brown leaves scattered about, it was a maple.

We bit into our sandwiches.

"This is good," Peter said. "Beef, cheese—no mayo, but it's tasty."

"I used suet instead."

It was a pleasant idyll. In another two months, Boston would be warm. The only good thing about the cold was that it kept my chocolate from melting. I had one small piece left.

I studied Peter out of the corner of my eye. I felt safe around him.

You don't need a man.

My mother's words. My father hadn't stuck around for long, and maybe that had turned her off all men. But maybe it was her own eccentric ways—hiking in Vermont in the summers and writing grants for obscure projects in winter.

As I stuffed the last bite of sandwich into my mouth, a figure approached. For a split second, I thought it was Winthrop, but I soon realized my mistake. The angular face, unkempt hair, and scuffed coat were the antithesis of the neat governor's appearance.

Peter rose, attempting seventeenth-century civility. "Care to partake of our victuals, Mis—"

"Philip Ratcliffe. At your service." The mousy man glanced at me dismissively, then returned his gaze to Peter's face. "I thank ye."

He took a seat on the grass nearby and I cut Winthrop's sandwich in half. I wasn't going to give this fellow all of the governor's lunch.

Ratcliffe received it with some grace while I struggled to place the name. *Rat. Ratcliffe.* So familiar. It was in Winthrop's journal, I was sure. And I had a bad feeling about both the name and this man.

As he ate, he exchanged pleasantries with Peter. They noted the weather. Peter made a comment about the angle of the sun, which was very Peter-ish of him.

Rat cut a glance at me. Then he took a long drink of the cider. "Ye are servants of the governor?"

His question felt like a statement.

Peter nodded but did not explain.

"Then ye know Winthrop's machinations. And the new minister will bring trouble on all our heads."

Machinations? My heart began a familiar thudding. I took a slow, deep breath.

Ratcliffe. A bad name. It was coming to me.

"Heard what the minister says? That we should have no truck with the king."

Peter said nothing.

"All the long noses are such fools and spoilsports. They will get their comeuppance now. Traitors they be, the lot of 'em."

"Fools?" Peter's tone held a warning note.

"Surely you cannot see it? Hypocrites, establishing their own kingdom, delighting in their harsh rule, and thumbing their noses at the monarch himself!"

He seemed to be studying us. "Perhaps I speak too plainly. Thou seemest a fine gentleman, thy waistcoat no mere rags. A reversal in fortune? Or a misunderstanding with the bishop?"

Peter shrugged agreeably. I frowned. This man was dangerous, I was sure, even though my memory was playing me false. I longed for the cider to ease my dry throat, but I wasn't going to touch the flask after that rat had drunk from it.

"'Tis wise to have friends. Even the scriptures say so, do they not? I have friends, strong friends. Winthrop may lose favor with his friends, and what then? He has no favor with the king, that be certain."

"Mayhap we will speak of this again," Peter said in a neutral voice.

I remembered everything now. Ratcliffe would be brought before the court and punished.

And that wasn't all. He did have friends, important friends.

Peter didn't know what he was doing.

Chapter 11

Another Crisis

"...our times are all in the Lord's hand, so as we need not trouble our thoughts how long or how short they may be, but how we may be found faithful when we are called for."

— John Winthrop

MARCH 15, 1631

Journal

Hey Scott, I never kept a journal, this feels more like a letter. My last entry was about Williams's separatism, and while on that subject, I am gathering a sense that separatists are viewed as extremists. I never thought of the "Pilgrims" in Plymouth that way. Who knew?

I have been serving as secretary to the governor, mainly copying his letters. He needs an extra for himself and in case a missive goes astray. (The rest of the time I spend in hard labor—surveying, raising houses, and next week, plowing.)

Copying his letters has given me a unique window into the situation here. Gen always wants to know (while we are safely in our room at night) who he has written to or from whom he has received a letter.

Winthrop does correspond with William Bradford of Plymouth, mostly over prosaic matters. This tells me that Winthrop does not view separatism as some kind of fatal heresy. He respects Bradford.

The governor also corresponds with friends in England. These letters are informative in a different way. Winthrop writes in a veiled fashion, hinting at things he cannot spell out. It's like reading the messages of a spy, coded with terms known to each party but perhaps not obvious to others.

Clearly, the mails are routinely opened, at least of people like him. Once William Laud is elevated to archbishop, King Charles will be fully capable of harrying the Puritans from all positions of influence. Or even killing them. Gen feeds me with bits and pieces of the history.

Meanwhile, Winthrop faces opposition. Last year the Company (Winthrop and the "Assistants") ejected a number of people from the area and sent them back to England. Some of the offenses included flagrant drunkenness. A certain Thomas Morton erected a "pagan" Maypole. According to Mrs. Alcock, "There were Indian maids..." She would not explain, only lifted her eyebrows meaningfully. The population was scandalized.

Winthrop has a good amount of support, and last year the Charter was amended. "Freemen" elect the Assistants, and qualifications for Freemen have been changed to include more of the population. The government is something we would recognize—representative in nature, with truly widespread suffrage. It gives me shivers to see American constitutional government in seed form.

Anyway, Gen tells me that the main problem will be the ejected fellows. They will cause trouble in England. Which makes me wonder about our thesis again. Can anyone believe they came here for riches?

Tell Candy I've had to use an awl to cut more holes in my belt. We have sufficient food—most of the time. Some days it's just corn mush and salt pork. Gen works hard to make it palatable, but everyone works from dawn to dusk, and no one is fat. A few have left. It was just too difficult.

It is true, one of the stated goals in forming the Company was acquiring land. To an Englishman, land was prized. It was a goal King Charles would understand. They can't exactly say, "the king and his minions have made things intolerable, hence we leave," can they?

I laid out Winthrop's piece of land along the Mystic two weeks ago. My shoulders hurt for days from hauling the chains around. It's a modest acreage but large by English standards. If you look at it—trees, scrubby clearings, a muddy riverbank—you realize the huge amount of labor necessary to improve it.

Nobody is looking for gold here. They just want to live a normal life —in peace.

Peter

P.S. Tomorrow I'll write about the latest rumor—candle almost gone.

Three days later, we got to spend time with Roger Williams. I'd labored all morning making a nutritious broth for the sick which Winthrop took to several families.

I felt filthy. Changing my chemise once a week and keeping clean linen next to my skin helped, and the men didn't stink as I thought they would, but still. Maybe we could bathe tonight. I'd have to make it happen. I had a fire and a kettle.

Yes, I would make it happen. But I had another problem. The mercury was slowly inching up. My chocolate.

"Peter?" He stumbled inside, looking tired after a morning's labor plowing. He had taken over Dixon's labor now that the other man was clearing Winthrop's property on the Mystic. "Here. Wipe your hands on this." I handed him a damp towel. We couldn't be totally hygienic here, but I did my best. "I need help."

He straightened. "You okay?"

"I fare well." Not *okay*. "But my chocolate will melt soon—I mean, betimes."

He didn't scoff but pursed his lips. "Oilcloth," he said finally. "Or paper." He brightened, then crossed to the desk in the parlor and extracted a piece of paper from a drawer.

"I have ruined several sheets of paper but hesitated to throw anything away."

The colony wasted nothing and recycled before it was even a word.

I studied the paper, half-covered in ink. Blots festooned the script. "Thank you. This is perfect."

I wrapped the chocolate in the clean half, then covered that with a bit of oilcloth.

"How about another picnic lunch?" he asked.

"I will leave the governor a sandwich."

I prepared the basket, donned my cloak, and we were on our way. We avoided the outcropping we'd sat on previously and changed direction. We made our way past a few clumps of trees. Beyond a stand of birch, a small clearing was marked by disturbed areas of soil. Rocks littered the ground.

No. They were *headstones*.

It was a burial ground. We stopped several yards from the nearest grave, neither of us speaking.

One of the graves was fresh, but most seemed older. I remembered the deaths of 1630. This was where they were buried.

Lady Arbella, after whom Winthrop's flagship was named. I searched for her stone but didn't see it. Was she buried at Charlestown? The settlers had first arrived at Salem. Then they tried Charlestown, but it was not an ideal location either. Next, they'd split up, many settling where Boston is now, because of a freshwater spring. Roxbury, Watertown, and what would eventually be named Cambridge were satellites of the main town.

Today, the burial site was lonely.

"What is this?" Peter asked. "I mean, in our time?"

"In the eighth grade, we went on a field trip. We stopped at several cemeteries. Roxbury, downtown Boston. I think this might be..."

A chill ran down my spine. One day John Winthrop would be buried here.

"Hallo. What cheer, Brother?"

I turned to see Roger Williams approaching us. He was mildly disheveled. Probably helping someone else build a house.

"Hello." Peter gave him a firm handshake. "Share our repast?"

Repast? I couldn't stop a smile. Peter was doing well.

"You are kind."

We all sat on the ground as there was no log or rock suitable. I distributed the food, cutting the larger submarine-style sandwich in half with my eating knife. I handed the smaller, intact sub to Williams. He examined it and smiled.

"Sensible. Meat, cheese, and bread together."

For a few minutes, conversation died as we chomped. I relished the fresh food—real food. I was proud of my mustard. I'd soaked ground mustard seed in vinegar and lavished it on the bread.

The minister eyed me. "Perhaps you might give my wife your receipt."

"I'd be glad to."

Then the men began to discuss theology. I followed along for a while, but the afternoon was warmer than usual—that is, above freezing—and my mind wandered.

Here... swee-tie. Here... swee-tie.

I searched for the bird, entranced by its delicate song. But I didn't see it. I did notice another bird, large, dark, and unafraid. I think I'd seen its descendant along Quincy Street. Some birds, I suspected, survived everywhere. Everywhen.

Something in the conversation drew my ear.

"The first table should not be enforced by the magistrate?" Peter asked.

Williams took a drink of cider. "Think of the horrors we have experienced in England. Queen Mary burnt brave Christians at the stake. Methinks Bishop Laud would do the like if he could. And what prevents him? Parliament has been dissolved."

What were they talking about? The first table?

The Ten Commandments. The Commandments were divided into two parts: the first table, the commandments having to do with God, and the second, having to do with other people. Like murder or adultery.

"I see your point." A line appeared between Peter's brows. "Enforcing the first table involves enforcing worship."

My mind sped over the list. *Thou shalt have no other gods before me...* the first commandment. I couldn't remember the second and third.

The fourth commandment had to do with the Sabbath. Keeping the Sabbath was on that list.

Williams plucked a long stem of grass and placed it in his mouth. "One of the men Winthrop and the assistants decided to send back to Britain two weeks ago is accused of being Catholic."

"Sir Gardiner? That wasn't the main reason."

"He's a bigamist and general scoundrel. But to clinch the argument, they label him papist. This plantation is for the orthodox—and Winthrop and the others decide who and what is orthodox."

Peter circled his knees with his arms. "But not in any wise independent of the Confessions. The Articles."

"Indeed. But what about the ungodly?"

"You are saying that the Company has no room for unbelievers."

"It is worse than that. There is no room for those who disagree. All must attend our worship on the Sabbath, even if it go against conscience to do so. Baptize their children."

Peter's expression shifted. "What of Baptists?"

"Anabaptists? Those lawless renegades?" Williams's tone was wry, almost sarcastic. "Mention not Anabaptists nor their doctrine to

Winthrop." He rose and brushed off his clothing. "I must return to Mr. Pollard's property. He raises a house."

"Fare thee well," Peter said.

I watched Williams walk away.

"There goes another spark on the kindling," I said.

"The first table?"

"Exactly. If he expresses himself publicly, Winthrop will not understand. No one will."

The next day, I felt cleaner after a sponge bath without a sponge, but I was still mulling over the discussion we'd had with Roger Williams.

He seemed to understand the inflexibility of Winthrop and the others on certain theological issues, yet I knew it would not stop him. He had cautioned us, but he would not heed his own advice. These concerns weren't dry things confined to the Archives anymore. I couldn't help myself. I cared about what happened to this man.

I had little time to speak to Peter alone. I still had concerns about Ratcliffe. But our conversations were mostly confined to whispers in the dark.

After supper I scrubbed the iron pot, scouring it with sand as Mrs. Alcock had suggested. My shoulders ached. My hands were red and chafed, despite all the care I took, moisturizing them with a bit of grease morning and night. Truly, it was the worst part of this Trip.

Nights were better now. The temperature had risen, and our wash water no longer froze. One of our neighbors had even broken up ground for a garden. But we still slept side-by-side rolled up in wool. It wasn't *that* warm.

I peeked over my shoulder. Governor Winthrop was at his desk, writing by the light of a single candle. He rarely wrote at night as candles were dear. It was either a letter to his wife or a journal entry.

I shivered. Centuries later I would read that journal. And practically memorize it.

I took a deep breath and released it slowly. Soon the pot was clean. I tidied the kitchen and secured the foodstuffs. Now that the weather had moderated, I was seeing evidence of mice. According to Mrs. Alcock, they would hunt out anything not behind an impenetrable barrier. I kept the bread and other leftovers in something that looked like a cast iron dutch oven.

The door creaked open, and cold air swirled around my ankles and up my skirt.

"Peter!"

Winthrop turned. In the dim light I could see his raised eyebrows. "Mr. Tuttle."

"Calf. Another one. I helped Sir Saltonstall butcher the remains." A small, wrapped package nestled under his arm. Meat? I wondered hopefully. We could use it. We had visitors frequently, and Dixon ate voraciously.

"Wolves?" Winthrop asked.

"Yes. The neighbors heard them, chased them off with musket fire. I was nearby."

One of the first acts of the government was to create a bounty on wolves. But the creatures were still plentiful.

Peter washed his face, neck, and hands, and we prepared for bed. There was so little light in the tiny bedroom that I stripped down to my loose chemise with no embarrassment. We wrapped up and tugged the counterpane over everything.

I was exhausted, but my mind was still fully awake.

"Peter, are we getting anywhere?" Both of the theses we were supposed to gain evidence for were stupid anyway. I loved living in the same house as John Winthrop, but that was personal. We would have to create a report on our return. The second thesis was problematic.

"We've certainly collected enough to disprove the first. The second is—"

"You're on Williams's side."

Peter snorted. "Maybe. Maybe he's a modern American living in medieval times."

Medieval. "Peter, you're a genius."

"And here I try to be humble."

"We are still in the Middle Ages, kind of." Thoughts clicked into place like dominoes falling. "The Reformation, from a theological standpoint, did what?"

"Rediscovered justification by faith. Salvation by grace. Through faith."

"But what didn't change?"

Peter was silent for a moment. "I'm a physicist. Not a historian. But my guess is a lot of things stayed the same."

"The nature of the church and baptism."

"And the church-state relationship."

"Precisely. Charles is the Defender of the Faith. *Fidei Defensor.* Head of the Church. To get into the Church of England, you are baptized as an infant."

"And the Anabaptists?" Peter's voice was sober.

"Sadly, some of these groups were extreme in all kinds of ways including their theology of salvation itself. Or they rejected the authority of the civil magistrate. Probably gave the rest a bad name."

"I wonder. Perhaps they were simply like Roger. Thinking through what was appropriate for the civil magistrate to enforce."

"I told you, Peter, you're a genius."

My eyes began to grow heavy. Despite the itchy wool, it was a cozy sleeping arrangement. It would be unworkable in warm weather. We'd figure something out.

Summer would be here soon. Then we'd leave.

I was going to miss our whispered conversations.

~

Mar 26, 1631

Journal

Scott, wolves took a calf yesterday. Chasing off the creatures felt unreal, like I was in a vid. Then today we had visitors, several Indians. The Native Americans here sometimes wear English clothing but in a haphazard fashion. One might wear a shirt with native leggings, another might wear breeches with a leather cape. The leader of this small group was adorned with what I believe is called wampum, in the form of decorative jewelry. I spotted one bracelet and one armband.

Governor Winthrop spoke kindly to these men, and they were all quite civil in return. One of the Indians (I am not sure of the tribe— Wampanoag? Massachusetts?) spoke English fairly well, and so we were able to communicate. There was some problem with an Englishman who had cheated them, and Winthrop dictated a letter for the first time. I scrambled, having almost forgotten my shorthand, but managed to get the gist of it, and I shall write a fair copy—two copies, actually—in the morning. They seem to respect him as a man who is interested in justice for both the red man and the settlers evenhandedly. I am convinced that Winthrop is no hypocrite. The sermon on Christian charity is something he truly believes in and strives to put into practice.

Which brings me to the rumor I alluded to, which has just been confirmed: Roger Williams questions the right of the magistrate to enforce the "first table" of the Ten Commandments, the things between God and man. For this time period, it is a radical idea. The state enforces the correct religion, the correct way of worship, and you conform accordingly. Winthrop et al don't think of this as tyranny, Gen says. Anything else feels like either anarchy or antinomianism to them.

Scott, I wonder if this is the default setting of mankind. Control over worship.

Gen is sleeping. She couldn't keep her eyes open after laboring all day, serving in the evening, and then cleaning up. I am thinking about her. There is so much here, so much we are learning. She's always wanted her PhD. Wouldn't "Doctor" Fielding garner some respect? I cringe when I see Dr. Howard look down his nose at her.

She could do any number of things for a thesis. I'll bet there aren't many studies on the importance of Winthrop's good relations with the Native Americans... oh, I am just rambling, letting the candle burn down.

What I really want to say (you will have to delete a good part of this entry) is that Candy should know going back as a married couple is harder than it seems. It's convenient in some ways. Especially in this culture. BUT.

Dare I say it? You're a man. Perhaps you can just imagine what it's like sleeping three inches from a beautiful woman every night.

A woman I can't have.

And you know very well why.

Chapter 12

Rain

"No distance of place or space of time can sever us in respect of our true and fervent affections to each other."

— John Winthrop to his wife Margaret

Mrs. Alcock stood at the door, clutching a bundle of blankets to her bosom. A swirl of cool sea air came in behind her.

"Come in." I escorted her to the kitchen, relieved her of her burden, and gave her a chair near the fire. Her eyes were red and watery. She didn't look well.

"There's a pillow in there," she said. "Goose down."

That pillow had probably come all the way from England.

"Thank you, the governor is sorely in want of bedding."

In the parlor, the conversation ebbed and flowed. The governor had guests, and I had my hands full. Sir Saltonstall and his family would be staying overnight. At the moment, the men were discussing the various changes that the departure of certain men would create.

Mrs. Alcock sneezed. As I wondered what to give her for a handkerchief, she wiped her face on her sleeve. I winced but said nothing.

These Puritans were not dirty people, by and large, but some things moderns took for granted—like showers—simply did not exist. What this woman did need was hot soup and fresh produce.

I filed away that observation for later. Right now I had house-keeping duties. Mrs. Alcock left, and I went upstairs to make up beds for Saltonstall's daughters. One was older, quite marriageable, and the other maybe ten years old. The family was to set sail on the *Lyon* from Salem in a day or two.

Mr. Wilson, the minister, was also leaving, and the pulpit needed to be filled until he returned. I thought of his preaching I'd heard in the drafty meetinghouse every Sabbath.

I knew theology and knew all the terms. I could probably write a thesis on the Reformation in England. But what I heard in John Wilson's voice as he spoke Sunday after Sunday was like Tollers's first lines as he spoke seventeenth-century dialect. Not quite compre-hensible.

Peter soaked it up. He occasionally made comments on the sermons as we walked back to the house. I was thankful Peter was here and not Dr. Howard, who would have more in common with Ratcliffe than Mr. Wilson.

The sermons were logical but heartfelt. One theme Wilson often hammered on was to heed the authority of God rather than man. If it wasn't in the scriptures, it could be set aside. But his tone was never bellicose. He never thumped the pulpit.

Some of his arguments seemed technical, heads and subheads supporting a thesis. Other times, his words were warm-hearted and even poetic, as when speaking of Christ as the "fountain" of life.

Theology I knew. But Christ a fountain? I felt like I was standing looking inside a room where folks were gathered around a banquet, enjoying themselves. I could catch a whiff of a savory aroma, but I could not taste it.

It bothered me. I was missing something.

I turned back to the hearth and fruitlessly waved away the smoke.

On one side, a pot of beans sat in the hot ashes. On the trivet, still centered over the red of the smoldering wood, a kettle simmered, a simple recipe described in the Archives as "Indian pudding." The settlers still ate mainly wheat and barley from England, but "Indian corn" had made its appearance in town. The Indians visiting last week had gifted us a whole barrel full of a strange bluish meal I finally deduced was ancient cornmeal. I'd already made a pan of only slightly scorched cornbread.

Real food, even if overdone. Kitchen duties completed for now, I finished making up the pallets and went to find Peter. He'd gone to chop wood.

I had to go almost all the way to what was the Boston Common in my day to find him. Many of the trees in the hamlet were gone, and I suspected the entire peninsula would be denuded in a couple of decades.

Peter lifted and swung an axe into a section of beech with a *clunk*. He swung again, and the length of wood split in half. The tree he'd felled was a modest size; those he'd left standing were much larger. One was sixty feet high if it was an inch.

He wiped his forehead and spotted me. "Gen."

A crude wheelbarrow waited to one side. I helped him load it. "Mrs. Alcock is sick."

He threw another chunk inside and looked at me with a raised eyebrow.

"Help me gather greens?" I asked.

Peter turned and scanned the trees as if looking for a pharmacy. "Candy gave you simples."

"She needs fresh food. Vitamins."

"Ah. I doubt if we'll find anything like that."

It was the tail end of March. No, not much was growing, but there was something. Some trees were swelling with buds. In a few weeks there would be a thin wash of green over all the branches.

"If I don't find much, I will look for rockweed at the beach."

We pushed through the densest thickets, finding little. What we did discover, I could not identify. Useless.

Finally, we sat together on a half-decayed log to rest. My throat tightened and I blinked.

"She's going to die."

"What are her symptoms?"

I told him.

"Sounds like a cold."

"This is 1631. It can be a death sentence."

Perhaps I was overreacting. I knew I was. But Peter didn't point it out, and I was glad. He was a true friend.

After a few minutes, we stood and returned to the wheelbarrow. As we made our way back to the settlement, the wind picked up, causing Peter's curls to dance. It came straight from the east, bringing a familiar smell with it. I'd lived in Boston most of my life, and I knew what this meant.

A storm. I picked up the pace.

The next morning was just as busy. Peter helped the boys fetch wood and water, and I stoked the fire. Outside, a gusting wind brought loud splatters of rain. I hoped the *Lyon* would not be affected. But of course, Captain Peirce would do nothing foolish. And Mr. Wilson would be safe. He'd get to England and return with his wife.

It was all part of the historical record.

At some point, I needed to see to Mrs. Alcock and help her somehow. But my chores came first.

The men had risen early, but the girls came down just before breakfast. As I ladled out porridge, I peeked at their faces.

Little Anne's eyes were red. Had I heard her crying in the night? Between the wind and occasional showers, it was hard to hear. But seeing her, I knew the truth.

I didn't know anything about Mr. Wilson's family, only that he had a wife. I suspected it might be a second wife—Puritan families were occasionally cobbled together to give a full set of parents to a mishmash of children. Women died in childbirth, or men were taken by sickness.

I could only guess why Anne had been crying. Was it the trip she was facing?

By now the men had washed, and if my eyes were not deceiving me, had trimmed their beards. Winthrop was wearing the white falling band that he normally only wore on the Sabbath or on Court days. Even Stephen looked neat, though Adam was his usual smiling, careless self, his stockings puddled around his ankles.

Winthrop led a blessing over the food and everyone pitched in. Anne picked at hers, but her father simply frowned and said nothing. Stephen and Adam cleaned up every bit of their porridge, as usual.

Afterward, I asked the girls to help me clean up.

"Anne, I suppose you are all ready for your trip," I asked.

Rosalind, the older girl, answered. "Our trunks have been packed three days hence." She cut a glance at her sister, who kept her eyes on the cup she was drying.

"I was very frightened on my voyage here," I confessed.

Anne's eyes widened slightly but her gaze remained focused on her work. Puritan children, I noticed, were not allowed to be foolish. On the other hand, they were allowed to be children.

"I had faith in the captain." I was floundering now. I didn't know what to say to give this child courage and comfort.

What would Mr. Wilson say? What would any preacher say?

Looking unto Jesus the author and finisher of our faith...

Mr. Wilson himself had delved into this verse, translating the Greek for "author" as "captain."

"Jesus is our captain," I said, pulling the last bowl out of the sudsy bucket. "If Jesus is in the boat too, how safe are we?"

"Perfectly safe," Rosalind said, casting a knowing look my way.

"But it's okay to be a little afraid," I said. "The waves can be quite large."

"O-kay?" Anne asked. She finished the last cup and we set all the crockery on the rough-hewn shelf where it was kept.

Oops—when was the word *okay* first used?

"We had great cheer on our trip here," Adam said from behind us, rescuing me. "Enemy ships came and we had to ready the cannon." His chest puffed as if he had given the order himself.

Rosalind cut a look at Adam. "They were not enemy ships."

"We thought they were."

I raised an eyebrow of warning, and the young people dispersed.

Grateful for Adam's interruption, I resumed cleaning. Soon it would be time to begin lunch.

Peter appeared at my shoulder. "We have a few more for the noon meal."

I put off the thought of soup for Mrs. Alcock and stared at a bucket where a wild turkey soaked. Yesterday I'd gutted and plucked it. Now it looked pitiful, not like the fat creature finding its way to American Thanksgivings. I'd brown it over the fire and then braise it with a little pork fat. Otherwise, the turkey would dry out. I had to avoid that somehow.

I had some of the Indian pudding left over. The gooey bluish mixture had received praise. I didn't have time to soak and cook beans, although I could do that for supper. I had two pints of wheat flour from the stores and a large ball of fresh butter Sir Saltonstall had brought as a gift. Cows were beginning to calve and give milk.

I rationed butter in my cooking, using tallow or suet when I could. But it was just begging to be used.

My mouth watered as I remembered the chocolate croissant I'd eaten before the Trip. My last bit of chocolate was safe in my pocket, held against a dire emergency. I couldn't use that. Instead, I reached for a small crock.

Currants. I would mash them, add a little sugar, and just maybe...

I got to work.

~

April 2

Journal

Scott, I have had very little time to myself before I collapse into bed. Hence the gap in my entries. Exhaustion solves one of my problems, at least for now. Well, almost.

We sent off the Lyon and her passengers with a good deal of fanfare, including firing cannons. I remember watching vids of the first space-ships to carry ordinary passengers. It was a big deal back then. Like-wise, a single ship crossing the ocean at this time is a big deal—and there are so many coming and going. I am trying to grasp it all. Having experienced the North Atlantic myself, I understand the danger. Still grappling with the motives of the settlers.

To that end, I have been cultivating the acquaintance of a certain Philip Ratcliffe. Gen looks at him like a veritable rodent, and his own words mark him as a troublemaker. But Gen is clear that he is connected to both Morton and Gardiner, men of influence, and so I am trying to plumb the depths of Winthrop's need to stay on the good side of the king. How powerful are these men, or is this paranoia?

Gen is so busy cooking and cleaning that she has had little opportu-nity for investigations of her own. Her culinary experiments are occa-sionally successful. A recent attempt at croissants failed, in my opinion, but the governor and his guests enjoyed the buttery lumps. Truthfully, if you didn't know what they were supposed to be, you would like them.

Recently she has also been caring for a neighbor who caught a bad chest cold. Gen braved a hard rain to discover the woman alone in a fireless house. She fixed her soup and tea from Winthrop's stash.

As soon as the rain let up, Gen dashed to the beach, returning with two buckets of clams and a satchel full of noxious seaweed. She made a nutritious soup, and we were all blessed, not just Mrs. Alcock, though

Winthrop's sons made faces at the rockweed. The governor squelched the rebellion with a frown.

Tonight Gen asked me, What if Mrs. Alcock is supposed to die, and I save her?

At this moment I feel marooned, as on a desert island. Far from the certainties of math and software. But are those things certain, really? These are metaphysical questions. I can only find relief in one place.

Everything is known from the foundation of the world. Nothing is random, is it?

Chapter 13

The Letter

"We ought to account ourselves knit together by this bond of love and live in the exercise of it."

— John Winthrop, *A Modell of Christian Charity*

THREE DAYS LATER, I plunged into my morning chores, desperate to get to Mrs. Alcock. Yesterday, she'd finished a whole bowl of my hot broth—nothing as good as the cook's onboard ship, but at least hot—and the one-room hovel she lived in with her coughing husband was now warm.

She had a chance.

In the gray dawn light outside, I grabbed a piece of kindling and gasped in pain. A fat splinter had run into my hand. I squeezed my wrist and plucked out the offending needle of pine. A drop of blood emerged, and I sucked at my hand, thankful the thing hadn't run into my implant.

The device was impervious to damage. At least, I thought so. I resumed filling my basket and went back inside the governor's house.

Water, wood. Water, wood. Peter did most of the fetching and chopping; I tended the fire and used much of the water in cooking and cleaning.

"Peter," I asked one day, "what am I doing wrong? The fire gives off so much smoke!"

We lived in a perpetual haze, our clothes perfumed with it.

He didn't know, but the question interested him. The next day I overheard him discussing chimneys and fireplaces with Winthrop.

I did not know there were problems besides smoky hearths until I finally visited Mrs. Alcock and discovered her cold house. Several families had lost their homes when poorly made chimneys caught fire. Mr. Alcock had decided that with the coming of spring (such as it was, it wasn't warm), he could dial the fire back and not risk burning the house down around them.

Seeing this situation, I snagged Peter, and with Winthrop's advice, we came up with a plan to re-mortar the Alcocks' hearth and chimney. The governor also told me to draw from his store of wood to help keep the couple warm.

In between making soup and tea, I begged clamshells from my neighbors, ground them, and gave them to Peter, who made a mortar out of them. For the inside of the house, mud was sufficient. Yesterday, he'd started on the outside, using a paste made with shells.

But all this work was pointless if Mrs. Alcock succumbed.

Was she supposed to die?

I shoved that question to the back of my mind. Peter didn't look worried.

I focused on my kitchen fire. Last evening's fire had gone out, but the ashes still radiated heat. I poked them with a stick of kindling and added a few tiny twigs. Starting a fire from scratch with flint and steel wasn't easy, and most mornings I was able to restart the fire from the embers of the old.

Orange glowed in the ashes. *Yes!* After ten minutes, fingers of flames danced about, and I slowly layered some heavier chunks of oak and pine over the twigs.

Over this, I placed the trivet and a kettle full of spring water.

I dashed out the door, ready to repeat my morning chores for Mrs. Alcock.

I crossed the lane with a basket full of wood and tapped on the Alcocks' door. I did not hear an answer.

I unhooked the simple string latch and entered. Mrs. Alcock was dozing in her chair while her husband still slept, wrapped in a blanket, on their bed. It was early, after all, and I felt only a little embarrassed at the scene. The fire was cold.

She erupted in a noisy chest cough. But she was sitting up, and then she opened her eyes and smiled.

"Good morning, Mrs. Tuttle. A pleasure to see you this day."

I felt her forehead. Her fever was gone.

Tears sprang to my eyes. "Let me get your fire going."

This time, coaxing would not work. I stuck my hand in my pocket and withdrew the flint and steel, but my heart was light.

Mrs. Alcock was going to live.

Back in the muddy lane, I paused and took a deep lungful of the clean sea breeze. Pale pink and delicate orange painted the sky above the ocean, the rising sun just barely visible between the tiny, thatched houses. Even the raucous caw from a gull sounded happy.

Tapping drew my eye. Standing on a huge barrel, Peter was perched halfway up the Alcocks' chimney, a pail of mortar in his hand.

I wandered over. "Can—might I build the fire high now?" I had more questions, but they could wait.

His mouth twitched. "Thou mayest."

The settlers only used *thee* and *thou* when they were being formal or serious. "Thy diligence is commendable, Sir Peter."

He smiled as he reached higher. "'Twill be good enough. The

flames will not leap higher." He laid another scoop of the mortar onto the chimney and smoothed it out. "We must needs speak."

"After breakfast." I'd get my chance.

I put another log on the Alcocks' fire before attending to breakfast. A large scoop of cornmeal had soaked all night, and I set it on the fire for mush—they'd call it porridge in this time period. We still had molasses for flavor. Should I add butter? These questions occupied me while Peter's statement hovered in the back of my mind.

We must needs speak. What about?

Governor Winthrop thanked me for the bowl of yellow sludge when it finally emerged, hot and butter-less. I'd used tallow instead. Milk would have been wonderful, but at the moment, we didn't have a cow and depended on the occasional gifts of neighbors. Winthrop was arranging for more livestock to come over—every ship brought cattle, sheep, pigs, and sometimes even a few horses.

By the time his wife came, he'd be set. I wish I could meet his wife Margaret, but she would be joining him later in the year—after we returned.

We were supposed to Travel again in 1635 for Roger Williams's banishment. I hadn't wanted to—surely there was a way out of it—but now I was unsure. I would love to meet Margaret.

Peter came inside, glanced at me, took a bowl, and filled it himself. "What's up?" he asked after the governor left for errands unknown, closing the latch behind him.

"Just thinking about the second Trip."

Peter nodded and blew on the hot porridge. Finally tried a bite. "Not bad," he said.

"Don't keep me in suspense." I stirred my own breakfast with a wooden spoon.

He downed another bite. "Roger Williams has disappeared."

My shoulders sagged from relief. This was not a surprise. "Salem is my guess." I began to eat. Suddenly I realized I was ravenous and emptied the bowl quickly.

Our diet was monotonous. Bread, "Indian corn," salted meat, seafood. I was hankering after something fresh. Fresh vegetables, berries.

Anything. I struggled to make everything palatable and was happy when simple foods tasted good.

Peter scraped his bowl clean and dunked it into the wash bucket. "Let's take a walk."

The dishes could wait.

I sucked bits of cornmeal from between my teeth as we strolled down the muddy lane, avoiding the worst spots.

"Remind me," Peter said. "What happens on the second Trip?"

A woman was feeding chickens about fifty yards away. Not a problem. She couldn't hear us. "The ministers will try to get Roger Williams to change his mind on the first table and the matter of the king's authority to give them the patent. When they fail, the General Court will act."

"To banish him."

"Yes."

"I remember a winter exile."

I kept my eyes moving, alert to eavesdroppers. "Actually, he would be banished to England, like the rest of those sent away, but the mother country was not a safe place for him. He ran off instead."

Or would run off. I felt a little dizzy. Which reminded me. Mrs. Alcock. Had I saved her life? Had I changed history? And how would we know?

"Peter, about the funding. Our reports. What kind of information—"

Peter slowed, and I looked up. Before us on the road, Winthrop stood talking to Dudley. They didn't notice us, and their conversation looked intense. Winthrop's stance was rigid, though he hadn't raised his voice. I couldn't make out a word, only the murmur of speech.

We drew closer. Dudley's wooly eyebrows dashed up and down as he made his points. Winthrop's jaw worked. He was a calm man; something must truly be disturbing him.

Dudley noticed us, and Winthrop turned. He smiled, but it was strained. He made a motion for us to join them.

"Mr. Tuttle," the governor began. "We shall hold a meeting tonight... " His gaze shifted to me. "Have we any venison? Turkey? I know not the number coming, but it will be large."

Large. All the assistants? Hopefully no more than eight. The dinner table could seat no more.

"Fret not, Governor Winthrop," Peter said politely. "I will assist my wife in preparing the meal."

Even Dudley's expression softened at this. Peter could wield an axe with the best of them and had the calluses to prove it, but he was willing to do woman's work.

I might have thought Puritans would be calcified in regards to women's roles, and perhaps in some ways they were, but I knew Winthrop had a kind heart—and he appreciated it in others.

I bobbed a curtsy, and we returned to the house.

How was I going to feed twelve people? We had no turkey or venison. I had to make sure I had plenty—and not disgrace Winthrop. I couldn't feed them cornmeal mush.

Once in the kitchen, I stared at the shelves and barrels. The largest one was the cornmeal the Indians had brought. Another container held a good amount of pork, enough for several pies. But only two onions and a single sorry-looking turnip were left on the shelf.

I sat on my stool and took ragged breaths. The currants were gone too.

Peter peered in the cornmeal barrel. "Plenty of this."

"We have no bread. Mrs. Alcock has been sick—"

"Cornbread?"

"Not without eggs." Hard hoecake was not an option. I could make baking powder biscuits, but baking powder hadn't been invented yet. My store of wheat flour laughed at me.

I spotted the tiny sack of beans. I could soak the last of the beans, and bake them with the last cup of molasses. But I couldn't seem to move.

"Cheese? I thought we had cheese."

"Winthrop gave away our cheese."

"To the family whose house burnt."

"Yes."

I couldn't think.

Organizing a meal was impossible.

Peter crouched in front of me. "Gen. Breathe."

I obeyed. I breathed.

In, out.

"Slowly. In again."

In, out.

After a minute the haze cleared, and I had a thought. "Money."

"Winthrop will pay for anything we need."

"Not enough time. We need ingredients now."

I struggled to my feet and staggered to our tiny room. The leather cape Candy gave me was full of shillings. It took the work of only a few moments to rip the seams. Soon I had half a dozen shillings in my hands.

Peter's face told me he understood. We both grabbed our cloaks and went to the community storehouse, where a tired, wiry man of uncertain age greeted us.

His gaze sharpened as he seemed to recognize us. "The governor needs supplies?"

Peter spoke to him while I looked over the barrels, crates, and sacks. Such a small amount of food for hundreds of people, everything sold at premium prices. I was now glad we had a garden behind the house. Peter had done much of the physical work while Winthrop himself took charge of sowing the seeds.

The governor knew what things were cold hardy and which were not, and he didn't mind getting his hands in the dirt. But for now, we had a limited diet.

I located some peas and asked for ten pounds.

The master gave me change for the price. "Wheat is dear. I can give you—"

"I will return for wheat. I need eggs."

"Ah, well, I can let the goodwives know when they come around on Thursday. Mayhap one will have pullets too."

Thursday was market day. I nodded and left, feeling claustrophobic. Peter joined me.

"I can make pease porridge. It might be enough." I was tired and it wasn't even noon.

"Perhaps... "

I guessed he hoped some townsfolk would come with something to sell or trade, but it wasn't market day.

"Perhaps we should pray."

I looked at him. He was serious. I shrugged.

"Father, you—thou seest our need and had knowledge of it before we knew ourselves."

Peter fit right in here. The praying was a great bit of theater. But I didn't see anyone around to hear.

"Wouldest thou provide what we need for this day, as thou hast promised. 'Give us this day our daily bread.' So we do pray. Amen."

He blinked and looked at me. "What are we in want of, exactly?"

"We could use some meat. I can make a pie with the salt pork, but we need more than that."

A pork pie would feed only about four hungry men.

A murmur of voices came from around the building. Two men appeared, carrying a bloody carcass. Dirty white puffs and cloven hooves resolved into a sheep. The throat was torn, and there were several ugly gashes on its flanks,

"Halloo," Peter greeted. "How might I be of service?"

We returned to the house two hours later with several choice pieces of mutton wrapped in burlap. The fresh meat was dripping all over Peter, and it was going to be a nightmare to get it all out of his clothes. But seemingly, his prayer had been answered.

Probably random.

We arrived at the house just in time to see a woman I knew by face but not by name. A large basket was hooked over her arm, its contents covered by a cloth.

"What cheer, Goody Biggs," Peter said.

"Good day to you both," she said. Her gaze fell on me. "Mistress Alcock tells me you succored her in her illness."

I nodded stupidly. "'Twas my pleasure."

She tugged on the cloth. Inside were several large loaves of bread.

I gaped.

"Mrs. Alcock asked me to bring the governor bread in her stead, as she has been unable."

I was stupefied. Everything I needed was here. "Thank you."

Surely this was random too. Wasn't it?

In the end, we used the table as a sideboard for the food that Peter and I served. Everyone sat around the parlor and balanced plates on their knees.

Five assistants had come, including Simon Bradstreet, who brought his wife Anne along. She greeted me with a wink, saying she'd help me wash up.

Anne Bradstreet? The first American female poet. I recognized her from church, but I hadn't known who she was. She was young, fresh-faced, with dark hair and eyes, the same coloring as her father, Thomas Dudley.

She was certainly much prettier than he. She was also educated in the classics, and from what I'd read, I suspected she'd outscore every freshman in Cambridge.

Two men I did not know also joined the group. One of them had preached on Sunday. Roger Williams's offense was also theological, so I was not surprised.

Governor Winthrop, Thomas Dudley, Peter, and me brought the number up to a dozen. No, thirteen, as Dixon would show up soon. He would need a plate. Stephen and Adam ate almost as much as full-grown men. Make that fifteen.

We had enough food. The mutton was tough, but I'd basted it with drippings and the last of my mustard. Edible. I lavished the rest of the butter on the bread and sliced it, created a stew thick with peas, and though my pork pie was burnt, the onions on the inside were caramelized and sweet.

The men ate with gusto. Peter did too. We'd even have leftovers for the next day.

The men got down to business, Peter ready with quill and paper to serve as recorder. As I worked in the kitchen, I listened intently. The first topics were mundane. Anne joined me, and though she worked heartily, she glanced back once, revealing that she was also interested in the men's business.

I was drying plates when Roger Williams's name was spoken. I forced myself to continue working, but all my attention was on the other room.

Thomas Dudley's voice was gravelly. "He is a threat to the Company."

Other voices insisted that what the minister had done was grievous.

"The question is Salem," Winthrop clarified. "They have called him to the post of teacher. Do Endecott and the rest even know of his views?"

"Surely they know not of his heresy, or they'd not call him." I didn't recognize the voice.

"Is this a church matter?" Winthrop asked.

Dudley cleared his throat. "How can that be? Salem falls within the Company Charter. It falls within our jurisdiction."

"The church has her sphere, the magistrates have theirs."

"But we punish heresy."

The voices confused me. I could only pick out Dudley and Winthrop in the mix.

"'Tis insulting! He declines to join the church here. We are not good enough for him."

"Aye, these are proper concerns," Winthrop said. "We are to restrain the evil of heresy. And his views touch on the magistrate as well. But I counsel a middle path. Allow the church at Salem to rethink their decision. By suggestion, not by commandment."

"By a strong suggestion," Dudley said.

Anne turned her head. Her expression was keen.

The others seemed to concur with the deputy governor.

Winthrop took a deep breath. "Mr. Tuttle, take a letter to the church at Salem."

Peter dipped his pen in the inkwell.

I knew what the letter said, or at least the gist of it. I grabbed a broom to make it look like I was a normal woman, cleaning.

"Heretofore we have dwelt in mutual Christian love and unity of spirit. But we are disturbed by the news that the church of Salem has chosen a man, to wit, Master Roger Williams, who has created controversy by proclaiming Boston to be no church, on account of it not having separated...."

John Winthrop hesitated. He continued his dictation, each word measured.

I felt the governor's mood. If there was to be strife in the colony, he did not want to be the cause of it.

Chapter 14

Peter

I am obnoxious to each carping tongue
Who says my hand a needle better fits.
A Poet's Pen all scorn I should thus wrong,
For such despite they cast on female wits.

— Anne Bradstreet

PETER WAS AVOIDING ME. At least, that's how it seemed. He'd been so kind in helping me with the food last week for the important meeting.

But now I rarely saw him.

At mealtimes, Winthrop led with a blessing on the food. Peter was there to eat. But then he would slip out after breakfast or the noon meal and claim he had tasks to do. He also participated in evening worship. But then we all went to bed.

The Lord's Day rolled around, and I struggled to make myself presentable. I'd worked all Saturday cleaning the governor's boots and Peter's clothes. His red jerkin was looking sad. I could still see a mark where I'd thrown up on him onboard ship. I spot-cleaned everything and brushed the dirt off as best I could. One day I was going to put everything in the iron pot with some lye soap and really wash it. I kept saying that, anyway. But I feared to ruin the wool.

This morning I was alone in the room, Peter having slipped out before dawn. I combed my hair and flipped it into a bun. Then I tugged on my cap, leaving the ties dangling as so many did.

I fastened my leather cape, repaired after the money raid, and we were off to meeting. Peter smiled at me briefly at the house but ignored me after that, strolling with the governor ahead of me. His red jerkin puckered in the back—it hadn't shrunk, had it?

Maybe Peter had grown more muscles with all the heavy work he did. I wouldn't be surprised.

The sermon was boring until the fellow started talking about the "covenant of works." That piqued my interest because it was a big deal in the 1630s. In a couple of years, Massachusetts would explode with the Anne Hutchinson debacle. That whole affair was largely fought over "works" vs "grace."

I decided to pay attention. Not that we'd be back for Anne Hutchinson's trial. But I had to help prepare those that did come. Sooner or later a proposal would be written. It was a popular topic.

And Dr. Howard would probably be the one to come. Ugh.

"The covenant of works, is God's covenant, made with the condition of perfect obedience, and is expressed in the moral law."

The preacher's Adam's apple bobbed as he spoke. "The Decalogue, or ten commandments, is an abridgment of the whole law, and the covenant of works."

Okay, that made sense. *Do this and live.*

"Why then the law if it cannot save? To lay open sin in the heart..."

It began to come together. Law and grace were not at war. I knew these things, didn't I? In the quiet of the Archives, I could have explained it all, but I don't think I'd truly grasped it until now.

It was all about the heart.

I was a little dazed when service ended and we were all dismissed. I greeted Anne Bradstreet, then hunted down Mrs. Alcock to make sure she was truly recovered and not just making a good show.

"Mr. Alcock still has a cough," she revealed. "Many thanks for your kindness. We are quite well."

I turned and froze.

Peter was talking to Philip Ratcliffe.

We had to talk—but when? Whispered comments at night would not suffice.

My chance did not come till several days later. Governor Winthrop was sending Peter to the Mystic River property to join Dixon in working the land. Peter's job would be to select the homesite and start felling the trees.

I'd spotted them after supper, heads together near a candle, pointing at a parchment. Plans for the house, most probably.

In the end, Winthrop was happy to send me along, saying that the men had to be fed. "Mrs. Alcock will see I want not."

The garden behind the house had been sown, and tiny green cabbage heads dotted several rows. The radishes would be ready first, and I couldn't wait for their tangy crunch. But we'd be gone before the beans were ripe.

Behind the garden was a line of small saplings, apple trees if they survived. Every few days I checked them for signs of life. It seemed a miracle to me that trees could survive the North Atlantic, but almost every ship brought some.

The nights were still cold, and the trees seemed to know this. The swellings on their branches had not yet shed their dark coverings. Flowers would wait.

But elsewhere, maples were covered in pale green gauze, a beacon of hope. The hard grip of winter had loosened, and we were on the precipice of spring.

Up at the Mystic River property, Dixon had cleared and plowed a field for corn. I stashed foodstuffs in Winthrop's small wagon as we would be staying at least one night. I added our wool blankets and a length of oilcloth for bedding. Plus kindling and anything else I thought we'd need.

Peter coaxed the pony as he approached with the harness collar. "Come now, sweet Bella."

Employed for both plowing and pulling the small wagon, Bella disliked the sight of the collar. He opened his hand, and her rubbery lips made short work of whatever treat was there.

He'd bribed her. In any case, it worked, and we were shortly on our way. It was a long trip up to the property on the Mystic River, and we'd have plenty of time to talk. I let Boston vanish behind us before I said anything.

"Peter, about Mrs. Alcock."

"You worried about changing history."

"Yes."

"Remember the waves?"

We'd had this discussion onboard ship. Somehow it had seemed more theoretical then. "Maybe she was supposed to die."

I wasn't a physicist, but cause and effect were linear, weren't they? My present depended on all the events of the past.

His forehead wrinkled. "She's past childbearing age, isn't she?"

"I think so. Her children are grown. Still back in England."

"Well, then. Even if she 'should have' died, her life will be like the tiny wavelets. Or—"

"Or what?"

"Maybe it was meant to be. That we were meant to come here. That you were meant to save her."

I stared at the pony's ears flicking back and forth ahead of us.

Meant to be. I liked that idea. But I had no real reason to believe it. How could something transcend ordinary cause and effect?

And I did not know how to frame my most important question.

We gained the crest of the gentle rise at the top of the neck and headed right, toward what would one day be Cambridge. Deputy Governor Dudley had claimed his rightful four hundred acres there—our college campus, Peter said. Houghton Library and the Archives would sit on his land one day. Thick, naked oaks stood forbiddingly to either side of the track we followed, and tiny bits of green peeped out in the undergrowth. Hard to believe this wilderness would be tamed one day, the only greenery confined to the geometric confines of the space between buildings.

"Peter, you fit in really well." I toyed with the strings of my cap. "Almost like you're a Puritan yourself."

There. I'd said it.

Peter said nothing for a long moment. "I-I told you I'd read the Bible."

Nobody just "read" the Bible. "Was it your grandmother in Salem?"

"Who got me to read it?" Peter shifted on the hard wagon seat. "No."

I tied my cap strings, yanked them apart, then tied them more loosely. Peter sat stiffly beside me, hands on the reins, silent. There was something he wasn't saying.

Finally, his shoulders eased. "Do you know that church way up on Beech Street?"

"I know the old stone church near campus. The museum."

"There's one to the north a few blocks. Red brick and pillars."

"I remember now. I saw a tour group exit the building one Sunday."

"That wasn't a tour group."

I stared at Peter. "A registered church? That close to campus?"

"Yes. One of my professors attended at one time."

"A physics professor?" The thought made me dizzy. How could a physics professor believe the Bible?

Peter nodded but didn't say more.

We were in dangerous territory. I was allowed to study and teach the theology of the Puritans because I didn't truly believe it.

I'd signed a form to that effect. A legally binding form.

I did not press Peter as we continued our journey. Instead, I absorbed the scenery, hoping for a glimpse of wildlife. Once, I spotted a rustle of black-and-white fur, and before I could recoil in shock, the skunk was gone.

Good.

But there was little else to distract me in the landscape. Peter's admission—such as it was—was troubling.

Had he signed a similar form regarding his beliefs? What did he believe, anyway? If he simply "knew" these things he wouldn't be averse to talking about it. But if he was a Christian, that was another thing entirely.

Christians were registered, controlled. They had to be. The ideas in the Bible were dangerous. Hadn't they torn England apart in this time?

I cut a glance at Peter, quietly guiding the pony, his strong yet graceful hands on the reins. His dark curls lay innocently on his brow.

Could I get him to explain?

The rest of the journey felt awkward, and finally hearing the *thwack, thwack* of an axe biting wood was a relief. The trees fell away to reveal a half-cleared area about the size of the Yard. Random stumps formed an obstacle course for the wagon.

"Halloo!" called Dixon, his lanky arms surrendering the axe. He stretched. "Have ye victuals? Cider?"

I liked Dixon. His ears stuck out to either side of his head, giving him the appearance of someone who could hear well, but the opposite was often true. Dixon had highly selective hearing, but a mention of food would not go ignored.

"Plenty," I declared. "Cold pork pie." I also had cornbread. Always the stiff, chewy cornbread—even with eggs it was barely palatable. Mrs. Alcock was teaching me the knack of making wheat bread. At least with wheat, you had the chance it would rise.

"I hooked a bass this morning," Dixon said.

Peter released the pony and tied her so she could reach the best grass. Dixon built a fire and we cooked what proved to be a large fish. Peter led in prayer, and we dug in. At the end of the meal, we were replete. Stuffed, even.

"Dixon," Peter said. "The governor desires me to select the site for the house."

Dixon wiped his mouth with his sleeve. "I know a fair place."

Leaving the pony to graze, we tromped about, our first destination the river. The Mystic's broad ripples were calm, the brackish estuary smell speaking of the ocean. A bright white spot proved to be a swan, perched on a stack of sticks on the other bank. Overhead, a hawk cruised.

And it was quiet save for the chirping of birds and insects. In my time, it would be noisy and smelly, the lone trees refugees from their past dominion.

Dixon led us to a flat area between the river and the field. Beech and red oak circled the small clearing.

"How far is it to water?" Peter asked.

Dixon pointed. "A few yards that way is a stream."

"Perfect."

The rest of the afternoon we worked to clear the area. Peter gave me a hoe, and I chopped rather ineffectually at the underbrush. Finally, Dixon offered me fishing gear.

"Thank you!" I dusted off my hands. This I could do. Maybe.

In the end, I was successful, because the estuary teemed with life.

By now I was game to do anything, and I stuck my fingers in the mud for worms or grubs with no hesitation. The instant the bait touched the water, a ripple or a tug resulted. Often I lost the bait entirely.

But a few times I jerked a fish onto the bank. We'd eat well tonight.

A shape dropped to the bank beside me. Peter.

The light was low and long, golden against the tree trunks on the other side of the river.

"I couldn't tell you everything," he said.

"You're a Christian," I blurted.

He looked at me, his dark eyes shadowed. "I meet with others to read the scriptures."

I opened my mouth and closed it again.

"We call ourselves the Way." Peter's voice was low. Not that he'd get in trouble here.

"That sounds kind of familiar."

"The book of Acts. Before they were called Christians in Antioch they used that term."

I tossed the fishing line out for a final time. "So. You're a Christian."

Peter watched the river silently.

"Look, I won't tell. I won't tell if you're unregistered. I know you're not dangerous."

"I will be caught one day. Many of us are."

The line tugged, and the rod almost slipped from my grasp. Peter helped me drag in a huge bass, five pounds if it was an ounce.

I'd cover for Peter. I had to.

Chapter 15

Ratcliffe

"...no King, nor Caesar, have any power over the consciences or souls of their subjects, in the matters of God and the crown of Jesus."

— Roger Williams, *The Bloudy Tenent of Persecution*, 1644

MAY SPED by in a flurry of showers, hard work, and new settlers. Every few weeks a new ship docked with new people. Each time, livestock limped down the gangway, and men hefted crates of supplies to the community store. The rat-tat-tat of hammering sounded almost every day. Some folks put up hasty shelters, but the governor did everything in his power to get decent housing built. He knew what winter was like.

One night, I woke feeling strange. Alone.

I reached for Peter, but the blanket entangled me, and I flailed briefly to get my arm loose.

No Peter.

The night was young. After so long without artificial light, I could sense the passage of time at night. I knew when it was almost dawn, and this wasn't it.

I got out of bed and felt my way to the rickety door. I pulled it open carefully and slipped out into the black space of the kitchen.

The banked kitchen fire glowed, and the fire in the parlor formed a second blob of light. Their pale glow revealed shapes. I took several steps toward the parlor.

My suspicion was confirmed.

Yes, someone was sleeping on the parlor bed.

Idiot Peter. Just like onboard ship, where he ended up sleeping on the deck.

I couldn't deceive myself any longer. Despite our long days and exhaustion, it was too weird to sleep together, and in another week or two "bundling" would begin to get too warm anyway.

Despite his beliefs, Peter was the wise one.

I sighed and went back to bed. Tomorrow I'd make sure he had enough bedding.

~

May 15

Journal

Scott, the corn is planted. Last week, I went to the Mystic River homestead and helped Dixon plant and chop wood for fencing. Then we worked on the foundations of the house but didn't get far. We need a copious amount of stone for the foundation and the hearths. Dixon had saved what emerged from the soil in his plowing, and we went to the river for more.

I'm back in town, but my arms and back are still aching. I sleep in the parlor now, a better situation all around. It's not as cold now, and in any case, I rise early, so Winthrop hasn't noticed. I write my entries in the privacy of the room first, and by the time I finish, Gen is usually asleep.

She is amazing. Pay no attention to Dr. Howard. She has not complained once, and there is plenty to complain about. The work, the smell, the diet. As servants Winthrop treats us gently. He believes we are of the "better" class, not used to such labor, and his commands seem mere suggestions.

My respect for these people grows exponentially. True, some flee bad situations, but those situations would instantly improve if they would only conform. Toe the line.

But they won't.

For Roger Williams vis-a-vis John Winthrop, it seems only a matter of degree. On top of which, Winthrop is the chief magistrate. Whatever he decides affects more than just himself. One of the perennial arguments is what constitutes a true church. Winthrop maintains that there is a difference between a false church and an impure one. He regards the Church of England as merely impure. Just as David would not harm Saul, Winthrop will not speak against the king in his role as head of the Church.

Roger Williams may still be in Salem, but Gen tells me he will go to Plymouth any time now. You would think it would be ideal for him, but from the little I was able to study before we left, he won't reside in Plymouth all that long either.

We are doing well, but I am counting down the days to our return. With one caveat.

Gen knows. But just about me.

In my defense, I can only say that she guessed. And when asked, I could not lie.

Something was going to happen on Court Day coming up in a week. I remembered Winthrop's journal said something about Ratcliffe. Peter had confessed to speaking to the man a time or two.

"At first, I thought Winthrop might just be paranoid," he

explained. "But some of the letters he writes to friends in England make me wonder." He paused. "They don't burn anyone at the stake, do they?"

I scratched under my cap. I hoped I was just imagining the itch. A shipload of passengers had emerged from the latest ship infested with lice. The delousing had just begun.

"No, Peter. They don't burn people at the stake in this century. Branding, whipping, the pillory are more likely. Hanging for capital crimes like murder."

Murder—and treason, and witchcraft, and heresy. But who defined heresy?

"But you said—"

"Yes, some of these ministers are fleeing for their lives. They were afraid things were reverting to the nasty days of 'Bloody Mary.' But only a few ministers were actually killed."

"Parliament is dissolved, you said."

"Yep. These men have no idea what will happen. The winds of change have shifted against them, and they only know of Bishop Laud's hatred. Once he becomes archbishop, he is that much more powerful. They have no security, no idea what they will face if caught."

Peter seemed to hesitate. "Gen," he said softly, "have you any chocolate left?"

I searched my pocket. The packet of chocolate emerged with some difficulty, the oilcloth having been jammed into the seam. Lint covered the surface, but the insides felt intact. I brought it to my nose.

The aroma flooded my brain. I was wrenched back to my own time, walking on a modern Boston sidewalk with a chocolate croissant. Dizziness blurred Winthrop's house.

"You okay?"

I nodded. "I've almost forgotten modern food. The modern world."

"Just two more weeks. Hang in there."

Peter slipped out the door, and I sought to focus. I glanced at the stairs, thinking about the musty rooms. It had drizzled for weeks, but today the sun had come out. Tomorrow I would air out the house and beat the bed rugs.

I was becoming a housekeeper. I actually kind of liked it. I pondered the upcoming Court once more. I couldn't remember the issues they'd discuss. Only Ratcliffe. But I'd get the house ready.

Then we'd go home, and everything would go back to normal. Except I knew something about Peter I couldn't unknow.

I'd deal with it later.

By the time the day for Court rolled around, the house was clean. Peter had given me gloves, and I was even able to wipe down the stones of the fireplaces wearing them. I had no true furniture polish, but I scrubbed the dining table with vinegar and then rubbed it with linseed oil till it gleamed.

I swept the parlor floor, then poured little puddles of vinegar at discrete intervals, wiping the pine planks with burlap. After an hour the dirt was gone, and there was a crick in my neck. Someone needed to invent a mop.

But we were leaving. Mops were the least of my worries.

The assistants began arriving shortly after the noon meal. Men I recognized from church—and some I didn't—milled about outside. Borrowed chairs filled the parlor, and the long dining table had been placed in front of the stairs as a courtroom bench. Behind it sat Winthrop, Dudley, Bradstreet, and another one of the assistants.

A man I did not recognize entered the house, tracking in dirt, but any ire I might have felt quickly faded. His clothes were not flashy, but something about the way he dressed and walked made me think of pictures of Sir Walter Raleigh. A late medieval man, wearing a wide falling band and a jerkin like Peter's, only green. But unlike Raleigh, his hat was plain, a simple dark cap. His facial hair was sparse, a mustache and a simple goatee. But there was energy in his bearing.

His dark gaze swept the room and lingered on several faces.

"What cheer, Mr. Endecott." Winthrop gave him a hearty greeting, and the others echoed the sentiments.

Endecott. Former governor and leading man of Salem. A Puritan of the Puritans, perhaps more radical in his positions than Winthrop. A better match for Roger Williams than Winthrop himself, which is why Williams had gone there.

Was Endecott angry about the letter?

As I fetched ale and heated water for tea, I gauged the atmosphere of the room. Endecott was a magistrate, not an officer of the church in Salem, and yet, I wondered. He'd probably read—or at least heard about—the letter. His face was peaceful enough.

So why was there tension in the room? Men of the town had filed in and now stood along the walls—there were not enough seats for all —and gossiped among themselves. I watched their faces and discerned that Endecott's presence was like a stone thrown in water. They knew something I didn't.

The door was propped open to let in light, and I spotted several men outside. One I recognized. Philip Ratcliffe. He stood unbound between two hefty men, essentially a prisoner ready to come before the judge.

Peter fetched the portable writing desk and sat on a stool not far from the open door, a good place for light. He'd be serving as Winthrop's—and the Court's—secretary.

Several minor matters were dealt with first, then John Endecott was summoned to stand before the now-shiny dining room table and the man sitting behind it.

"Governor Endecott." Winthrop gave him his former title, out of courtesy, and I had the suspicion that whatever was coming, Winthrop wanted to tone it down, cut a deal. "I have heard a grave rumor regarding a certain Thomas Dexter."

"Indeed, Governor, I was too rash in my actions. I am a hasty man, and I struck him. The insolent fraud well deserved it"—here he smiled briefly and glanced at the assistants—"but as a Justice of the Peace I should not have beaten him. It was unlawful." He dipped his head to Winthrop. "I bow before the mercy of the Court."

Assault. Endecott, despite his smiles and bearing, was guilty of assault, and I knew Winthrop aspired to be evenhanded in meting out justice. Rich and poor received the same punishments, save for the fact that sometimes the poor could not afford fines. They received other punishments in those cases.

Other punishments could include whipping. Boston had no jail, not yet. In fact, Endecott could be stripped of his office as magistrate in view of the nature of the crime. But would Winthrop and the others dare do such a thing? Boston's relationship with Salem was already fraught because of the letter.

The room was silent except for the creaking of a chair and the *scritch* of Peter's pen.

Winthrop took an audible breath. "Brother. I know you for a just man. However"—he sat back in his seat—"the assistants concur on punishment." He turned to Simon Bradstreet.

"A fine," the latter read from his notes. He gave the amount.

The whole room seemed to sigh. Endecott had gotten off lightly. No public humiliation, no physical blows. Just a fine. A reasonable fine, in fact.

It was a light sentence.

I was still pondering the implications when the next case was called.

"Philip Ratcliffe, approach the bench."

Philip Ratcliffe was not a "mister," and even the more common courtesy title "goodman" had been omitted. Perhaps because of the irony.

Ratcliffe stood before the table, dirty, his hair standing at angles. Those men outside may have roughed him up, not intentionally, perhaps, but simply in order to get him here. Ratcliffe straightened his wiry frame and stared at Winthrop.

"Philip Ratcliffe," Winthrop said. "We hear grave charges against you. But we will not pass judgment without the testimony of two or three witnesses."

Ratcliffe smirked, but I read nervousness in his stance. Winthrop called the first witness, a man I did not recognize, who proved to be from Salem.

"This man has brought calumny against our settlement and especially our church." The man began a halting list of charges. Some of the things were merely foolish name-calling, the things I'd heard myself. But in an era where heresy could be mixed up with treason in one nasty legal dish, it was serious enough.

Winthrop leaned forward. "Is he a drunkard or a fornicator?"

The man shook his head. "Not to my knowledge."

The next witness was called, Mr. Pond of Watertown, who looked like a scrawny student, all knees and elbows. Winthrop asked a few questions, and the young man answered. It was all the same complaint. I kept my gaze on Ratcliffe, who like Tolkien's Gollum, was surely capable of significant mischief.

When Pond finished, Ratcliffe said, "This is all hearsay. And this court has no authority, forbye. The Charter is a fraud."

My mouth hung open. He had just condemned himself. The sound in the room swirled around me. I took a deep, steadying breath. Blew it out gently.

Winthrop stood, his expression grave, and after a few seconds, the room quieted. He sat and his gaze swung to Peter.

"Next witness. Mr. Peter Tuttle."

Chapter 16

The Implant

"That from henceforth for ever, there shalbe one Governor, one Deputy Governor, and eighteene Assistants of the same Company, to be from tyme to tyme constituted, elected and chosen out of the Freemen of the saide Company..."

— *The Charter of Massachusetts Bay, 1629*

PETER ROSE, gave the writing desk to Winthrop, and returned to his seat near the door. "I am ready."

The governor squinted at the shorthand on Peter's paper but neglected to give the record-keeping task to anyone else. "What know ye of Philip Ratcliffe? His character? His speech?"

Peter began. Much of what he said echoed what I'd heard that one picnic day. I shifted my attention to Ratcliffe, who scowled at Peter.

I didn't trust him.

"I asked him about the situation in England. About Morton, Gardiner, and the others he called his friends. According to him, the Charter is not valid because of competing claims."

Winthrop lifted a hand. "Mr. Dudley, will you explain these claims for the information of the Court?"

"Sir Gorges claims to have an interest here. His company was disbanded in 1624. But his grant was to the region north of the Merrimack River. North of our boundaries."

"Continue, if you please, Mr. Tuttle."

"Ratcliffe has confessed to me his plan—"

"Hearsay! Hearsay!" The Rat's red face twisted in anger.

Peter seemed to falter. Then he took a breath. "His plan is to meet with 'his powerful friends' as he terms them. He wants to see the Charter revoked and all the assistants punished by the king." He paused. "I saw Ratcliffe pass a small object, possibly a letter, to a ship's captain."

"False! He speaks falsehood!" Ratcliffe cried, taking a step toward Peter, but one of the sturdy men nudged him back to stand before the bench.

Murmurs around the room grew as the assistants gave each other meaningful glances.

Next to the governor, Simon Bradstreet scowled and rubbed his forehead. "What a tangle."

But Winthrop had made up his mind. I could read it in his face. Ratcliffe was doomed.

The scoundrel's expression told me he knew his fate. He jumped for the door, evading his escorts. Metal flashed in his uplifted hand.

Peter stepped to intercept him, hands raised.

"No!" I heard myself cry.

Then Peter was on the floor, the Rat was out the door, and the roar of tromping boots and men's shouts filled my brain. Endecott launched himself over Peter in order to reach the door.

Ratcliffe's guards followed, joined by Bradstreet and some of the bystanders.

A cup hit the floor and spun, flinging drops of ale.

Men dodged both the cup and Peter's body on their way out. I dove for Peter and was clipped on the shoulder by one of the exiting men.

No one wanted to see Ratcliffe escape, but Peter was injured.

I helped him sit up. His forearm was bleeding, and his left hand was covered in blood. I tore off my apron and grabbed my eating knife. I hacked off a long strip of cloth.

"Vinegar," Peter prompted, gripping his forearm. His face was covered with droplets of sweat.

I was barely aware of Winthrop as he crouched nearby, a line between his brows. As I dribbled cider over the ugly slice on Peter's wrist—vinegar sounded too harsh to use as a disinfectant—the governor nodded approvingly.

"I will leave you in the loving care of your wife," he said to Peter and returned to the table, where Dudley remained alone of all the assistants. The parlor was almost empty.

Peter winced as I bound his wound. "The implant. It popped out. It's gone."

"What?" I knotted the linen bandage. It should do for now. "Your implant? What? Where? Where did it go?"

Peter slid to his knees and began to search the floor. It was filthy after the gathering and the stampede out the door. Lumps of dried mud clustered near the door where he'd fallen. But I saw a tiny glimmer.

I snatched it up. It was too small. It was only a piece of the implant.

Oh, no.

Peter and I continued searching. The expanse of pine floor loomed forbiddingly, the dirty boards forming a puzzling landscape. Which lump was a piece of the implant?

Slowly, the hum of conversation behind me resolved into words.

"A wise decision," Dudley was saying.

Would we ever get back? Could Peter and I return on the strength of one implant?

How did they work, anyway?

"The Almighty overruled. I could not strip him of his office, that would be an unseemly overreach. Bless him, Endecott is a man prone to temper. All saints may fail."

Peter lunged, picked something up, and placed it in my hands. A mere shard.

I closed my eyes, thinking of all the vigorous men stomping out the door. No one in my century had tested the implants under the force of multiple hobnailed boots.

"And now Endecott will support us." Dudley's voice.

"He ought to in any case. He is a good man."

"What of Williams?"

But Dudley's question was not answered, for Endecott marched in just then.

"The miscreant has escaped."

Behind him, the other assistants filed in. Peter joined me in a corner of the kitchen.

I held out my hands, revealing the collected pieces of twenty-first-century technology. Shattered.

Peter took a deep breath. He was pale. In shock, and not just from the injury.

"Come," I said. "Let's take a walk."

I led the way to the new stable, rubbing my bruised shoulder. The building smelled of pine and fresh manure. The horses were out in the fenced yard, nibbling on whatever green bits they could find.

Peter hesitated at the stable doorway, then turned toward the animals.

Bella the pony lifted her head. She took several steps toward Peter, and he met her in the middle of the paddock. She nuzzled him, and he stroked her neck.

I wished at that moment that I could be the one comforting Peter.

Why was he more open, more affectionate, with an animal?

My chest ached. Maybe Peter just didn't like me. Not *that* way.

We were colleagues only.

~

June 13

Journal

Scott, it has taken a whole day to digest what has happened.

I was attacked. With a knife. Right at the place where the implant had been inserted. It popped out, and that would not have been a problem, but in that instant, it was trampled by a score of heavy feet.

We collected the pieces.

We have not been exposed in any way. Everyone was too distracted by the event to notice. This happened during June's Court at which Philip Ratcliffe was tried. I testified, and the "Rat," as Gen calls him, took out his wrath on me before he fled.

According to her, he will have his ears chopped off and will be shipped to England. In the meantime, they are looking for him. I know, chopping off someone's ears sounds barbaric. But if you had been here, you would have feared for his life. I am convinced of Winthrop's brilliance and moderation as a magistrate.

But now we are unsure of our return. In only seven days we will try it using only a single implant as the tracking hook to bring us home.

I tried to explain to Gen that the implant was merely a locator beacon. It's more than that, but the mathematics only obscure the reality. We do have a good chance on just one implant, especially as both our energies belong in the twenty-first century. Going back takes less energy than coming.

Like releasing a coiled spring. Or rolling down a hill. I used both analogies with Gen.

But the fact is, even a stone going down a hill needs a nudge to get going.

Scott, if I don't survive the return, do me a favor. Take care of Gen.

She is so capable and vulnerable at the same time. Just be there.

Encourage her in her hopes. I know she would do great defending a thesis. She's born for that sort of thing. I know you and I regard a sheepskin as a means to an end, but in her case, it's that and more. She'd enjoy it. It would be a validation, an affirmation, and maybe even a bulwark against Dr. Howard's comments.

I don't know what she believes, exactly. But she knows a lot. In her head. I don't have to tell you to be cautious. I know you are.

I will give Gen the journal to carry back.

If I don't see you soon, I will see you later.

Peter

The days crept by. Or sped by. The final week seemed alternately to go by fast and slow. We attended meeting on the Lord's Day and planned for a trip to the Mystic the next day to work on the house.

"This is perfect," Peter said as he harnessed the animals after breakfast. Winthrop now had two ponies and a mare. The latter had arrived gaunt and dispirited after the trip over the North Atlantic, but care and plenty of grass had perked her up. Her ribs still showed, but her coat was beginning to shine. "Perfect for our exit," he continued. "The Mystic property is our recommended departure site anyway."

I knew what he meant. We couldn't just walk down a Boston lane and vanish into thin air. Someone would see us.

"We can go foraging."

"It should be easy."

I could tell he was still trying to comfort me after the loss of his implant, the shards of which were still in my pocket. He'd explained that returning was like rolling downhill.

Rolling downhill could be dangerous, in my view. Without an implant, I'd have to grab him and hang on. And hope for the best.

He was putting a brave face on it.

Winthrop saddled the mare while we stocked the wagon with

boards, kegs of nails, and sufficient foodstuffs for a three-day expedition. Stephen and Adam were assigned to help with a neighbor's garden, and soon we were on our way.

The sun came out from behind the clouds. It was cool when we started, but it promised to be a warm day. Finally.

"Peter, it's June. Why isn't it warmer?"

"The Little Ice Age."

Winthrop rode ahead of us on the barely visible track. We kept our voices low.

"What's that?" I wanted to encourage him and get him talking.

"The climate was warm when the Vikings settled in Greenland, about a thousand years ago. Over the centuries it cooled. They left Greenland, and the Thames River in Britain froze solid in the winter. Things didn't really get warm again until the Victorian Age."

"Valley Forge." Things were cold for Washington.

"That was the tail end."

I should have known this. I wonder if Candy did. No wonder the settlers wore wool all the time. And no wonder so many had died. It wasn't just the lack of central heat. It was actually colder then. Now, that is.

"Thought of a dissertation topic?"

Peter was so kind. "I'm mainly thinking of our reports." Truthfully, I hadn't been thinking much about either. Looking at Winthrop's back while discussing our reports made me feel discombobulated. It seemed impossible now to write a dispassionate thesis about this man. He was a flesh-and-blood individual, a complex man living in a different time.

Tomorrow was our official return date. But Peter had explained that the exact date wasn't as important on a return. Travelers could return at any time without adding much risk.

So today, tomorrow, the next day. Whatever.

The trees thickened on either side, their leaves blocking the sun. It was beautiful here, and I would miss it.

We arrived around noon, judging by the sun, and I dove into meal preparations. An hour later saw us at the house site. The governor discussed building plans with Peter and Dixon, while I sat and enjoyed the breeze and the hum of insects.

"Mr. Perkins will help with the framing next week," Winthrop said.

Soon Dixon got to work on a root cellar while Peter mortared stones into place on a chimney. I went to the river for more stones. After ten trips, I was exhausted. I found a grassy spot and lay back. The afternoon sun felt good at first, but after a while I was baking. I got up and wandered through the trees, inhaling their crisp, woodsy scents.

"Mrs. Tuttle." It was Winthrop, wiping his forehead with a kerchief. He must have been looking for shade as well.

"Hello."

"I want to thank you for your labors." His tone sounded hesitant, awkward. "Mr. Tuttle—and you—have eased my straitened circumstances in diverse ways."

"I-I feel privileged to serve, Governor."

"Your hands."

My left hand, reddened from work, rested on the bark of a huge red oak. I snatched it away. "Mrs. Alcock gave me a salve which has helped greatly." I found nothing else to say, but simply stood silent for a moment, enjoying the canopy above our heads. "This country—these trees—are beautiful. Wild, but breathtaking."

Winthrop simply looked at me, and I babbled. "I never enjoyed botany, I preferred other subjects. I never considered how beautiful trees could be. But now? 'I thought all the trees were whispering to each other, passing news and plots along in an unintelligible language.'"

Winthrop raised a brow. "I know not the writer."

Oh, no. J.R.R. Tolkien was not born yet. "An unknown fellow."

"I like it. 'Passing news.' The Psalms portray trees as living beings in the most poetical parts. Tell me, Mrs. Tuttle, was it worth coming here?"

I thought of the North Atlantic, the vomit, the fear. "There have been moments—"

"Only moments?" John Winthrop was smiling, and I rejoiced to see it. He rarely smiled.

"Long moments."

He laughed then, a hearty guffaw. He wiped his eyes. "Long moments. Thank you. This has been a very long year indeed, but I confess that you and the gossiping trees do cheer me." He sighed, but it was a contented sigh that gladdened my heart. "Now I must commune with my wife."

He turned and wandered off. Late afternoon was a set time he tried to set aside to think of his wife, a mystic communion I used to find weird when reading about it. But knowing the man—the real man —I didn't think it strange anymore.

I walked back to the clearing, where I discovered a sweaty Peter drinking from the cider jug.

He offered it to me.

"Thanks."

"I have a present," Peter said. "From the Bradstreets, actually." In his hand was a wrapped lump. "Soap. Good soap, I mean."

Did good soap exist in this time period? "Like French soap?"

"I don't know. European, most probably."

I felt the tiny paper-wrapped package. Slightly squishy, but only slightly. "I am so filthy."

"The Mystic River is still cold."

Winthrop would be meditating for a while.

"I don't care. Let's go."

We left a smiling Dixon with his fishing tackle, in charge of supper. "I'll catch a big 'un."

"Let's go upstream a bit," Peter said. "Out of sight."

I couldn't disrobe entirely, but I could at least peel off the wool and wash myself and my linen shift. I must smell ripe. Many in the colony did now that it was warmer. So did Peter.

He led the way a few yards above the Mystic River beach, keeping his eye out for a secluded spot.

"How far does Winthrop's property extend?" I asked.

"Just a little farther. Mr. Craddock's place is somewhere beyond it."

Craddock. That was a familiar name. An investor, a good guy, but there was something bad associated with him too. I couldn't remember the problem.

We circled a thicket.

"There." Peter pointed. A rocky outcrop extended into the river, interrupting the current and forming a pool of water behind it. The gleaming mud of the bank was interrupted by only a couple of rocks. Perfect.

My feet propelled me down to the river. I tugged at the strings of my bodice as I took the last few steps.

"Wait." Peter's voice was low and urgent.

Then I saw him.

Ratcliffe.

Chapter 17

The Return

"At this court one Philip Ratcliffe, a servant of Mr. Cradock, being convict, ore tenus, of most foul, scandalous invectives against our churches and government, was censured to be whipped, lose his ears, and be banished the plantation, which was presently executed."

— John Winthrop, *Journal*

I STOOD ON THE WET, muddy bank of the Mystic River and took a quick breath of briny air. Ratcliffe's beady eyes were fixed on me. Then his gaze shifted to Peter behind me.

"Trespassers, methinks I see." Ratcliffe's smile was chilling.

Half-hidden by saplings, a small boat floated next to the bank. Apparently, the Rat had been up and down the river.

Peter joined me. "Are we indeed on Mr. Craddock's property?" He touched my elbow.

"Tellest thou me, mister surveyor man." Ratcliffe secured his craft to a sapling and turned back to us. "Perhaps it is a happy chance that brought us together."

Happy for whom? I focused on my breathing.

In... out. In... out. It wouldn't do to get worked up now.

"We hunt for a place to bathe," Peter said. "We will leave you now."

"I think not." The Rat's face twisted. "You spied on me. Lied to the governor."

Peter's hand hooked my elbow more securely, and he took a step away from the water. But he didn't answer Rat.

It all happened so quickly after that.

Ratcliffe jumped for Peter, and I stumbled. Peter swung his fist, but the Rat ducked. They sprang apart and shifted warily for a few moments.

Then Rat pulled out a glinting object.

The knife.

What could I do? I thrust my hands into my pockets and felt the shards from the implant. My eating knife. Flint and steel for fire. The soap, and below it, my chocolate.

Grinning, Ratcliffe took a wide swing at Peter with the knife, and Peter jumped back. The villain sidestepped and did it again, like a cat toying with a mouse.

I couldn't use my eating knife against a strong man. Frantically, I pulled out my chocolate and clutched it stupidly.

Ratcliffe lunged, and they grappled a moment. Peter stumbled and slumped to the ground.

I held the wrapped chocolate aloft as a talisman. "I warn you, O miscreant! Thou cursed of the Lord!"

I stepped over Peter's sprawled form. "I have the second sight! I see thee, Philip Ratcliffe—"

"A witch, I knew it!" His finger flew out in accusation.

"O, worse than that. I know your future." I was making it up as I went.

Sudden doubt shaded his expression. I pressed my advantage.

"Flee, lest a worse thing befall thee!" I curled my lips in a snarl. I might as well look the part.

Ratcliffe hesitated, then turned and jumped in his boat. He pushed away, but I did not watch him leave. Heart hammering, I knelt in the mud at Peter's side.

Was he hurt? He was lying partially curled, his face hidden.

"Peter, Peter."

I gently turned him over. His eyelids fluttered, and he made an effort to rise.

"He's gone. We're safe." I didn't see any blood—oh.

There it was.

Ratcliffe had stabbed him in the gut. I hadn't seen it at first. Peter's jerkin was red.

There wasn't much blood, but it was increasing, spreading, a darker red against the red.

I took a deep breath. Then another.

We had to leave. Right now.

"Just lay back, Peter." I stretched out on top of him, and he groaned. I hooked my arm around his neck and grabbed the wrist with the implant. I pressed the implant three times, my cheek against Peter's face.

"Return, now."

I woke to the bright light of Quarantine. A medical biosafety suit hung limp on the wall. I was on a bed in one of the bedrooms. I pushed myself up, and the room started spinning. The cold smell of disinfectant made me nauseated.

I lay back down, and the sheet underneath me crackled. Peter— where was Peter?

I sat up again and ignored the spinning.

"Lie down," spoke a robotic voice. "Lie down."

A RoboMedic stood at the foot of the bed. I hadn't noticed it when

Peter had given me the tour. Like Tollers, it looked slightly disreputable. Probably refurbished.

"Medic," I spoke firmly. "Tell me where Peter Donatelli is."

A green light flashed in its eye ports. Clicking, robotic arms bent and swung, accessing drawers in its boxy torso. Steel fingers readied a hypo before my eyes, a green fluid filling the glass chamber.

"What's that?"

"Nothing you need be concerned about," wheedled the machine. "Something to help you relax. You are clearly upset."

I slid off the bed. "I refuse treatment." I felt tired and filthy, but I didn't need a shot.

"You were hysterical on the launchpad," the medic informed me.

I didn't remember that. The last thing I remembered was pressing the implant.

"Quarantine AI," I said. "Locate Peter Donatelli."

"He's in the hospital," a voice said—a real voice, only slightly muffled.

I turned. Inside the biosafety suit was a familiar face—Scott Rice. His dark face was such a welcome sight my vision blurred with moisture.

"Oh, Scott. You are such a sight for sore eyes. How is Peter?"

"He'll be fine. They took him in a biosafety bubble to the hospital. He's being stitched up."

"The journal—"

"I got it—everything's uploaded."

I sat on the bed. Everything would be fine. Peter would be fine. Relief trickled through my body. "What happened to me? I don't remember the launchpad."

"The RoboMedic got to you right after the disinfectant protocol. You were calling for help, and the medic decided that not only did Peter need help, you did too. It injected a sedative."

He turned to the robot. "Medic, list the treatments given to patient Geneva Fielding."

The green lights flashed. "Ambiance, 10 mg by injection. Sodium ascorbate solution—"

"Thank you. Diagnosis?" Scott asked.

"Mild scurvy, parasites. Skin irritation. Panic disorder."

I snorted. "What? How is being concerned about a serious injury a panic disorder?"

The machine did not respond.

Scott spoke. "I'll make sure you get something decent to eat."

"Thanks, Scott. Thank you." Tears of gratitude returned to my eyes.

He left.

"Weeping is a side effect of Ambiance," the robot announced.

"Oh, shut up."

The Quarantine bathroom was complete with a counter, toilet, and shower. Inside, I found some clean clothes: a T-shirt and a pair of sweatpants with a drawstring, both men's medium in size. At least I'd be covered.

My clothes were not only filthy, they were stiff with the disinfectant we'd been sprayed with upon our arrival. I didn't know if Candy would be able to rehabilitate anything.

Peter's red jerkin was definitely ruined now. My heart contracted at the thought.

I unpinned my partlet and took it off, unlaced my bodice, removed the outer garment, and folded everything on the CarbonLam counter. The pockets hung on me, tied by their strings around my waist.

I didn't want to relinquish everything. Without trying to analyze my feelings, I extracted their contents.

The smashed implant could go, but I decided to keep the rest. The flint and steel, the little knife, the soap, and the lint-covered wrapped morsel of chocolate. I slipped these items into the pockets of the sweat-pants before removing my chemise.

The shower felt wonderful, but even so, I thought of the Mystic. The river was cleaner then. Full of life. Even the mud looked welcoming. Dunking myself into that flowing water would have been awesome.

I stared at the sterile walls of the bathroom and sighed.

And what about Winthrop? Was he looking for us? We'd told Dixon what we were doing. They'd have searched.

And searched. And searched. Would they think we had drowned?

It was painful to think about, and only Peter would understand. As soon as I got out of here, I needed to find him.

I emerged clean and confused, surrounded by gleaming walls and eye-piercing light. Everything was strange, foreign. I was shell-shocked, a refugee from another time. I had never heard or read of such a phenomenon. I couldn't imagine Dr. Howard needing tranquilizers or counseling to decompress.

The Quarantine apartment had a tiny kitchen. I opened the white cabinet doors to discover ready-to-eat meals. Soups. Drinks. Coffee and tea. No chocolate.

I fixed a cup of tea and pondered the food selection. I was hungry.

On the wall, a light flashed. "Incoming."

I reached for the knob next to the light. Inside a little cupboard was a bag. I pulled it out.

It was a crusty loaf of bread. It looked like something from the French café near my apartment. Scott had come through. How did he know?

I grabbed it and tore it apart.

I should give thanks, shouldn't I?

Winthrop's blessings at the table overshadowed me.

"Thank you... Lord God. Creator of heaven and earth." My whispered prayer sounded feeble to my ears.

But I couldn't deny it. I was thankful.

Peter was going to be okay.

~

"Quarantine AI, calls and messages."

After the bread, I felt brave enough to face the world.

The tinny voice responded. "Seventeen missed calls and messages. Ninety-five emails."

"Send emails to Lucy to sort."

"Done." The AI didn't scold me for that. My confidence rose.

"Sort messages by sender."

"Twelve from your mother, one from your father, and four requesting you purchase an extended warranty."

"Delete warranty calls."

I frowned as I realized I needed to listen to my mother's messages. Twelve was a lot, even for her. She had a problem she wanted me to solve. Or a grant she wanted me to write. She imagined that since I was employed by a university, I had some kind of pull in academia.

That was a laugh.

I decided to listen to my father's message.

But first, another cup of tea. I hadn't seen my father for a long time. He'd come to my college graduation four years ago. His calls were rare. Occasionally I missed his calls and felt guilty when I didn't call him back.

My mother had a strange way of avoiding the entire topic of my father and his absence from our lives. She'd say, "He's a good man. He's part Oneida."

It was a strange response. Granted, she was into Native American interests, and when those interests coincided with her own, she was happiest. I remembered a grant to establish a Seneca Nation business. Something about maple trees and maple syrup. So, the Oneida part was praiseworthy in her universe.

She wouldn't say anything bad about him but did not explain our fractured family. Maybe my mother simply enjoyed a freewheeling lifestyle, hiking and camping in the woods during the summers, doing events for disadvantaged groups the rest of the year, and a husband would interfere with all that.

I felt sorry for my dad, but the fact was, I barely knew him.

I sipped at my tea, waiting for the bravery of the beverage to soak in. Finally, I could wait no longer.

"Quarantine AI, play my father's message."

I was so distracted by the sound of his voice that I barely registered what he said. Something about a visit.

I finished my tea. Might as well return the call. It didn't sound like I could put it off.

"Quarantine AI, connect me to my father."

"Voice or video?"

"Voice."

"Dialing." While the call went through, my father appeared in my mind's eye. Unlike Scott, with his Mohawk complexion, my father was ordinary looking, with calm brown eyes and tousled mousy brown hair. Granny's fair skin and blue eyes had watered down the Native genes of my father's father.

"Hello? Is this Geneva?"

"Yes, Dad. How... how are you?"

"I'm fine. I'll be in Boston tomorrow. I'll be there a week."

"I get home in a few days." I thought quickly. "There's a French café around the corner from my apartment."

"Sounds wonderful."

"How about this L—" I stopped myself. "This Sunday afternoon."

"I'll be there."

This Lord's Day, I'd almost said. I really had to be careful about my speech.

It wasn't as if I were a Christian. But still, I knew I needed to be careful. Even with my family.

The next day, I whiled away my time in the Quarantine apartment by catching up with my work in the Archives. Lucy had done a wonderful job holding down the fort.

"We did get a new document from the Historical Society," Lucy said over the video chat. "A letter from Thomas Dudley to somebody in England."

Chills went down my spine. Dudley's wooly eyebrows were so close in my memory. But this new find was undoubtedly yellowed and damaged by time. I'd never applied for a license to drink alcohol, but it sounded tempting right now. One way to deal with the discord in my head.

"Thanks, Lucy. I'll get to that next week. Can you do me a favor? Find out how Peter's doing."

She promised me she would.

"And I need clothes." I described what I wanted from my apartment. "I'll instruct the apartment AI to let you in." I'd never named the AI, and I resisted talking to it. But sometimes it came in handy.

After the call ended, I sagged. I'd be released in another day and a half. But I didn't know when Peter would get out of the hospital. I needed to talk to him.

I ate lunch. Then I couldn't put it off any longer. I called my mother.

"Gen, you're back from your trip!"

Trip? Had somebody told her? "I got my messages, but I won't be back until this weekend."

"Oh. Lucy told me you were out of town." Probing. She always told me I needed to "get out."

"Yes, it was for research."

"Hmm. Speaking of which, I need to write a grant proposal. I'm terrible at it."

"Mom, you have a virtual assistant."

"Oh, yes. Roger Two."

Her AI was named Roger. Then he'd gotten an upgrade. "I bet Roger is a whiz at this."

"I hate computers."

It was one of two things I shared with my mother. A dislike of computers, and gray eyes.

"Just tell it what you want. Like you're talking to me. But specify academic style. Otherwise, AI uses way too many adjectives."

I hardly ever used it myself. But I wasn't going to write any more of my mother's grants and legal documents. It was ridiculous.

"But—"

"I'm sorry, Mom. I just can't. I'm much too busy right now." I forced myself to not add any qualifiers. Otherwise, I'd be stuck for sure.

"Has your father been in touch?"

That came out of left field. "Yes, as a matter of fact. I got to talk to him just yesterday."

"Remember, Gen, he's a good man. And he's part Oneida."

I concluded the call with a sense of relief.

Finally, my stay in Quarantine was over. My blood tests had come back negative, and I was ready to escape.

The vid buzzed. It was Lucy.

"Scott managed to get an update on Peter," she said.

I tensed. "Is he okay?"

"Yes. The knife nicked a small artery, but the RoboSurg stitched it up. He's getting out this morning and wants to meet you. The Yard."

I thanked her profusely. Then I thanked God silently.

I put on the clothes Lucy'd brought yesterday, a thick cabled sweater and a midi skirt. I put my hair up using the reproduction seventeenth-century pins, which had been left behind, the rest of my costume having vanished.

Had a robotech cleaned while I was sleeping?

I shifted the contents of my pockets to the skirt pockets. They bulged. One thing I liked about ancient pockets was their size. They were meant to hold stuff, not like these modern afterthoughts. No wonder some women still carried purses.

I took the elevator to the ground floor, left the building, and made my way toward the Yard.

Peter was going to meet me there. He'd left a message. A brief message. It didn't tell me anything. But at least he was well enough to get out of the hospital.

The red brick Houghton Library loomed ahead. Wet brown leaves squished and slipped under my feet, the detritus of the autumn month we'd been away.

One month here, six months back there.

It was nippy. My sweater was warm enough, but the skirt flapped uselessly around my knees, nothing like its seventeenth-century woolen counterpart.

I turned the corner into the Yard, the green space between stolid, ancient buildings groomed and manicured past any resemblance to Dudley's wooded tract. Under a half-naked elm, Peter sat in a wheel-chair, talking to someone sitting on a bench facing him.

Dr. Howard.

Chapter 18

Reports

"After God had carried us safe to new England... one of the next things we longed for and looked after was to advance learning and perpetuate it to posterity; dreading to leave an illiterate ministry to the churches, when our present ministers shall lie in the dust."

— *New England's First Fruits*, 1643, on the establishment of Harvard

I HESITATED, then walked slowly into the Yard. The two men didn't notice me at first. Dr. Howard gesticulated, making some point. Peter nodded in response, and then he saw me.

"Good morning, Gen."

"Miss Fielding." Dr. Howard's expression was bland. "I see you made it back unharmed."

Everything he said always sounded like an accusation.

"Peter, why are you in a wheelchair?" I asked.

Dr. Howard answered. "The hospital. Rules, you know. I picked him up." He rose and indicated the bench.

I sat, the stone cold beneath my thighs. The modern fabric did little to insulate me, and I wished for my wool skirt. I glanced around the Yard. The trees seemed too tame. Like weaker, domesticated versions of the grand specimens I'd seen less than a week ago.

"A bit wobbly?" Dr. Howard's gaze was fixed on me. "Coming back, it's like jumping off a people mover. The ones at shuttle ports. You have to step on it just right. Then you get accustomed to the speed. When the end approaches, you have to be careful getting off or you'll stumble."

Was he being nice? Was it even possible?

"Tomorrow I'm getting a chocolate croissant."

Did Dr. Howard crack a smile? I wasn't sure.

"Miss Fielding, tell me about the men at Roger Williams's trial. Who will be there."

Was he taking our place? "Winthrop and Dudley, of course. But not Endecott. He's been stripped of his office because he'd defaced a flag in his zeal. He viewed the cross on the British flag as papist." I thought about 1635. "Winthrop is no longer governor—his office is now held by John Haynes."

"Haynes?"

"This man tended to side with Dudley in thinking Winthrop was too lenient. It may be important that he was in office during Williams's trial."

"Hmph." He looked off at the trees. "What about the ministers?"

"Maybe a dozen or more from the entire area attended. John Cotton arrived in 1633, he's influential. He preaches at the Boston church, he's highly esteemed. Thomas Hooker will take the lead, though. They refute Williams's views with the hope of convincing him of his errors. They aren't judges."

Dr. Howard was not convinced, I could see it on his face. "When did they decide to exile him, exactly?"

"Officially, he had six weeks to leave. But they let him alone until January. At first, they did nothing because he was sick, then he must have recovered, because people started meeting at his house to hear him speak."

"He became dangerous again."

I shrugged. "Basically, yes. Looking at the timeline, it seems they wanted to be lenient, but were pushed into a decision."

"I would hardly call them lenient."

I held my peace. In any case, this was Dr. Howard's task. He'd be going back. Not me.

"Miss Fielding," he said. "Since Peter can't go, I'd like you along."

"What?"

He waved a hand. "Not that you're my first choice. But clearly, Peter can't come. And it's a short Trip."

My breathing accelerated. I swallowed.

"We'll leave next Tuesday. Can you be ready?"

I nodded reluctantly.

He turned and walked away. A single brown leaf spiraled down behind him.

I took a slow, deep breath. "Peter..."

"I know. He's not all bad. At least he's honest."

I focused on the wheelchair. "How are you?"

His mouth traced a lopsided grin. "Still hurts when I move suddenly. But I'm fine." He gestured to the chair. "Never mind this. I get a week off from work."

"Wh-what were you two talking about?" I blurted.

He shrugged. "The second Trip. Obviously, I'm grounded for the time being." He glanced at the path Dr. Howard had taken. The Yard was almost empty. A lone student carrying a backpack trudged along one diagonal. I approved. Most carried only a StudyPad.

"Is Dr. Howard—"

"Yes, he's been cleared to go back for the trial."

"Just the trial?" There was a space of time between the actual trial of Roger Williams and his exile—or escape, however you chose to look at it.

"That's the plan. Dr. Howard is scheduled to go to 1862 Virginia in a month. So you'll go back next Tuesday for the trial and come back with that report. We'll give all our reports together."

I slouched, trying to process this. "But the theology test."

"He passed. He wasn't idle while we were gone."

I was going to ask Lucy his score. I had a lot of doubts.

"He was asking me questions about our Trip. About the political mood."

"I can't fault him there." Everything overlapped. Theology, relationships, politics. "You think he's ready?"

"I think he will be. He's a Traveler, remember."

Peter accepted my help to get home, and I returned to my apartment. I calmed my mind by thinking of the next day—meeting my father at the café. But picturing the café's menu made me hungry.

"Apartment AI," I said reluctantly, "What is there to eat?"

"Tuna. Beans. Moldy bread."

I did need a name for the thing. "Apartment AI, you now have a name." But what? I didn't take long to decide. "Ratcliffe. Your name is Ratcliffe."

"Ratcliffe?" The AI sounded dubious.

"A historical reference."

I investigated the kitchen. I found some nuts and a Meal-To-Go. I hated prepackaged food. Before, convenience sometimes trumped sense. But now I was used to cooking. After dumping the moldy bread and the instant meal in the trash, I ate some nuts, cleaned the kitchen, and made a list.

Somehow Ratcliffe knew what I was doing. "I can place the order. Delivered in one hour."

The whole apartment felt stuffy. "Go ahead, place my order." I read to him the list. I couldn't wait for fresh fruit, and I needed to clean. "And unlock the windows."

"The outside air is dirty," complained Ratcliffe.

"Do it anyway." I remembered why I hated AIs. Peter had explained that the software behind personal AIs was peppered with cautions. The same way most software was: *do you really want to delete that?*

I'll make my own mistakes, thank you very much.

Soon fresh air was flowing inside. Mainly I needed to keep myself busy to avoid thinking about Peter's revelation. Plus, I had a habit now. Months of housekeeping had created an itch for homely tasks.

As I went room to room cleaning, I thought of Winthrop's house. I'd developed a system, taking care of sanitation needs first (only gross the first two weeks), then bedding, then the kitchen. The floors I saved for last since they weren't as critical. Plus, they got dirty again almost instantly.

My apartment floor was dirty. Most people subscribed to an automated maid that came to clean every week or month. I didn't. Well, sometimes I caved and paid for a yearly deep clean.

"Ratcliffe, locate the mop."

"You have no mop."

I did have a broom and soon had the floor reasonably clean. I put in an order for a mop and a houseplant and then had an idea.

"Ratcliffe. I have a job for you." The AI might as well work for me. "Oh?"

"I need a skirt. Preferably wool." I listed size, style, and price parameters, and then was inspired. "Perform a continuous search of Boston-area estate sales. I want an antique wooden entry table. Hardwood, not CarbonBoard. And less than..." I thought about my account and named a price.

"Working. But for that price, don't get your hopes up."

Perhaps it had been a bad idea to name the AI Ratcliffe. Or maybe it had always been snarky.

I turned the corner, my stomach curling into a ball. I was looking forward to seeing my father, but nervous too.

As I walked the last few steps to the café door, wonderful smells enveloped me. Coffee—ground fresh—and luscious bakery aromas. My mouth watered.

My apartment was clean, I was clean, my clothes were clean—though a little loose—and my hair was neatly put up. I'd even used mascara.

"Geneva?"

I searched for the source of the familiar voice. My dad was sitting in a chair next to the window, in front of a tiny table. I took the other seat.

"Hey, Dad. You look great." He did. Maybe a little older. More lines around his eyes. But he looked healthy and not as thin as when I'd seen him last. He had a cup in front of him.

"Want me to order for us?" I wanted a croissant, and I wasn't going to stop at one.

"I'll follow your lead."

I bought two chocolate croissants, one to take home, and a tart. A *tarte aux brumbelles*—blueberries. Yesterday I'd eaten a peach, an orange, and a handful of cherries.

"You've got an appetite," my father observed.

"Where I was, we didn't have fresh fruit. Only dried." Mother would have made a remark like, "You're too thin." I was glad my father didn't.

We dug into our treats. The taste of the croissant brought me back to the Archives and my work. Tomorrow, I needed to face it. I used to love it. Maybe I would again. And I had to write up a report.

I'd think about that later.

"So, you're a librarian?" My father finished his drink and set down his cup.

"Not exactly. An archivist. I deal with historical documents. My assistant Lucy is trained in library science and deals with published works as well as keeps everything in order."

"I would have thought everything would be"—he gestured—"online. In the Cloud."

"A lot of it is. But every once in a while, we discover a new document. Houghton Library, next door, is a famous repository for original materials. We're kind of... connected... to the library." Of course, I couldn't reveal our true purpose. Many people knew experiments in time travel were done, but few had a clue as to how successful they were or to what use they were put. It was a need-to-know technology, and all personal AIs were pre-programmed to curtail searches for information on it.

"I always liked physical books," Dad said. He scooped his crumbs into a napkin.

"Me too. I always felt that touching real documents was like touching history. It's why I do what I do." The croissant and the tart were gone, and I was full. I took a sip of cappuccino.

"And the old buildings," he said. "The cemeteries."

I set my cup down and studied my father's face. He was ordinary and quiet in manner, and yet there was a particular watchfulness about his gaze I hadn't noticed before.

"Some people know a lot about those old buildings," I said. "There are a number of old ones around campus. Old churches. One is a museum."

His eyebrow twitched. "Museums are safe."

"Not the one on Beech Street?" I tried to be offhand. "Not sure when it was built."

He leaned forward, his voice hushed. "Avoid Beech Street. Avoid it at all costs."

I could think of no response. "How is your coffee, Dad?"

~

I spent the next few days working on my report and preparing for the Trip. I tried not to contact Peter too often. What I really wanted was time away. Time out of the Archives, time with Peter.

Alone.

We'd been jerked away from 1631 and plopped back into our jobs, and I had so many unanswered questions. I had questions I didn't even know how to ask.

On top of which, I was going back—into a new situation.

Roger Williams versus John Cotton. That's how historians remembered it. The reality was, their main clash was later, via an exchange of written documents. Other ministers were involved at this point. And the magistrates made the decision. Magistrates like Dudley and Haynes, hard-liners both, though Haynes later regretted the choice to send Williams away.

I needed to know more. But first, my report on the first Trip.

Commercial elements of John Winthrop's expedition. I jotted down a short list. It really was short: land. Each of the principal investors received a portion. Two hundred acres had been amended by vote to four hundred. I'd seen Winthrop's portion and broken my fingernails there.

I knew to refute a proposition you had to list all the things that would support it. Then tear those down. It seemed easier to write a counter-thesis instead.

I leaned back. I could turn it into my PhD thesis. I had the credits. I just needed a sponsor. And the time to flesh it out.

A sponsor. It would be an uphill battle, writing a thesis that went against the established narrative. Puritans were supposed to be hypocrites, exploiting the resources of the New World for their own purposes.

I couldn't think of Governor Winthrop, Roger Williams, Mrs. Alcock, or Anne Bradstreet that way. I'd have to find a sponsor who would sympathize. Did any academics exist who would stick out their neck like that?

My shoulders sagged, and my mind drifted.

Mrs. Alcock.

I reached for the StudyPad and began to type. I had more than enough to do, but I wanted to know what had happened to Mrs. Alcock.

Where to look? I wasn't exactly a historian. But my skills did overlap. I fed an extended search into the Archives AI and soon had my answer.

"Result. Hartford Ancient Burial Ground. Died July fifth, 1647."

Hartford, Connecticut. Apparently, Mrs. Alcock had gone with her brother, Thomas Hooker, when he'd left to found the new colony. But there was no way to know if she would have died if I had not helped her. It would be one thing if I had intervened in Winthrop's life. I knew all the facts of his life. If I'd come back and seen them changed, I would know.

But Mrs. Alcock was a very minor player in history. Was Peter right? Was her life like one of those tiny wavelets that were lost in the larger swells? Or was all of it simply meant to be?

Was I meant to go back and save her?

I rubbed my forehead. That was a question of meaning. A question of God's Providence, and to go there, even in my thoughts, seemed dangerous.

I punched my comm screen. The comm listed Peter on the top of my contacts list, knowing my propensities. The buzzing didn't last long.

"Gen. What's up?"

"Do you know the Riverfront Park near the Fellsway Bridge?"

"Sounds familiar. I can find it."

"How would you like a picnic this Saturday?"

Once we found a good spot, free of trash and wet leaves, I laid down a sheet of waterproof CarbonFilm for us to sit on.

"Good idea," Peter said, stretching his legs out.

"How do you feel?"

"The doctor has cleared me for work on Monday. Says the internal tears are healing well. Just no extreme sports."

I scanned the park and the water. It was drab compared to what it had been. I spotted a white speck on the water.

"Is that a swan?"

Peter squinted. "I think so. Some kind of bird."

My throat seemed to swell. Finally, I could speak. "I never thought the Trip would affect me the way it has."

"I know what you mean."

I busied myself with the food to avoid speaking.

"Where did you get this bread?" Peter asked.

"That café near my apartment."

It was cold, but I was used to temperatures like these. The skirt I was wearing was from Costumes, with Candy's blessing.

When my sandwich grew small between my fingers, I realized I needed to get to the point. There were several things we needed to discuss.

"The report?" Peter asked. He'd read my mind.

"I'm working on it." I explained my dilemma about a thesis.

"You can save those ideas for later. Just write down your observations. The rest is a matter of historical record. The report is for your observations and impressions, whether they support the proposal or not."

That made it sound easy. "And the second one, about the mistreatment of Roger Williams? That's even harder. My mind is divided on the subject."

"What if we divide the load? I'll take Roger Williams and you take Winthrop. Dr. Howard will undoubtedly give the trial report."

"Perfect."

I felt better until I remembered the second thing. "I saw my dad."

Peter regarded me, concern in his dark eyes. "Everything all right?"

Peter didn't know much about my family. I'd mentioned my mother a time or two. "Yes, we met at the café." I didn't know what to say—or what not to say.

Or even what my question was.

"He warned me against going to the church on Beech Street. I mean, we were speaking of historical buildings—"

"And his comment sounded out of place?"

"Yes. Like he was speaking in code."

Peter scanned the park. No one was nearby. He got to his feet.

"Have any breadcrumbs? There are some ducks over there."

We strolled along the bank, stepping around rocks and muddy spots, tossing bits of bread to a couple of apathetic mallards. I waited for Peter to speak.

"My professor attended that church," he said finally. "Every Sunday. Said he would worship publicly no matter what."

"He was registered?"

"Yes. Registered and tracked. But when you are registered, even your speech is monitored. There's a lot of fine print associated with registration, and of course, if there's a doubt about the law, it tends to go against the Christian."

"That doesn't seem fair," I said. Another species of duck bumped in between the mallards and went for a floating crumb.

"It's why most of us are not registered. My professor eventually crossed a line and was arrested."

"What?"

"The whole point of registration is control. Christians are only allowed to say so much, do so much. They may attend church on Sunday and that's about it."

I saw my dad's face in the café. "Was my dad warning me not to register?"

"Maybe. An oblique warning that would mean nothing if you weren't already a believer."

"But I'm not—"

"He doesn't know that. I'm surprised he said what he said. Maybe you will take an interest one day."

"He can't know that."

"But God does."

Chapter 19

Back to the Past

"If our heavenly father be pleased to make our yoke more heavy than we did so soon expect, remember I pray thee what we have heard, that our heavenly husband the lord Jesus... called us into his condition, to deny ourselves, and to take up our cross daily, to follow him."

— John Cotton to his wife, *letter,* 1632

"Lucy, what do we have on John Cotton?" I grabbed an old-fashioned pencil out of a ceramic cup on my desk and stuck it between my teeth.

"I'll check. Might have to find it in Houghton."

Houghton Library was a gold mine, but the library's AI was fussy about sharing with the Archive's. Almost as bad as Ratcliffe.

It took over an hour, but eventually I had more than enough on this minister so important to the Bay Colony. And only a day to soak in whatever I might need.

Tomorrow was Tuesday. The day I would accompany Dr. Howard to 1635. John Cotton would be there. Thomas Hooker would take the lead in the argument, trying to persuade Williams of his errors, but I had no doubt Cotton would be influential as well. He was highly respected, at the peak of his popularity.

I skimmed over the material downloaded to my Pad. By noon I had a headache, and I wandered over to the cafeteria.

Candy's bright red dress, circa 1940, caught my eye. I joined her in the line.

"What looks good?" I asked.

"Fried chicken."

Misshapen lumps testified to the anatomical parts of real chicken. I chose a drumstick and thigh and asked the robot to add a scoop of coleslaw to my plate.

We found a table and tried the chicken. Not bad.

"Tell me," she asked between bites, "how goes the prep?"

What could I tell her? John Cotton's life flashed before my eyes. He was a prodigy as a child, at Cambridge by thirteen, a resounding success at his studies, but unhappy. Then he was converted, received a happy assurance of faith, and his sermons were altered forever. No longer grandly eloquent, he preached a simple gospel. But I could speak of none of that.

"John Cotton is hard to understand." I picked up the drumstick. "His theology is changing a little, year over year. At first, he's very much a Church of England man, they all were. They were Puritans, not Separatists. Cotton spent his youth walking a fine line, believing it could be done."

Candy made a motion with a drumstick for me to continue.

"By 1640, he is for all intents and purposes a Separatist. They all were. I saw this with Winthrop. The act of moving three thousand miles away was just the beginning."

I swallowed another bite. "Cotton was the one to finally work it out theologically. Independent churches, congregational rule."

"Congregationalism."

"Yes, the churches were already functioning that way when

Cotton arrived. But they wouldn't admit to being Separatist. They were Church of England, but it was in name only."

"Why would such men find fault with Roger Williams? Wasn't he Baptist or something?"

Baptist. How familiar was Candy with theology—and why?

"Williams's search for purity seemed extreme to them." I pointed to my plate. "Like a person who throws away his food if his coleslaw touches his chicken. And he was popular and influential. If he'd been a quiet farmer, nothing would have happened." I finished my coleslaw. "Tell me about my persona."

"Obviously, you've already been there. They'd recognize you as Jane Tuttle. So, you'll be her sister."

"Don't tell me. Dr. Howard is my husband."

Candy chuckled, seeing my face. "No, I think I'll make him your brother or half-brother. And look. Dr. Howard takes everything very seriously. Worries a lot." She finished her chicken and licked her thumb. "Do you know there was a betting pool? Dr. Howard bet you wouldn't last the whole six months of the first Trip."

"That I'd come back early?"

She nodded. "The rest of us made money. Including Madeleine."

My shoulders relaxed. I'd made it six months—tomorrow's Trip was only two days in length. "Cosmetics?"

"Yeah, we'll have to give you some slight changes to your appearance. Your brows, hair color. Definitely eye color. Dr. Howard has brown eyes, that will be easy to change." She wiped her fingers with a napkin. "You'll be fine."

Maybe.

The next morning, I went to Medical for my final prep. My antibiotics, my implant, and my cosmetics. I understood temporary hair color and colored contacts. I couldn't imagine how they'd change my eyebrows realistically.

It took over an hour of sweaty palms. First the nasty drink, then the implant, then my brows and hair. We were leaving at noon. I wished for Peter, but he was holed away, working on a report.

I'd be back soon. It was a short Trip, just a few days there and a few hours here. I tried not to think of trains or math. Just the hour I'd spent with Tollers yesterday afternoon, refreshing my accent.

And John Cotton's biography. He'd written a letter to Williams after the trial. In January, just before the exile. Was he just being argumentative, wanting to prove a point? Or did he really care? What about the rest of the ministers? Were they all so judicious and kindly as Cotton's descendant, Cotton Mather, depicted them?

"Okay, tilt your head back." The nurse, gowned and gloved, opened a small container. My contacts. "Just relax."

Easy for her to say.

"There. Take a look." She handed me a mirror.

A stranger stared back at me. "Brilliant. The way you did my eyebrows. They look natural."

"Thank you."

I could pass for a sister—or even a cousin.

I went to Costumes. An hour later, I left the warmth of Candy's friendliness for the elevator. Once below, the gleaming white walls shrouded me as I walked to my doom.

Peter wasn't going. Only Dr. Howard, who'd bet against me.

A jumble of stuff covered the launchpad. I was surprised. Dr. Howard stood near the console, talking to Chamar, so I walked to the pile.

It wasn't actually a lot, just several satchels, a chest, and a box—probably tools. But a big roll of canvas lay on top.

"A tent," Dr. Howard said, behind me.

"Candy warned me we were camping out."

"It's easier. Fewer questions." He frowned. "Did you get all the details? Our backstory?"

I tapped my head. "All right here."

Ugh. I'd be sleeping in a tent with Dr. Howard. I looked at the clock. Twenty minutes to go. I went to the bathroom in Quarantine and checked my appearance. My hair was neatly pinned under my cap. The cape over my partlet was thick and warm. All beautiful wool. Dr. Howard's persona was wealthy, and our clothing reflected that. My shoes were sturdy and well-made, tied with thick silk laces instead of leather.

I shoved my hands into my pockets.

My eating knife, my flint and steel, my chocolate.

I returned to the launchpad and Dr. Howard.

He eyed me. "You okay?"

"Absolutely."

I fell into a pile of new autumn leaves, dizzy from the sudden shift. Cambridge—I was in Cambridge. Or as they called it then, New Town. We were on ground that belonged—would belong—to the university.

I gasped, trying to catch my breath. The air was cool but not frigid. It was October 1635. I got to my feet unsteadily.

Dr. Howard was standing next to me, his posture rigid and alert. Trees surrounded us like soldiers—oak and elm and birch. My heart thundered in my chest, and I took a deep, calming breath.

And another. I focused on the trees. Here and there a red-cloaked maple. Green peppered the area—pine and perhaps cypress. The warm, variegated color calmed my heart.

Sunlight cast afternoon shadows, and a single bird called *chick-a dee-dee-dee.* A familiar sound, a comforting sound.

Dr. Howard glared at me. "You okay? We'll reconnoiter," he said gruffly. "Then we'll make camp back here."

Logical. We couldn't haul all our stuff around. Not easily.

I nodded and followed Dr. Howard, who consulted a compass. He pointed out a direction, and we moved slowly through the trees, the only sound the humble rustle of leaves.

In thirty yards a fallen tree blocked our path. An elderly half-dead elm had blown down, roots still fresh with clinging dirt.

Dr. Howard frowned a question.

"A big storm blew in several months ago, damaging Winthrop's house and ruining crops."

He grunted an assent, and we skirted the roots. Twenty yards past that was another obstacle. A fence. Split rails, not the stone I associated with New England. Beyond it, several sleek, red-coated cattle chomped on dry corn stalks, remnants of the recent harvest.

To the left, a path ran along the fence line.

Dr. Howard pointed to it. "The market square and the meeting-house are southwest."

It was hard to picture. I remembered a historical marker southwest of campus, but I was just going to have to trust Dr. Howard and the compass.

We got back to the pile of supplies and spent the next two hours pitching the tent, building a fire, and eating a simple supper. Thankfully, Scott had sent a keg of cider. I was not really keen on fetching and boiling water. Not on this kind of Trip.

Dr. Howard's grumpiness had subsided.

"Tell me about the ministers," he said. "Peter explained some of the political aspects."

"Thomas Hooker will be in charge. He's the pastor of the New Town church. John Eliot is from Roxbury, John Cotton from Boston —"

He waved a hand in the fading light. "How many?"

"About a dozen."

"Sounds like they're ganging up on Williams. Why would they need a dozen to try to change his mind? Sounds like the Inquisition."

I looked for something I could use as a napkin and failed. I licked my fingers instead. "I am not sure as to their motives. Generally speaking, they are honest men, desiring truth above all. Kind men."

"Exiling Williams doesn't sound kind."

I suspected he was acting as a devil's advocate. He'd been briefed by Peter. He knew the stakes. "That's why I'm not sure. Even the best men can be harsh."

We cleaned up and prepared for bed. The ground would be hard, but at least we had oilcloth to keep us dry and wool blankets for warmth.

I dreaded sleeping in the same tent as this man, but strangely, he made it easy. He rolled himself in wool and lay facing one canvas wall. Soon I heard soft snores.

On the other side of the tiny tent, I lay on my back and breathed a sigh. The forest whispered gently all around us.

Kay-tee-did... kay-tee-did... kay-tee-did...

I'd survived the arrival. And Dr. Howard's frowns. My limbs relaxed.

An eerie howl woke me. A wolf? I stiffened. The half-banked fire still glowed at the entrance to our tent. Surely we wouldn't be bothered. I found the eating knife and kept it clutched in my hand, just in case.

Kay-tee-did... kay-tee-did... kay-tee-did...

My eyelids grew heavy, and I slept.

Morning slammed into me with the force of an overdue paper. I sat up and surveyed the tent. Dr. Howard was gone. I needed to use the restroom desperately. Too bad the forest was losing its thick mantle of green, for I'd need a living screen. I pushed open the flap and eased myself to a standing position, my back sending a twinge of protest.

Autumn chill nipped at my cheeks. Tiny sparkles of dew illumined the leaves of a nearby rhododendron. Dr. Howard was bent over the chest, rummaging inside. He drew out a portable writing desk.

"I'll be back," I said.

He looked at me blankly.

"Need to use the facilities."

A strange expression washed over his face. Embarrassment? It was hard to imagine Dr. Howard embarrassed or flustered. Angry, yes. And maybe frustrated, but not human.

Without waiting for an answer, I found a cypress with thick, heavy green limbs and skirted behind it. When I returned, I found Dr. Howard with spectacles on his face, nibbling a chunk of bread.

I grabbed my own breakfast, and we ate on the way through the forest and along the narrow path. The writing desk was tucked under Dr. Howard's arm. He looked like a scholar, and that was consistent with his persona.

I was a mere sister, no list of accomplishments necessary. Although Candy had suggested, with a wink, the sister of an educated man would know a few things.

Perhaps not as educated as Anne Bradstreet, but I was certainly literate. I couldn't fake Latin. Cotton Mather littered his history, his *Magnalia Christi Americana*, with Latin and even Hebrew. I'd cracked open a primer once.

Amo, amas, amat...

My gut tightened around the ball of my breakfast as we walked through the cool morning. We passed a homestead, and the smell of woodsmoke grew thicker.

Ahead, gray smoke curled above the trees. More houses—and the center of town. The scent of manure and chamber pots joined the perfume of the morning, and then I heard clattering. Horses and wagons. Or oxen. We turned a slight corner and entered a square of sorts—people and conveyances and voices and smells, all gathered about a large log building.

Women tended a crackling fire. Older children helped, and a few younger boys tussled or ran races. Men clustered in small groups, talking. A couple of them wore starched white falling bands above their sober outfits. Some were smiling, but others wore a more somber expression.

And several I recognized.

John Winthrop. And Roger Williams. They were talking.

Williams looked a little older. The skin had settled on the planes of his face, and his complexion was slightly sallow. He was moving well, his gestures sure, but he had lost the glow I remembered.

If only I could eavesdrop on their conversation.

The clatter of a wagon jerked my attention away. Two sturdy chestnut horses pulled a simple vehicle driven by a woman, another woman beside her on the wagon seat. The driver was horse-faced, to be honest. The other was prettier, but they seemed to be of an age, mature but not gray-headed. Fortyish. Behind them, a child's head emerged, tousled with sleep. As the wagon pulled to a stop, he clambered out from the side, came around to the front, and grabbed the bridle of the near horse.

"Mind Bushy, Dean." the horse-faced woman warned.

"Yes'm."

Bushy was the horse's name, presumably, who rolled an eye before submitting to the child—I judged him to be about twelve—who worked at the harness with nimble fingers. As the horses were released from the harness, the prettier woman descended from the wagon seat and pulled out a basket from the bed.

The driver stepped down and began to unload items as well. I took a deep breath to quell my nervousness and approached the wagon to greet the horse-faced woman.

"Mr. Cotton!" The prettier one was hailing one of the ministers.

John Cotton. I turned. What did he look like?

The woman closed the gap between the parking lot—as I thought of it—and the milling ministers before the church. One short older man faced her, puzzlement on his face. His bushy hair was tinged with silver at the temples. He had the soft, saggy look of a man who tended to corpulence but through suffering had lost weight.

"Mistress Hutchinson? Good day to ye."

She offered him the basket, and he received it graciously but then remained there for a moment, looking bemused.

A clatter drew my eye back to the wagon, but my mind spun.

Anne Hutchinson. The American Jezebel, Winthrop had called her. My heart thumped wildly. I felt like I was in a bad dream. I was supposed to be here for Roger Williams's trial, and so I was. But here *she* was, too. To steady myself I looked at the other woman, the horse-faced one, realizing with a start that her animals were the best—the most expensive—in the trampled yard.

Who was she?

My heart still raced, but I forced myself to speak, to act normal. "May I help you?"

For she did need it. She'd dropped several chunks of wood. Her son was away tethering the horses.

She turned, saw me, and smiled, a smile that lit up her face and softened her strong features. "Why certainly. Margaret Winthrop, at your service."

Chapter 20

The Trial

"I have no way to manifest my love to you but by these unworthy lines, which I would entreat you to accept from her that loveth you with an unfeigned heart."

— Margaret Winthrop to John

I ARRANGED the wood from the wagon in the fire pit, careful not to extinguish the infant flames. As Mrs. Winthrop directed and spoke to the other women, I recognized preparations for a noon meal for the twenty-plus men as well as women and children. Visions of my struggles to feed a smaller number flashed through my mind.

But Mrs. Winthrop seemed unperturbed by the task. After fetching a second armful of wood, I looked for Dr. Howard. He was talking to one of the ministers, but he wasn't too busy to toss me a glare across the yard. I wished I could ignore him. But I needed his endorsement if I was ever to get a thesis topic approved.

"Mistress, I fear my brother is needful of my assistance."

Margaret looked toward the men. A tiny, brief smile hinted at a sense of humor. "By all means."

The minister speaking to Dr. Howard wore good clothing, including a hat and a seventeenth-century version of a tie. As I drew near, I began to catch snippets of their conversation.

"Where will ye settle?" The minister asked.

"We are looking for property. I had thought New Town, but I found it settled. 'Tis a worthy place, with a fine minister," Dr. Howard said.

"You flatter me."

Thomas Hooker. It had to be. New Town's minister and host of this gathering. He saw me and nodded a greeting.

Dr. Howard extended a hand toward me. "My sister, Miss Howard."

"Pleased. Thomas Hooker at your service."

Another minister drifted over. This man was young, perhaps even younger than Roger Williams. He waited patiently for introductions, which Mr. Hooker soon gave, including the tidbit that Dr. Howard was a schoolmaster—or at least, his persona was.

"John Eliot at your service." He fixed his gaze on the bespectacled Dr. Howard. "A schoolmaster, you say?"

"Aye. Although, I confess my Hebrew is nonexistent. I teach lads to prepare them for college. History is my great love."

"We need schools," Eliot said. "Schools and schoolmasters."

"And a college for ministers," Mr. Hooker said with a sigh. "We are all mortal and must be thinking of the next generation."

Eliot slid his gaze to me. "Is his sister learned as well?"

I smiled. "My Latin is nonexistent."

"Indeed?" Eliot was a cheery sort.

"*E pluribus unum?*"

Dr. Howard's eyes seemed to bulge.

Eliot was nonplussed. "'Out of many, one.' What a beautiful—and godly—sentiment."

"Let us pray we be unified today," said Mr. Hooker.

An unspoken signal seemed to pass through the crowd, and one by one, they went inside. I hung back with Dr. Howard. Through the doorway, I could see rough-hewn benches aligned in a purposeful way to create a courtroom. It reminded me of Winthrop's parlor, with the dining room table as a judicial bench.

We slipped inside and took places along the back wall. Anne Hutchinson sat nearby, but I did not see Mrs. Winthrop. She was probably busy with the fire and the food.

A man I guessed to be John Haynes took the place of prominence at the front. He was even more finely dressed than Mr. Hooker, with an actual ruff around his neck. He was governor, after all. Light from small glass-paned windows at the far end of the church illumined him and the other men at the front. To his left sat Thomas Dudley, but I did not know the man on his right. At the end of the row, in a shadowed corner, was John Winthrop.

"Mr. Hooker," Governor Haynes said, "please take the meeting."

I swallowed. I was watching it in real time, the ministers' examination of Roger Williams, one last attempt to dissuade the man from his opinions. To convince him of what they viewed as right and true. Every gaze fell on Williams, and I could feel the tension in the room. There was very little noise, even from the few children who were present.

"Mr. Williams," Mr. Hooker began. "All know you for a good and godly minister, and we shall not attempt to besmirch your character, only your mistaken opinions."

Mistaken opinions. Ouch.

Roger Williams's face revealed little. Like a prisoner in the dock, he sat on a lonely bench across from the other ministers who were arrayed on the other side. There were no fireplaces, and it was cool in the room. I spotted a few charcoal braziers.

Hooker went on to list Williams's infractions. The first, and one of seeming great concern to them, had to do with public oaths using the name of God.

The first table. The first four commandments, the commandments involving God.

As Hooker and Williams exchanged comments—some rather pithy and pointed—the rest sat erect or even leaning forward, attentive.

"You cannot compel worship," Williams argued. "Taking God's name is worship, and worship must come from the heart. A wicked man must not be compelled to swear or pray."

"We compel the sixth commandment, we protect the community's property. Even the property of the wicked."

It was like watching volleyball or tennis. Hooker would make an argument, then Williams would respond. Back and forth, back and forth. Some things I couldn't follow.

"God needeth not the sword of steel to assist the sword of the Spirit," Williams argued.

I liked his words, but they didn't convince these ministers. Men took oaths in my day, but they no longer placed their hands upon a Bible. They simply made a "solemn promise." Roger Williams had insisted—was insisting—that civil oaths using the name of God were improper.

The arguments droned on for several hours. John Cotton asked several questions of his own, and Mr. Wilson spoke up once. John Eliot remained silent.

The bench was hard under me, and once I saw Williams shifting uncomfortably.

Finally, Governor Haynes banged a gavel, and we were dismissed for the noon meal. I eased my way past Dr. Howard and made a beeline for the door, eager to help Mrs. Winthrop.

Soup bubbled in a huge kettle over the fire. She handed me a basket of loaves and a knife. "How went the meeting?"

"Long," I said. "I did not understand all the arguments."

She smiled. "Thou art an honest woman."

We labored to feed the men, passing out hot soup, bread, cheese, and fresh apples. Once that was accomplished, we served the children and each other.

I found a place to sit next to Margaret. "It was the first table."

"Yes."

"He has not changed his mind."

Margaret Winthrop nodded but said little. A discreet woman. I suspected she knew more of the issues than most. I sipped the soup. It was thin but tasty. And best of all, hot.

"Is this cheese from your cattle?" I had a professional interest now. I was a housekeeper too—or was.

"This particular cheese came from Devonshire," she said. "But our two cows are giving me more than enough for my family, and I have tried my hand at cheesemaking."

We spoke of the craft while I watched the ministers. John Eliot stood alone, leaning on the building, studying the inside of his bowl.

"I will gather some bowls." I rose and walked over to Eliot.

"How fare thee?" I said. "I am collecting bowls for the mistress."

I took his bowl but did not move away. He glanced at me, trouble in his eyes.

"Roger Williams possesses an amazing gift," he said. "Languages. He can speak modern languages, even Italian, with skill, and his Hebrew—" He motioned helplessly.

"I have heard something of his proficiency."

Eliot nodded. "And—" He opened his arms wide, trying to express what he clearly could not find words to say. "His heart. He has the greatest heart for the savages. Indeed, they are not savages but men, men with dark veils over their sight. All they need is the Word of God."

I fought to hold back my emotions. Eliot would later enter a voluntary exile to preach to the Indians—and translate the scriptures into their language. "You think Williams can give this to them."

Eyes misty, he nodded. "His faculty with translation exceeds my own—I am a child by comparison."

"You fear the outcome."

He sighed and said nothing.

I nodded, then moved away and collected the rest of the bowls.

I slid back into my seat just as the discussion resumed. Dr. Howard eyed me once, then subsided and leaned against the wall behind us. Margaret found a place to sit next to Anne Hutchinson.

Mr. Hooker brought up the matter of the Indians. "I hear that—it troubles me to speak it aloud—that you reject the king's authority to give us land by means of the patent."

"I do." Roger Williams seemed revived by the meal—or perhaps by the subject. "God gives to all men their boundaries. For the king, whose jurisdiction is thousands of miles away, to give away the Indians' possessions is quite plainly a farce."

A murmur rose. The ministers wriggled in their seats. John Eliot frowned.

Governor Haynes struck his gavel. "Be careful what words you use in reference to the king."

I gaped. This wasn't the Inquisition. No one would be burned at the stake or even hung. But treason was serious, and it was the appearance of collective treason in tolerating Williams that made the position of the Colony so difficult.

Williams nodded to the governor. "I apologize."

I exhaled. I found myself wishing he'd retract more of his statements. Exile was bad enough—it was a wilderness, after all.

Hooker continued. "Rejectest thou the authority of the governor?"

"I honor all—the king, the magistrate, the common man in his place. Even the poor, benighted Indian."

"The governor's authority is based on the Charter. The Charter granted by the king."

"I accept his authority. I say only that the king is wrong regarding the Indians. The Natives are the true owners of this land and ought to be compensated."

The ministers were quiet but restless, shifting in their seats. Eliot turned to his neighbor, and Governor Haynes spoke in Dudley's ear.

Hooker frowned. "We ought to submit to authority, whether in our families, churches, or the state. If the king pronounces that the land is part of the patent, we must consent."

Eliot spoke. "But Williams is correct about the Indians. The scriptures are clear that we must not steal."

Voices rose in protest.

"I have not stolen one farthing nor one ell of land from the Indians," someone said.

"'Tis a valid argument," another man said.

The noise grew. My hands clenched and opened, clenched and opened.

Governor Haynes struck the gavel. "Let us be clear. We have not taken from the Indians. We only occupy uninhabited land. Mr. Hooker?"

The disturbance subsided as quickly as it had begun.

"Rejecteth thou the king's authority to grant us the land?" said Hooker.

Williams rose to his feet. "I reject the king's authority where he bids us to sin against our fellow man in claiming another's property. I further believe that the king must repent of his actions. I believe the king must apologize."

Shock silenced the room. Slowly, a murmur like the buzz of bees filled the air.

Hooker rose and moved to a seat next to John Cotton. They conferred. Then Hooker retook his original seat.

"I leave the magistrates to decide whether you have spoken treason. But let us speak of love to our fellow man. Is it loving to break with the churches of the Bay, to insult them, to insult their ministers, and to put us all in danger?"

"Speak the truth in love," Williams replied. "If there is no truth, then there is no love."

Hooker seemed to deflate. "You have heard him. He repents not."

The ministers voted. One lone soul refused to condemn Williams. But it was not John Eliot.

The shadows were long in the autumn afternoon as the tired men and women congregated outside, talking. Tomorrow the General Court would issue a decision. I came outside and watched the crowd, wishing Peter could be here.

Roger Williams walked around the corner of the building, and John Winthrop followed him. I scurried to eavesdrop unashamedly.

They were speaking in low tones. I couldn't quite hear from my spot at the corner of the building, so I nonchalantly strolled a wide berth about the talking men, pretending I was on my way to do something around back.

Williams's eyes glanced my way, but he said nothing. Winthrop's back was to me.

"Go to the Narragansetts," the former governor said. "South of Plymouth, past the boundary of the patents."

Williams seemed to consider it. "It is hard what they do."

Winthrop waved a hand. "There has been no decision."

"The decision is made."

"No one wants to banish you."

"I disagree."

"If they make the decision, it is of necessity, not desire. Surely you can see that."

"They fear the king more than they fear God."

Winthrop sighed. "Down south the land is good. There is a harbor."

I had completed an arc to the far corner, and he spotted me.

"Mistress Tuttle?" His tone was perplexed.

I turned. "Miss Mary Howard. Jane Tuttle's sister."

"I thought—I thought—"

"Please trouble not yourself. There is a resemblance."

"I am so sorry," he said.

He must have thought that I—Jane Tuttle—had drowned.

"Oh, no. Jane is safe. Though she and her husband had quite a scare. A renegade attacked them, and they had to flee. They made it back to England, but 'twas a harrowing escape."

"A renegade?" Lines appeared on his forehead.

"At the time, his name reminded me of a rodent." I could not help myself.

Winthrop's face cleared. "Ratcliffe! Why, I should have known."

I curtsied and made my way to Dr. Howard, who was standing in the yard like a lost schoolchild.

"That's dangerous," he muttered and did not speak again until we came in sight of the fallen tree. "Women did not speak to men like that in this time period."

The light was fading, and the breeze picked up. "I'll make the fire. I'm cold. And yes, you're right. I was a bit forward."

Dr. Howard said nothing until the first flames were dancing on our pile of hastily gathered twigs. "Learn anything?"

I added a small piece of deadwood from the fallen tree. "A little. Mr. Eliot spoke of Roger Williams's gift of languages." I tried to explain what he was really saying.

"You wouldn't know that from the final vote."

That vote must have cost Eliot but I said nothing.

The fire snapped cheerfully as Dr. Howard rummaged for a snack. He passed me some cheese, rather bland after the Devonshire variety. But it was still real food, and I chewed it slowly.

"Anything else?" He passed me some cider.

"Winthrop suggested to Williams that he go south, to what is now Rhode Island."

"Already? He hasn't been banished yet."

"Tomorrow he will be given six weeks to depart, which won't be enforced until January. Winthrop knows or guesses what will happen."

"Why Rhode Island?"

My mouth was dry, and I poured another cup of cider. "He's trying to be kind in any small way he can."

But privately I agreed with John Cotton, who would say that Williams had brought his troubles upon himself.

<h1 style="text-align:center">Chapter 21</h1>

<h1 style="text-align:center">The Conference Room</h1>

"Liberty of conscience is for those who truly fear the Lord. A fundamental task of the state is the establishment of pure religion."

— John Cotton

I HATED LAUNCHPAD DISINFECTANT. I stood under the shower and washed my hair a second time. Added conditioner. Rinsed it out. Added more, rinsed it out.

I was back in my time, and I was clean, but I missed the woodsmoke and the funky, sweaty wool smell of the 1600s. I wouldn't miss Dr. Howard's companionship, but still. He hadn't been as grumpy as he could have been. We'd slept, rose with the tweeting of birds in our ears, and returned to the meetinghouse for the convening of the General Court.

As I dressed in the Quarantine bathroom, I mulled over the details of the second day's gathering. The banishment of Roger Williams was not even the only item on the agenda. Governor Haynes had even looked a little bored, much like Dean Hutchinson during a long meeting.

197

We made it back to our camp without incident, but Dr. Howard had made an interesting comment.

"Winthrop spoke to Hooker."

"I saw them." Alas, I'd been helping Margaret load the wagon.

"They weren't precisely arguing. But Winthrop insisted that Williams was sound in 'the root of the matter.' It seemed obscure. Is it a reference to some text?"

"I think it simply means Williams is correct in the most important thing."

Dr. Howard snorted. "Why would they exile him then?"

"What about the tent?" I'd said, avoiding the question. Everything else at the campsite we could take back in our arms.

"It's not real canvas. It's CarbonTemp." He looked at the sky. "It will disintegrate in a week or two, depending on the weather."

We pressed our implants and returned without a lot to contribute to the two theses on the table. But...

The root of the matter.

I determined to speak to Peter about it.

As I combed my hair in the Quarantine apartment—now a familiar place—I couldn't help thinking of Roger Williams, alone against the world. Brave. I admired him. Agreed with him—mostly. Why on earth had he proposed that the king apologize for his errors?

He was a danger to the community, and I couldn't understand why he didn't see that.

"AI, pull up my emails." Thankfully, we hadn't been gone long. Just a matter of hours here. Not long enough for things to really pile up.

I deleted most of the emails and forwarded a request from Cornell to Lucy.

"AI, pull up voicemails."

"One from your apartment, one from your mother, and one which I think belongs in spam."

"Spam?" Didn't an AI filter my communications? Did these artificial intelligences disagree on what constituted spam?

"Yes, well, it's an advertisement for a product. A *personal* product."

I snorted. "Delete product voicemail. Play voicemail from my apartment."

Ratcliffe's recorded voice filled the tiny Quarantine bedroom. "Greetings. I have been successful. I found a skirt for sale with the parameters you gave me."

This was good news. "AI, put in a call to my apartment."

"Ratcliffe. Tell me about the skirt."

"Ah, yes. It's in Salem. On clearance. Very nice, if I say so myself."

Who programmed these things? "Is it wool?"

"Sadly, no. But it's the very best faux wool. Thick. Heather gray. It will pair well with the blue sweater in your closet."

"How long? Below the knee?"

He recited the dimensions—when had I started thinking of it as a he?—and I told him to buy it.

I was strangely cheerful when I pulled up the rough drafts of my reports. Might as well make good use of my time here. The dean would schedule a meeting soon.

The cheerfulness soon wore off. I woke the morning of the meeting out of sorts. I dressed in the new skirt and the blue sweater Ratcliffe had recommended.

My hair was getting long, so I French braided it, a painful decision. I wasn't good with hair. Ratcliffe tried to help with advice.

"Tighten the strand on the right!"

Maybe I could get its voice reprogrammed. Right now, it was a reedy, irritating tenor. There was no way I'd agree to a whining female in my house. I already had a mother. Maybe a classic baritone. With classic vocab. It could scold me gently: "Perhaps a little more tightly?"

I dawdled over my makeup until I finally looked at the time and rushed out the door. Spotting a solar trolley, I plotted an intercept course. They were good about picking up random people. Many of their passengers were students on the way to campus.

The little trolley car slowed, and I jumped on board. The AI warned me to watch my feet, and I grabbed the bar attached to the next seat ahead of me. As the trolley slowly increased in speed, I enjoyed the fresh air sliding in from the open side. There were three other passengers—two students, and one older woman on her way shopping or visiting, presumably.

Then I rediscovered one reason why I rarely took the trolley. It was slow. Faster than walking speed, but not by much. Still, at least I wouldn't arrive winded and sweaty.

When I walked into the conference room clutching my StudyPad, my heart was pounding, but not from exertion.

Dr. Howard was responsible for the report from the trial. But I still had mine to give.

Candy and the doctor were already there. Candy looked glorious in a smart 1920s dress with long beads and a hat.

"Nice outfit," I said to her.

"I like the new skirt."

The dean entered the room. I sat down, and the doctor sat next to me. Scott circled the table and chose a seat next to Candy. Madeline appeared clutching Pads, which she passed out to the group. Perhaps the dean had gone over the department's quota of paper. I wouldn't be surprised. Dr. Howard arrived, followed by Peter, who was wearing his red jerkin.

The same red jerkin? How could it be? Yes, it was. A faint line in the front marked the place where Ratcliffe had stabbed him.

I cut a glance at Candy, and her gaze met mine. She lifted her brows in a secret signal. I widened my eyes to tell her I was impressed. The stained, damaged jerkin had been rehabilitated.

I wasn't sure what Peter's thinking was, but he had everyone's attention.

Dean Hutchinson opened the meeting. "Dr. Donatelli, may we hear your findings?"

Peter rose and cleared his throat. "Miss Fielding and I arrived safely on the Bristol docks before dawn." He sketched our Trip in outline, ending with Ratcliffe's attack on the bank of the Mystic. He traced the line of mending on his jerkin as a visual aid.

The illustration even kept the doctor awake. These reports were important. The department funding was at stake.

"With respect to Roger Williams's treatment, we observed the first months only. My tentative conclusion is that the magistrates were eager to give him the benefit of the doubt whenever possible, but they were in a difficult political situation."

Peter did not include all the details recorded in the journal. Of course, those were already available to the dean and Dr. Howard.

"As much as I sympathize with Williams, I had a glimpse of what the Colony was up against. The existence of the whole settlement was balanced on a knife's edge politically."

Peter finished and regained his seat. He'd spoken for perhaps fifteen minutes in total. Silence fell. I think everyone wanted to know the dean's opinion.

"Interesting. We will wait on Dr. Howard's report regarding Williams." His gaze shifted to me. "Miss Fielding? Your report on Winthrop's commercial interests."

My hands were clammy as I rose to speak. I felt like a clumsy schoolgirl. "The commercial interests of the Company are clearly spelled out in the application for the Charter," I began. "But the de facto situation I found to be much different from the de jure." I hoped the Latin terms sounded academic.

The dean raised an eyebrow. I didn't dare look at Dr. Howard.

I described the hardship I saw. Then I mentioned the focus. The Massachusetts Bay Colony was a community more interested in spiritual things than wealth. It was true they sought to improve their material situation. "They were planting apple trees, not looking for gold," I said. "Apple trees take years to mature. An orchard is an investment in the future, an investment in one's children."

Candy smiled, and I took courage.

I closed by quoting from Winthrop's famous sermon and explaining his vision of Christian charity. "I saw this firsthand. Kindness under duress. He meant what he said."

The silence when I sat down was strained. I felt everyone's eyes on me.

What was it? The apple trees had gone over well. Maybe it was the sermon. But wasn't that the proof?

I met Peter's gaze. It was the word "Christian." And the context. I had practically preached the sermon myself.

The dean cleared his throat. "Yes, well. Thank you. Dr. Howard?"

He stood, and his gaze flickered over everyone, landing on me. I couldn't interpret his expression.

"First, some background, which I included in my report. Both bad news and good news had come from England. A warship that would have attempted to prove Sir Gorges's claims on New England by force broke up before it even left the harbor. At the same time, rumor had it a letter was sent back to England proclaiming the Colony's humble obedience to the king."

I nodded. I knew about this letter. Winthrop was never going to return the Charter or give an inch. But he and the other magistrates made all the right political noises.

"Then Salem appointed Roger Williams as Teacher without any input from the other churches," Dr. Howard explained. "My impression was that folks were offended by this. Salem was off doing their own thing, in a time of great public danger. The oath Williams objected to was part of a civic-minded drive to get men united and prepared in case of attack. They even organized militias because of the danger from England."

"And the trial?" The dean asked.

"Apparently, Williams had already spoken privately with some of the ministers, and I had the feeling of stepping into a conversation midway."

His expression softened. "I liked Roger Williams. He was open and earnest in his manner. At the same time, the magistrates were facing enemies in England. I concur with Peter that the political danger was significant.

"It wasn't a trial like we would think of it. The ministers of the area took turns in refuting his views. In response, Williams conceded that it was the role of the magistrate to preserve civil order. But not worship. You should have seen the faces of the ministers. It was like you were telling them the moon was made of green cheese. I rather liked Williams's arguments, but the whole thing was a forgone conclusion. In any case, the ministers were just there to try and persuade Williams to recant." He hesitated. "I don't blame the magistrates, but my report will say that the evidence supports the second thesis. Religion is dangerous, and it led to Williams's exile as surely as night follows day."

The dean looked at me, then Dr. Howard. "Any concluding comments?"

"Yes," Dr. Howard said. "I would like to recommend Dr. Donatelli for full Traveler certification if he so desires. He managed a six-month Trip very well."

"I will take it under advisement," said the dean, nodding. The department had only two fully certified Travelers. Adding to the number was a good thing.

But any expansion would cost money. Did this mean the department was in the clear budget-wise?

"As to Miss Fielding," Dr. Howard said, "I had to take the lead every step of the way. She nearly fainted at our arrival. And she constantly skirted the behavioral rules of the time, speaking to men, endangering our mission."

Heat rushed up my neck. I didn't know if I was more embarrassed or angry.

"She was a great help to me," Peter said.

"I doubt if you are objective," Dr. Howard said. "Look in her records. She ought to be on medication."

My mouth fell open. "I have never—"

"Been diagnosed? Of course not. You avoid the doctor. Do you even know his name?" Dr. Howard sat down triumphantly.

I fled the room.

Chapter 22

Alone

"We daily confess that we have nothing, and can do nothing, without Christ..."

— Thomas Hooker

TEARS FOGGING MY VISION, I made my way to Costumes, yearning to breathe in the scent of leather and real wool. Candy hadn't returned yet, but I pushed through the lonely stacks, found a stool near the back wall, and sat.

It was a good place to weep.

Dr. Howard knew everybody. In order to get a thesis approved, I not only needed a sponsor, I needed to defend it before a panel of academics. My PhD was becoming more and more unlikely.

And I'd certainly never Travel again.

Why did that feel like a rip in my soul? That day with Peter on the launchpad so long ago seemed horrifying. Not to mention the storm on the Atlantic.

The vomit on Peter's jerkin.

Peter chopping wood. Peter with a quill in his hand, copying a letter of John Winthrop's. Peter's gentle snores while he lay next to me in the frigid bedroom.

He would be going back to observe Roger Williams's exile. I sniffed and wiped my face with the sleeve of my sweater. I needed to help him prepare.

It was a dangerous Trip, as Trips went. And he would be going alone.

Humming announced someone's presence. I half-rose and spotted Candy.

"Hey," she said.

"Hey." My makeup would be streaked, and I didn't trust my voice, but this was Candy. "I like the smells in here."

She found her way to my side and squatted, the beautiful dress pooling on the floor around her. "I've never Traveled, so this is as good as it gets for me. Sometimes I wander into Scott's shop and let my imagination run."

"What kind of things does he make?" Small talk was comforting.

"Everything under the shining sun. Pottery, tomahawks, leather products. Some things he hunts down for us. Specialty items. He's working on his master's in Native American history."

"I didn't know that." Scott was so quiet. I knew little about him.

Candy fished in her sequined purse and handed me a tissue.

"Thanks." I blew my nose. "I would have gone straight home, but I didn't want to face my AI."

She chuckled. "I feel your pain. Sometimes I just put mine on emergency mode. It only wakes up for fires or break-ins."

I imagined a burglar breaking in to steal my houseplant. "Help, help!" Ratcliffe's voice might scare the person away. I smiled. "I may try that. Thanks for the tissue. I'll go back to the Archives." I rose to my feet. "Lucy will wonder."

Or not. Everyone probably knew of my disgrace by now.

∾

The quiet of the Archives was solemn. Lucy had greeted me without comment and returned to her little office. I punched up my schedule and stared at it sightlessly. My stomach grumbled, and I realized that despite the catastrophes of the day, I still needed to eat.

I walked into the cafeteria and surveyed the choices. Cheesy chicken casserole, pizza, hamburgers, and—surprise—salad.

I lingered over the salad for a few minutes. The robot server made an inquiring noise.

"Give me half a serving of casserole and half of salad."

Purple flashed in the robot's eyes. "Half?"

A baritone voice intruded. "Multiply by zero-point-five. Both the quantity of food and the price."

Peter's warm presence was soothing.

The robot buzzed and moved quickly to prepare my lunch. Peter chose a hamburger, and we found a table.

"Robots." I filled the word with all the frustrations of the day.

Peter took a bite of his burger, chewed slowly, and swallowed. "Sometimes just a little tweak in input straightens them out. They are quite limited, really."

Tollers's red glare came to my mind.

"I'm sorry you had to be subjected to that," he said.

I poked at my salad. "I'm not a Traveler."

"Dr. Howard is driven. He strives to earn the trust the department has placed in him. I don't think he likes being shown up."

The casserole tasted only a little plastic. "I don't understand," I said after swallowing. "Shown up?"

"He recognizes your expertise. And your gumption. Not that he wants to."

"Candy told me about the betting pool." I got up and went to the drinks counter and retrieved two coffees, wanting time to compose myself. In some ways, Dr. Howard was right.

I handed Peter his coffee black, the way he took it. I stirred mine and watched the fake cream swirl about.

"No wonder Dr. Howard hates me."

"Maybe hate is a bit strong. Honestly, I think everyone in the room took it all with a grain of salt."

"But it's true, Peter. I have… issues. I—"

"I know. But you managed quite well despite them." He sipped at his coffee, looking thoughtful. "Perhaps it's only an imbalance. Something that can be fixed."

"Fixed?" Hope blossomed in my mind. "I don't want to take medication."

"I understand. But what if it can be fixed another way?" Peter smiled gently. "Let me look into it."

I nodded, dubious.

I took a trolley home, feeling wrung out from the day. Peter's words had affected me just as much as Dr. Howard's.

Cured, without medication? Scott couldn't Travel because he needed medication. I knew that subjecting myself to a doctor's care would almost certainly result in both a diagnosis and medication.

Not only was it hard to admit that I had a problem. I didn't want to be dependent on a drug for treatment.

Would I feel like myself? My emotions were part of what made me, me. Even the swirls of anxiety that pummeled me every so often. What would I feel like without them? Like an automaton?

The Archives possessed evidence of what had happened to the mentally ill in other ages. Asylums. Mind-numbing drugs. Ice baths and electric shocks. Like using a hammer to fix a delicate timepiece.

I had little confidence that things were better in my day.

I walked in the door and turned to my houseplant, ignoring Ratcliffe's greeting. The cheerful leaves of the philodendron remained healthy looking, and I forced myself not to water it. Once a week was enough.

"Are you sure you're all right?" Ratcliffe's words penetrated the haze.

"Yes, thank you very much. Please go to emergency mode."

"Ahh!" my AI protested. "Emergency mode activated."

The silence left a sudden void, but I was determined it would not bother me. I took out my StudyPad and began to search.

"Settings on private," I told the Pad. I didn't want the whole department to have access to my searches about my condition.

I learned a lot. But it all depressed me.

Peter was most likely chasing a rabbit.

The next day was Saturday, and I didn't know what to do with myself. The walls of the apartment seemed to close in around me. It was early, and the day stretched out before me.

Three quick raps sounded on my door.

"Ratcliffe, who's here?"

Nothing.

"Ratcliffe?"

Three more raps, more hesitant this time.

"Ratcliffe, unlock yourself. Normal mode."

"Dr. Peter Donatelli is at the door. Shall I admit him?"

"Yes." I went to the door.

Cold air swirled in along with Peter's form. He was wearing a brown coat and carrying a lumpy bag.

"Um... hello," Peter said.

"Come in, come in. Set your bag down here." I motioned to my tiny dining room table, which could barely seat two people.

I took his coat, and he started emptying the bag. Baguettes, cheese, tarts, croissants.

"You went to the café!"

"I confess I did a search for bakeries. My AI pointed this out. And I knew it was close to your apartment."

I almost threw my arms around him. "Isn't it a bit chilly for a picnic?"

"We can eat here and take a stroll somewhere." He shrugged. "There's a museum I go to sometimes."

"We can take a trolley," I suggested.

A strange expression washed over Peter's face. "I don't use trolleys."

My knife stopped its motion. "Why not?"

I had a single armchair and Peter sank down onto it. "They're solar powered, right?"

I laid the knife down and dragged a chair from the table to join him. "Sure."

"That's kind of true. The solar panels on the top power a storage battery on the driver's end. But it's not sufficient for the type of acceleration—and torque—a trolley needs."

"So how—"

He addressed Ratcliffe first. "AI, shut down and reboot."

"Certainly."

Maybe Ratcliffe responded better to a man's voice. Ugh.

Peter took a deep breath before he spoke. "People. Human power."

"Peter, you're making no sense."

"Think about a trolley. What it looks like."

Four double seats, front to back. A closed-off section in the rear, which I assumed was part of the electrical system. "There's a chunky part in the back."

"Like a big box."

I nodded.

"There's a man in that box. A prisoner."

"What?" It couldn't be true. Peter kept spinning my reality.

"There's an apparatus inside that looks like a bicycle. The man creates power by pedaling. There's significant resistance, and it's hard work. When the driver needs to accelerate, he depresses a lever. A signal..."

Peter halted, his face distressed.

I waited, absorbing the horror on his face.

"The signal gives the prisoner an electric shock."

"Rebooted," Ratcliffe announced. "No anomalies found."

Thankfully, the museum was close by. Peter didn't seem to want to explain further about the trolleys, and I wasn't sure I wanted to know anyway. We left the apartment and made our way on foot. A trolley passed as we walked, and Peter's jaw rippled.

The front door of the red brick museum creaked as Peter pulled it open, and warm, musty air wafted out, a smell I loved. The building was probably well over one hundred years old. Wood, brick, plaster, paint, and old wallpaper all gave off a unique patina of scents that CarbonPlank construction could not rival. No wonder these buildings were carefully preserved.

I'd seen this building before but never entered. Like many older buildings, the floor plan was subdivided into many rooms, and the ceiling was high. Several exhibition areas were carpeted, but our footsteps on the planking of the foyer produced large, roomy echoes.

One of the doors to the side rooms opened, and a familiar face appeared.

It was Scott Rice. All six-foot-four of him.

"Peter?" Did he know Scott was here?

"We meet here on occasion," Peter explained.

The room we entered was simply furnished with old but comfortable chairs and a couple of tables. There were no exhibits here. It was a place to visit or read or study.

Scott's dark gaze was upon Peter, his expression inquiring, though if I did not know him I might have missed it. Scott was not stoic, I decided, just quiet. Perhaps he was an introvert, like me. He wore a flannel shirt and thick jeans, a retro look but practical in this weather. A satchel sat on one of the tables. His?

Peter shut the door with a click, and we all found seats. Scott fumbled with the clasp of his satchel, then hesitated.

"It's okay," Peter said.

I meet with others to study the scriptures, Peter had said.

His wary gaze on me, Scott opened the bag and drew out a book.

The Complete Handyman said the cover. I frowned. That wasn't illegal or controlled.

He opened the book, revealing a type of paper I had last seen in 1631. Every evening, Winthrop had opened the scriptures and read a short passage before prayer. His Bible looked like this.

It was a familiar sight in an unfamiliar context. My mind spun.

Scott—a believer too?

How many in the department were secret believers? How many on campus? In Boston?

I had so many questions. And I remembered my father's admonition to stay away from the regulated church. Was my father a believer too?

"Gen?" Peter asked.

"I don't even know where to start."

"I have only one question," Scott said. "Will you report us?"

"No, no of course not. I-I'm confused about a lot of things, but I certainly won't report you."

Scott's shoulders relaxed. "It's difficult to find a place to meet. Old buildings work the best—they aren't prewired for AI."

In other words, no one here was listening to our conversation.

A signal seemed to pass between the men. Peter began to pray.

"Open your word of life to us, O Lord. Give us hearts to hear and receive. Give us wisdom and understanding."

Scott read a section from the Psalms. They seemed to have a sort of order to this thing.

"Questions?" Peter asked.

"Yes, I do." Scott stared at the Bible in his large hands. "In the journal, you recorded sections from the sermons there—which I deleted from the record, of course. I remember one about 'Christ the fountain.' Do you recall the scripture that was based on?"

Peter frowned. "Mr. Wilson quoted a lot of scriptures in that sermon."

Christ the fountain. I couldn't remember either. *No, wait.* "Z. The reference started with the letter Z."

Peter's face lit up. "There are two books starting with Z. Thanks, Gen. That really narrows it down."

Scott began turning pages, and for a few minutes the *shrush, shrush* of paper filled the room.

"Here," he said. "'In that day there shall be a fountain opened to the house of David and to the inhabitants of Jerusalem for sin and for uncleanness.' Zechariah chapter thirteen."

"The house of David," Peter said. "The Messiah?"

Scott nodded. "For sin... " He stared at the page, visibly moved. "It's here, it's really here. When you wrote about the sermons and the singing, it seemed like a dream."

I was forgotten as the men engaged in an earnest conversation.

"One question I had, one clue I sought as I was back there," Peter was saying, "was how these men could tease out the meaning of obscure passages like this."

"And what did you notice?"

My attention sharpened. The meaning of old documents was sometimes difficult to discern. There were rules, principles. In fact, the English Department had a course on this.

"I noticed Mr. Wilson took scriptures from various places to prove a point," Peter said. "There's a reason we readily identify this verse as Messianic. The Son of David. It's all over the place."

"Context," I said. "Immediate context and global context. Looking at a writer's opus, you can look at terms he uses in one place to unravel what he means in another."

They stared at me, and I shrugged.

Scott tapped on the page. "Wait. 'A writer's opus,' you said."

"Everything a certain person has written."

He lifted the Bible in his lap. "One opus? One writer?"

I had read the Bible through once. I knew there were many writers.

Peter smiled. "One author. Many writers."

I filed that concept away for later. "There do seem to be overarching themes. Law, redemption, grace."

They looked at me. Scott nodded slowly.

"I wish Professor—" Peter began to say.

Scott grunted, and Peter stopped.

"You said a certain professor had been arrested," I said to Peter. "Did he meet with you?"

Scott frowned. "How much did you tell her?"

Chapter 23

Preparation

"I shall leave the matter, and desire the Lord to show him his errors and return him to the way of truth, and give him a settled judgment and constancy therein; for I hope he belongs to the Lord and that He will show him mercy."

— William Bradford, of Roger Williams, *Of Plymouth Plantation*

THERE WAS silence for a moment before Peter spoke. "I've told her nothing, really. Except for the fact that a professor was arrested because of his connection with Beech Street."

I was sure the church in question had a name, but Peter seemed to be careful about using names, particulars, or even the term, "Christian."

Were such terms keywords for surveillance AIs?

"I didn't realize believers were arrested," I said. "Until now."

Scott's gaze fastened on me. "But they are registered."

"That just seems normal. Like getting a license to drink alcohol. Everything is regulated or licensed."

"We haven't heard from Professor Kiyoshi ever since," Peter said.

I thought of the trolleys. "What do they do—"

"We don't know much," Scott said, staring at the book in his hands.

"The professor knew a man who had a contact inside the Walpole prison," Peter said. "They try to reeducate believers. If that fails, they are punished until they submit."

The trolleys.

"Suffice it to say, we don't want to be caught," Scott said.

"We pray for Professor Kiyoshi every day." Peter's voice was tight.

"The Star Chamber," I said. "The 1630s. Prominent Puritans were brought before this ad hoc tribunal to answer for their crimes."

Scott looked up at me and nodded.

History repeats itself.

"It affects Peter, too," I said. "His Trip. Roger Williams is fleeing Salem in the winter of 1636 because he will be in trouble if he goes back to England."

Scott's brows drew together. "I knew the Puritans were persecuted. So it seems harsh that the Bay Colony would do this to Williams."

"They were in a bad spot," Peter said. "Without at least lip service to the king, they would lose their legal right to inhabit New England."

"At first, Roger Williams complied," I said. "He kept his comments to himself. He was discreet. But when the Salem church's pastor died, he took the helm, and became more vocal."

I explained Salem's role in the difficulties. "It was the last straw. The magistrates had to act."

"How does Williams survive? You said he went to Rhode Island," Scott asked.

"Not right away," I said. "The Wampanoag helped him, sheltered him. He would have died otherwise."

Scott's face creased as he regarded Peter. "Brother, you'd better dress warmly. When are you scheduled to leave?"

"Tuesday after this."

They looked at me.

Peter spoke first. "Sunday. Want to meet with us again?"

I nodded.

Then I wondered. What would happen if we were all found out? I wasn't a believer. Not really. Would they even care?

I already hated AIs. I had reason to fear them now.

Standing, I took a deep breath. "Do they put women in trolleys?"

Present Day

Journal

Scott, this is a good idea. Testing the new journal while I am still here. Getting the hang of the pen again—so different from typing or voice activation. But I've always loved the feel of pen on paper.

And it's a good safeguard to put an implant in the journal itself. I can send it back. Or it can be independently recalled. Especially for this Trip. Of course, if I meet with real trouble, I will simply come back myself, but for plotting Williams's course through the wilderness, it occurs to me we can establish both time and place by sending the journal. I may not need it much during a short Trip anyway.

Dr. Howard pretends the Trip is inconsequential. The reality is that it is dangerous. Not that he is a coward, but perhaps he thinks the data gained are not worth the risk. But I confess everything about Roger Williams fascinates me, and not just in an academic way. He is a brother, an earnest believer, who faces much adversity for conscience's sake. I don't need to explain more.

What to do about Gen. That is always the question for me. I am so worried about her. She has not professed faith in Christ, but in meeting with us, she exposes herself to the same danger.

We have tossed this back and forth so many times. "Go into all the world and make disciples" is not a suggestion. It's a command. I am convinced the Lord Jesus would have us act wisely. But when is "wisdom" a cloak for cowardice?

Professor Kiyoshi took a chance when he first spoke to me. He opened up the great metaphysical questions—why are we here, does life have a purpose? All perfectly legal and innocent. Then he slipped me a Gospel of John and asked me what I thought. The rest you know.

Geneva is coming at this from an entirely different angle. She could probably explain the gospel herself. She just doesn't believe it. I do have one thought. Sitting under the sound of Mr. Wilson's voice, I couldn't understand how anyone could hear it and not be as moved as I was. It may be that the Lord is preparing her—bringing her—to Himself, and our study is another part of that. We can pray He opens her eyes.

Scott, in case something happens to me on the Trip, will you look after her?

Peter

~

"Three?" Ratcliffe asked.

I took a bit of croissant, chewed, and swallowed. "What, are you counting? Who cares if I eat three croissants?"

"Each *pain au chocolat* contains approximately three hundred calories. Ten grams of saturated fat."

"Ten delicious grams." In actuality, I was getting full, but I wasn't going to give Ratcliffe any satisfaction. I took another large bite. I had put in a long, difficult, and seemingly fruitless day at the Archives, and I needed comfort.

"Do you know what your triglycerides are?"

"No." I avoided doctors. "French food is good for you. Just look at the French." They were skinny. All that bread and cheese, and they somehow never gained weight. "Lest you forget, I lost weight on that Trip."

"True. But still—"

I wiped my mouth. Peter had only a few days before his departure to 1636, and I was having a hard time thinking of ways to prepare him. There was little actual data on Roger Williams's movements after leaving his wife and children behind in Salem that cold January day.

I wished I could go too.

"Ratcliffe. I have a task for you." A hazy idea began to coalesce in my mind. And I really wanted to keep the AI occupied. Shutting it down looked suspicious.

Peter was canny, and that's how I needed to be.

"I need a primer on the Massachusett language, also known as Wampanoag. The Native language. It should be accessible in the Cloud. A phrase book, if you will, for Peter. I need you to assemble one."

"I am not a linguistics AI."

The strength—and weakness—of AIs had to do with their decentralization. Like flying cars instead of shuttles or larger craft. But it could be overcome to a degree.

"Can you talk to Tollers at the Applied History Department?"

Ratcliffe's voice sounded whiny. "I can try."

The AI fell silent, and I wondered. Well, Tollers *was* incredibly useful in training Travelers. Perhaps Peter could ask for some time with it as well.

Because Roger Williams was headed into Indian territory, and Peter would be too.

"But here?" I asked Peter. The alcove was isolated from the main reading room, but still. Houghton Library was a public place. There were always people about, even on Sunday.

Scott strolled in. Like Peter, he had a StudyPad tucked under his arm. No sign of the Bible.

"Hiding in plain sight," Peter said in a low voice. "It's an old building. We've done experiments. The building's AI doesn't respond to us in this nook."

I pulled a CarbonFirm chair closer to Peter's. The men opened with hushed prayers, and soon we were looking at the scriptures.

"The covenant of works," Peter tapped his Pad. "The Puritans claim Adam was part of this covenant. Are there scriptures to support this?"

"He was before the Law of Moses," Scott said.

"Adam was given a law too."

"When he broke it, he died," Scott murmured. "Life and death hinged on obedience."

I kept an eye on the doorway. We were in a place clearly designed for group study, set off from the main area, but not entirely private. Any random graduate student could overhear us.

"Adam pops up several times in the New Testament," Peter said. "I'm still grappling with the meaning of Romans five."

Adam was a problematic person, period. Adam's sin somehow spelled the downfall of all mankind. But it wasn't Romans chapter five that puzzled me.

It was the concept of sin itself. Sin was meaningless without the commandment. And the commandment came from God.

If God was real, I was a sinner.

I heard footsteps.

"What is this?" Dr. Howard's bulging face intruded, his facial hair fuller than I had ever seen it. Baggy trousers and an equally relaxed jacket concealed his frame. "Who is Adam?"

"The first man, according to the Puritans," Peter said. "We are reviewing some theology."

"And getting primed on the Massachusett language," Scott added.

I stopped breathing.

"Just in case," Peter said. "Roger Will—"

"I know, I know." Dr. Howard waved a hand, scowling. "The

Native Americans." He looked around. "This whole place needs an upgrade. Hardly any signal."

I tapped my Pad. "You're right. I can't connect."

He left, and I took a deep breath. The others were quiet.

"He's leaving tomorrow," I said. "For 1862. And he gets extra grumpy just before a Trip."

As it turned out, Peter was able to schedule time with Tollers the next day. I hid in the Archives until I knew Dr. Howard was gone. As I went through the trivialities cluttering my inbox, questions harassed me.

Peter was leaving tomorrow. My stomach turned over thinking of the dangers.

And the secret meetings. Was I now a Christian? What exactly made a Christian, a Christian?

Part of me had accepted the challenge to protect the men, to keep their secret. But I wasn't yet one of them. Not exactly.

The root of the matter. John Winthrop said Roger Williams was sound with regard to the root of the matter, the gospel itself. That was the key.

I shoved that train of thought aside. I needed to focus on practical matters.

Peter.

I went to see Scott. He was in his office, scrutinizing some coins. He looked up, saw me, and dropped several. A shilling spun on his desk and rolled to the floor.

I dove for it. "Nice coin," I said lamely. Then I looked at him.

"He needs money," Scott said. "But trade goods are even more important."

"Like what?" Trading with Indians evoked images of mirrors and trinkets.

In response, he reached for a knife. It was not much bigger than the eating knife I still had in my skirt pocket.

Why I kept all that junk I didn't know.

"Natives had no steel, only beaten copper." He placed the knife and several others in a small satchel.

"Food?" I worried that Peter wouldn't have enough to eat.

"He will be sent back with enough bread and cheese for seven days. And he's bringing a cask of cider to the Williams's house. Oh—" He grabbed a sack below his desk and pulled it out. "And this. Charcoal."

January. Yes. They'd need fuel.

"There's only one problem," Scott said. "The dates are uncertain. We don't know the exact day Roger Williams leaves Salem. We only know the authorities come knocking on his door three days later."

"So, Peter has a week to meet up with Williams and get to an Indian village."

"Or return."

I didn't like this plan at all.

I decided to take Ratcliffe's dietary advice. On the way home, I bought a few ounces of good chocolate in a specialty shop instead of stopping at the café for a bag of croissants. The chocolate was labeled *fair trade,* and though it was costly for such a small amount, I viewed it as an investment. I broke off an ounce and ate it slowly.

It was worth it.

I broke off a larger piece, wrapped it in CarbonFilm, and found a place for it in one of my pockets. Now I was ready to face the next day.

Perhaps.

I woke in the middle of the night, picturing Peter floundering in the snow. Could I pray? Even if God heard me, would it make a difference?

Peter said that perhaps certain things were *meant to be*.

That sounded like some fatalistic philosophy to me. I knew Puritan theology was not fatalistic, not at all. They pressed things like repentance and duty.

They also said God was sovereign over the affairs of man.

I was not going to square this circle tonight.

"O God, I believe you're there." Maybe. "Okay, I'm not certain about it. But Peter is. Peter knows you. Would you—"

Adam and the sinfulness of man loomed before me. My sinfulness. Like a giant boulder, it blocked my hope of being heard. Still. Peter was in danger.

"If you're as sovereign and all-knowing as they say, you must hear me. Please, help him. Not for my sake, for Peter's sake. If you're sovereign, you know he's in danger."

My throat closed and my eyes flooded with tears. "Please," I croaked.

Chapter 24

The Exile

"And for the season it was winter, and they that know the winters of that country know them to be sharp and violent, and subject to cruel and fierce storms."

— William Bradford

THE NEXT DAY I woke early, but there was nothing to do in the apartment except fret, so I left while the pink glow of sunrise hovered over the east. I'd seen the sun rise over the ocean in 1631. It must be doing the same right now, just beyond the buildings and haze of Boston.

I never took the trolleys anymore, and the late November air gusted against my face and swirled up my skirt. It wasn't as frigid as what I had experienced in 1631, but cold enough to remind me of what Peter would face today.

Halfway to work, the warmth of the market drew me inside. I wandered aimlessly through the aisles like a zombie. What could I give Peter to help him survive a week of brutal cold? Nothing here. It needed to be period appropriate.

Scott and Candy would make sure he was dressed warmly. But what about fire? The fact that he would be in a forest, surrounded by wood, was not necessarily helpful. Green wood did not burn easily.

I stared at rows of cheerful snacks wrapped in colorful Carbon-Film. Candy would make sure he'd have food. What he really needed was something he could burn.

Alcohol. Alcohol was flammable. It was also ubiquitous in the Massachusetts Bay Colony, even though the Puritans were mindful of the dangers of drunkenness. Winthrop chose not to make toasts around the table, knowing the custom could lead to excess.

Would ale help start a fire? I doubted it. I needed something stronger. But I didn't have a license to drink alcohol, much less purchase it.

Still, I wandered down the next aisle and spotted wine and brandy. Then a small dark bottle. Rum. *That might work.* I needed to ask Candy. Maybe they had some.

I purchased a bag of nuts, the only snack that looked like real food, and left the store. Now that I had a purpose, my stride lengthened, and I arrived at the Archives panting.

Lucy was still wearing her coat. She'd just arrived.

"Lucy, today's the day."

She scrutinized me. "Are you okay?"

"Fine. Any crises?"

"No, actually. Dr. Howard's gone, and—"

"Peter's leaving." Our prep work was essentially finished for the week. "I need to see Candy."

Lucy waved a hand, shooing me out.

She understood.

I ran into Scott in the hall. "Good morning," he said, his dark gaze questioning.

"Do we have rum? Can we send Peter with rum?"

"Maybe. Why? He can't bring much."

I shared my thoughts about fire.

His expression turned thoughtful. "Let's check and see if we have any. We always have things like ale and cider."

I followed him through his office and into a back storeroom. Pottery, tools, leather goods, and rolls of canvas and oilcloth crammed the shelves on either side.

"Over here." Scott indicated a corner crammed with kegs and jugs. "Ale. Here's cider." He sniffed a small jug. "Bingo."

He popped open the cork and poured a little into a cup. Sniffed again. Tasted and scrunched his face. "That is strong."

"Can we send him back with a small flask?"

More rummaging. "Here. This might work."

It was a gourd. A canteen of sorts. It held not more than half a liter —a pint, in old-style measurements.

"Perfect, Scott. Thank you."

A rustle made me turn. Candy stood in the doorway. "Scott. Help me choose a jacket." She noticed the gourd.

"Rum," I said. "For fire."

I followed them into Candy's domain. Slithering between the stacks, I discovered Peter in the back near the computer and the red coat on the wall. He was only partially dressed.

Well, partially dressed according to 1636 eyes. A baggy shirt hung over his breeches. His calves were bundled in fur, making him look bottom-heavy.

Candy motioned to a stack of clothing. Peter's red jerkin lay on top.

"I can't finish dressing him yet," she explained. "He'll sweat."

He was probably sweating already. But I understood. It would not be good to throw him into frigid weather all sweaty.

Peter stood patiently. He looked my way. "Gen. While we're

waiting for these two to sort out my clothes, can you drill me in Wampanoag?"

We found seats among the racks of linen and leather. I poked at my Pad and drew up the file.

"We found rum."

Peter's brows lifted.

"To help start a fire."

His expression shifted. "Good idea. But look, I'll only be gone a week."

"That's a long time in a January forest."

He looked at his furry shins. "My feet are warm. I'm sure the rest of me will be too. I'm wearing two shirts, and that's just the beginning."

"Friend. How do you say, 'friend?'"

"*Netop.*"

"How do you say, 'help me?'"

Peter frowned and scratched his head. "Remind me."

As we surveyed words and phrases that might be useful, I surveyed Peter. His dark curls. His eyes, their deep brown color like fine chocolate.

I would give anything to pile on skirts and warm clothing and go along.

In the Launch Room, I surveyed Peter's supplies. Charcoal. A satchel full of food. The cider. A pile of clothes from Costumes. Scott was rummaging in a cupboard.

Chamar was making funny faces over the computer screen. But the tech was like that. Funny faces were normal. He tapped and poked and spoke to the Launch Room AI. But he didn't look alarmed. Everything was fine. Hopefully.

I turned to him. "When does Peter return?"

"Our time? Tomorrow. At two." He tilted his head. "Of course, he is able to come back sooner, or send the journal back independently."

"The book?"

"Yes, it's been upgraded. It has its own implant."

I wasn't sure how that would be useful, but Scott must have asked for that feature, and I trusted Scott.

Peter walked in, rubbing his wrist. He hadn't added any more clothing. Looking pensive, he walked over to the launchpad and sat down on the edge.

I joined him. "Medical?"

He nodded. "All set. So, we don't know exactly where Williams is going?"

"Massasoit is eighty miles away. He's got to stop somewhere closer. The Massachusetts villages near Salem are governed by Wenepoykin. Sagamore George is how the settlers referred to him."

"I read the article you sent. But how far is he from Salem?"

"The closest village?" I plucked at my skirt, restless. "There is no way to know. Modern-day Reading is about twelve miles away. There might be a village there."

"According to the article, many of these people died in 1633."

I nodded. "Smallpox. Wenepoykin was disfigured by it, but he survived. The villages will be small."

"A dozen miles. Not far."

"That's the best-case scenario."

He looked at me silently.

I studied Peter's face. The left brow had a quirk in it unmatched by his right. His bottom lip curved just so.

"Gen..." His voice was strangely husky.

Movement caught my eye. Above us, Scott loomed.

"The journal." A funny expression washed over his face as he handed the book to Peter. "All set."

Peter scrambled to his feet.

I didn't know what he felt about me, but I knew how I felt about him.

~

My heels struck the pavement firmly as I walked home, a borrowed satchel swinging against my hip. I was acutely aware of the contents of the bag I'd begged from Candy, who was eager to help.

"Anything leather needs care. Storing it in an air-conditioned room for months on end dries it out. By taking it home you're doing it a favor. Take this, it's conditioner. Apply and buff every three months." Her blue gaze held mine for an extra beat. She hadn't witnessed Peter's departure but knew I had. "Lunch in the cafeteria tomorrow?"

Lunch. Two o'clock return. "Yes, I'd love that."

I doubted I could eat, but I welcomed the company as I whiled away the time.

I tightened my grip on the bag's strap. Even Candy wasn't aware of the cargo in the satchel, an item I'd borrowed from the Archives. "Borrowed" was a euphemism, as nothing could leave, nothing was checked out. Everyone read uploads or came to the Archives personally to study.

I skipped the café and went straight to my door.

"Welcome home," Ratcliffe said.

"Why are you so friendly?"

Silence for a beat. "Studies show when an AI is programmed to use social commonplaces, tension and anxiety are reduced in the human."

"You think I'm anxious?" I set down the satchel on the small dining room table. I rummaged for a snack, unwilling to give thought to actual cooking.

"I am charting chocolate croissant consumption as a stand-in for anxiety."

Spying on me. Well, I was not eating a croissant now, and my anxieties were off the charts. The contents of the satchel glowed in my mind like a bomb ready to go off.

Not to mention Peter. He was undoubtedly fighting a blizzard at this very moment.

Or had fought. Time travel messed with my mind.

"I have good news," the AI said. "I found a table."

Finally, I remembered. I'd asked for an entry table. "What did you find?"

"Cherrywood. Reclaimed, I think. Beautiful. An estate sale."

"How much?" I'd given him parameters already. I hoped he'd taken price into account—but he was a computer, he'd have to, wouldn't he?

He recited the asking price with a triumphant tone.

"Buy it. You have my account info."

"Offer sent."

My hostility ebbed, and I was able to think more clearly.

"Ratcliffe, the croissant thing is a stroke of genius." I found some jerky I'd bought last week. I brought the jerky and an apple to the table.

"Why, thank you."

"I am sure you represent the very latest in AI technology." I ripped open the jerky package.

"Not exactly." Did I detect hesitation?

"Rat, run a short scan of your operating system. I'd like to know."

I took a bite of my apple and studied the satchel. Thought about its contents.

"Working. Operating system installed seven years ago, number —"

"Stop. Review pending updates." I never installed updates, there must be a lot.

"Yes, absolutely. Working."

I inserted a piece of jerky in my mouth and spat it out. I was spoiled, in a way, by seventeenth-century food. You had to make sure it hadn't gone bad, but it was always real at least.

"There are nineteen updates available. Three cost money."

"How much?"

The amounts were small.

"Go ahead. Install all updates and restart when finished."

I gnawed the apple all the way to the core. That would keep Ratcliffe busy.

I took the satchel to the bedroom, unbuckled the latch, and drew out the book inside.

Holy Bible blared the front. Bound in russet-red fake leather, the copyright proclaimed it to be about sixty years old. *King James Version* appeared in small letters underneath the title. The edges of the pages were gold, and some of the patina had worn off. Still, it was in decent shape—there were no torn pages and no water damage. Overall, a good specimen.

I doubted it had been read much. I had used this volume to read through the scriptures as an adjunct to my study of theology. Some of the Old Testament was heavy slogging, though from listening to Mr. Wilson and even Peter, I knew there were treasures in those obscure places.

I wanted to pray. To persuade God to keep Peter safe. But my prayers clogged my throat. God seemed very far away.

As I set the book on my bed, my fingers seemed to burn. I was glad Ratcliffe was occupied. Oh, I could come up with an excuse for what I was doing, but I didn't want to. Not now.

Genesis. Quickly, I read the first page. The creation of the world. It seemed far-fetched, yet I knew God as Creator was an important thematic element of the Bible as a whole.

In the beginning God. I tucked that away for later. Ratcliffe would be distracted for only so long. I got up and went to the kitchen. I had a cookbook—my grandmother's—with a large cover. I grabbed scissors and tape and brought everything into the bedroom.

Fifteen busy minutes later, the Bible was disguised. I'd have to cook more, to fool Ratcliffe, but that was no hardship. Fake food seemed especially bad now that I'd drunk milk fresh from a cow. I even had fond memories of cornmeal porridge.

"Updates complete." Ratcliffe was back.

"Any new functionality?" I needed to know how dangerous my AI was.

"Quicker processing speed. Better video processing and auditory recognition. Enhanced security suite."

"What's a security suite?"

"Basic surveillance and anti-theft programming. Updated Homeland keywords and phrases."

"So, if I became some sort of dangerous person, you'd be able to tell?"

"For shame," Rat said. "You are not a bad person. I am programmed to protect you."

Likely story. But maybe at some point, I could use that. "You said keywords. I could trigger your surveillance and reporting functions accidentally."

A pause. "You are correct. There is quite a long list of phrases here."

"Can you give me a few examples?"

"Freedom of expression. The rule of law. Made in the image of God."

"Ratcliffe, some of those expressions could be used in innocent contexts. On top of which, I work with historical documents, which are replete with this kind of stuff."

I doubted if making an argument would help, but who knew?

"I see your point. I will give this to my logic subroutine."

"Thank you."

The AI fell silent, and I took a shower still thinking about the creation of the world. I had purposed to read about Adam but hadn't got to him yet. The fact—was it a fact?—of creation had a number of uncomfortable implications all by itself.

Had God indeed—immediately or in some secondary way—created me?

If so, what did that imply?

As I was dressing, the voice-over contact buzz interrupted my thoughts.

"Ratcliffe, who's calling?"

"Scott Rice."

"Take the call."

"Gen? It's Scott. You need to come in. We have a situation."

Chapter 25

The Rescue

"...God requireth not a uniformity of religion to be enacted or enforced in a civil state..."

— Roger Williams, *The Bloudy Tenent of Persecution*, 1644

WE MET at the entrance to the Launch Room. Hastily dressed, I stood before Scott clad in a mishmash of clothing. The wool skirt was from Costumes, the sweater was mine. I was even wearing seventeenth-century pockets, which held all the flotsam and jetsam I'd been clinging to since I'd returned.

"You said something about the journal," I prompted. The call had been brief.

"Come." Wearing a rumpled red plaid shirt and jeans, Scott led me inside. It was at least eight o'clock, and the building's lighting was subdued. The computer podium in the Launch Room was the brightest thing there. The AI was awake, of course, and kept track of Travelers.

"Peter sent the journal back?"

"The AI notified me. I read the journal, but there wasn't much." He tapped the podium's screen. "I uploaded it."

He stepped aside and I scrolled. There was just one entry.

~

Jan ? 1636

Scott, I am writing this late at night by the light of a candle. I found the Williams's home after asking someone for directions. That was interesting. The fellow seemed concerned that I would align myself with Roger Williams. "There be folks here who love his teaching," he said. "But we cannot have discord, ye see that, Goodman?"

It was a veiled warning. The men of Salem would not defend Williams. I did not know if they'd heard rumors that the magistrates' men were coming any day to haul him off to a waiting ship, but the tension was undeniable.

Mary Williams was tense and tired, but was happy to see me, and asked about my wife. There is only the most basic of food in the house, and the cider was welcome. Her house is cold, so I went outside seeking wood. I had arrived in the afternoon, too late to follow her husband immediately. Besides, she couldn't—or wouldn't—tell me where he went.

I asked, "Where is the nearest village? Where does Sagamore George live?"

Her face relaxed. I had guessed his destination. "I know not. I have not been there. But I believe 'tis a day's journey to the west."

I am leaving half the charcoal with her and her children, as I had not time to lay in much wood, and in any case, green wood burns poorly. I suspect between Roger Williams's sickness and the trips to New Town, he had not been able to prepare properly for winter.

I plan to leave as soon as I can see my hand before my face. Snow has been falling—lazy, fat flakes. Not a blizzard by any means, but still a problem. They will cover any trace of the man if I do not find him soon. I will send back this journal at some point on my journey, so you can get some data. Peter

~

"Scott. He gave away—"

"That's not the problem."

He closed the file. "Hal, overlay the time and location data from the journal implant to a map of the area around Salem, Massachusetts, in the early seventeenth century."

Hal was the Launch Room AI's name, presumably.

"Working," Hal intoned. "Finished."

A map lit up on the podium's screen. A red line jumped out at me. "What's this little circle?"

"That's the problem," Scott said. "Peter is wandering in circles."

"What? Why?"

Scott stepped back from the podium, his shoulders relaxing. He'd never gone home, that was obvious. He had no five o'clock shadow, but I didn't know how much of a beard Native Americans grew. "I studied tracking once. You know the week we get for cultural training and appreciation?"

"CTA. Yes. My mother says I should go to the Oneida Nation one year. They have camps."

Scott lifted his brows at this. I hadn't told him anything about my family. "I went to a camp sponsored by the Mohawk Nation. It was fun, and I learned a little. The value of a compass, and the tendency to travel in circles." A line deepened between his brows. "I should have explained. I gave him a compass, but..."

"He would need to keep checking it."

"Most people have a dominant leg," Scott said. "You may think you are walking in a straight line, but in a snowstorm or other situations without familiar landmarks, you will start traveling in a circle."

All my fears coalesced in my belly. I wanted to throw up. "We need to go."

Scott was silent for a moment. "He has an implant. He can come back at any time."

"Only if he's conscious."

I dashed to Costumes and grabbed what I needed to dress for an Arctic blizzard, including two heavy cloaks. I sped back to the Launch Room, my leather shoes making altogether too much noise in the dim, empty hallways.

I was dressed, but I couldn't go back without an implant, and the AI would have to cooperate. All these hindrances made it seem impossible.

But we had to figure out a way. Peter was in danger.

Scott was still standing over the podium when I returned. His face was shadowed.

"I might be able to get us an implant," he said, looking at me. "I should be the one going back."

"I wish we could both go. Can't you skip your medicine for a day or two?"

He shook his head. "Thirty-six hours at most."

His epilepsy was no ordinary kind. They couldn't fix it. It was certainly worse than mere anxiety. Scott was not averse to risk, that I was sure of. Anyone who studied the Bible illegally put himself in danger.

"I will go. But what about the AI?"

"Hal? I think I can swing that. Peter gave me the admin passcode."

Why would—but no, Peter and Scott were brethren in faith. It meant something. Peter would have trusted Scott with just about anything.

"Hal?" Scott's voice was confident—almost. "We need an implant programmed and a Trip scheduled."

"Sorry, Scott. I can't do that."

My breath caught in my throat.

"Passcode Peter Donatelli root command N-C-C seventeen-oh-one Enterprise."

"Accepted. What can I do for you?"

I took a big gulp of air. We were in.

A white cold slammed me, and I fought to gain my equilibrium. I was in the precise spot Peter had been when he'd sent the journal back.

But three hours behind him. Hal, the AI, had been insistent.

"I can't send you back any closer! Some safeties are hardwired!"

Scott had frowned darkly and found a sack of charcoal for me. Then he laid a rolled piece of canvas across my shoulders. "You'll be staying overnight, I'm sure." He handed me the journal. "You can send it back anytime."

I tried to see through the whirling snowflakes, a dizzying veil obscuring my vision in every direction. They were no longer the fat, lazy flakes of Peter's description. They were small and sharp. The weather had turned. The frigid air stung my nose and eyes.

I took a step and studied the ground. The snow was not deep. At least, not yet.

"Forget about seeing obvious footprints," Scott had said. "Look for other things. A depression. A twig out of place. And he may try to leave a trail."

I doubted that last possibility. On top of which, a man traveling in circles might set off in any direction.

I decided to search the entire area before setting off west. I was sure that sooner or later Peter would check his compass. Scott had given me forty-eight hours. He insisted I return. "We can't lose you both," he'd said.

No, that would not happen. I'd find him. I pulled out my compass and waited till the iron needle began to settle in a particular direction —north. I'd keep it clutched in my glove, ever conscious of the tendency to circle.

On either side, through the white, I made out trees, lifting menacing branches to an invisible sky. The sun was totally obscured behind clouds, and for a moment I panicked.

If there was shelter nearby—a farm, a warm barn—I'd never see it. I'd walk within a quarter mile and never know.

I took a steadying breath and resumed my search.

Tiny irregularities emerged from the thin blanket of snow. A rock. Other objects came into focus. A stick. A thick root led to an oak. No footprints, nothing even close.

I took careful steps south, then west, then north, eyeing my compass to stay oriented. Which way had Peter gone?

I returned to the west and took several steps. A depression caught my eye.

It could be anything.

I stepped to the side of the dip and scanned the ground. I didn't see anything, but I needed to go west eventually. I took a half dozen steps.

There. Another tiny dip in the three-inch snow. It looked the same as the first, and my heart leapt in my throat.

A footprint?

I followed the trail, such as it was. Soon the trees crowded in, their bare branches skeletal, and their roots white humps under the snow. I kept the compass in my gloved hand, checking my direction now and again. Peter must have consulted his own compass. He was headed west once again and, for now at least, was no longer walking in circles.

The snow continued, and I worried. At some point, the flakes would obscure the shallow tracks. Pushing myself to keep up a decent pace, I kept reasonably warm—all but my face. I couldn't feel my nose, and my cheeks stung.

How far could a man travel in three hours?

I made a calculation. About ten miles. I was ten miles behind him. I wondered about our guess of twelve miles to the village. Mary Williams had called it a day's journey. How far could a man walk in a day?

I made another calculation. In good weather, as far as thirty miles.

I glanced at the western sky and made out the sun's presence behind a bright patch of cloud. I only had an hour or two before I needed to make camp.

I increased my pace. My throat burned from the cold air. I could no longer feel my feet, but I forced myself to move.

It was no longer Peter I was concerned about. The snow and cold would swallow me up as well. And the dips and subtle tracks I was following were slowly disappearing, vanishing under a white blanket. The naked forest grew gloomy as the sun descended. The path I was following seemed a figment of my imagination.

A depression in the snow lay ahead. Was that a footprint? I could no longer tell. I glanced at my compass and faced west. Took several more steps—was *that* a print? No matter, I plunged forward—

And fell flat on my face. Powdery snow choked me, and my satchel slipped off my shoulder. My compass—where was it?

I got to my knees and searched. Without that compass I was lost. I could signal with my implant and return, but I'd purposed not to do so without Peter. He'd come this way.

He was in danger.

A shadow fell over the snow.

I looked up. A monster with coal-black eyes glared at me.

I scrambled to stand but instead fell back upon my rump in the powder. Not a monster, but a man, dressed in leather and furs. His hands emerged from slits in a dark fur poncho, and raccoon tails framed his face.

My breaths were short and panicked. I sought to remember words from the primer, but my mind seemed frozen as well as my body.

"I-I'm a friend. *Netop.*" Netop—friend. I hoped. I managed to stand. "*Muttae wunee.*" I couldn't remember what that meant. Maybe part of the "How are you?" exchange of pleasantries.

I thrust my hand into my pocket, looking for a gift. My fingers closed on a lumpy bag. Nuts. I opened the CarbonFilm—a no-no here —grabbed the man's hand and poured the snack into his palm.

The man tasted them, then threw the rest into his mouth and crunched. "I think you not well." He gestured and emitted a string of incomprehensible syllables. The meaning was clear. I was alone in a snowstorm. Not a good situation.

At least, he did not act like he was about to kill me just yet. "Roger Williams?" Perhaps the Indian could help me. "Sagamore George."

I pointed in the general direction of west—I thought. Then I bent and ran my hands through the snow. Where was my compass?

The Indian—I couldn't think of him as a "Native American" in this time—reached down and plucked something up. My compass.

The Indian studied the face of the device.

"I can show you how—"

He ignored me, shoved the object somewhere in his clothing, and grabbed my wrist.

"We go."

He jerked me along, and we sped through the woods. I had no idea if he'd understood anything I'd said.

And it was going to be dark soon.

I thought of nothing but keeping my feet moving after that. The cold had seeped into my bones, and my mind was sluggish. The quick march helped, but my lungs ached. Soon, my thighs began to burn. The man's grip on my arm kept me going, but my shoulder hurt— whenever I slowed, I received a sharp tug.

Slowly I became aware of a huddled shape up ahead. The gray light of dusk illumined two humps in the snow.

Two men, huddled side-by-side.

Unmoving.

Chapter 26

The Village

— Roger Williams, *A Key into the Language
of America*, 1643

"Peter!" I staggered forward, my limbs stiff. The Indian released me.

His eyes were closed, his body curled up like a child's. Roger Williams sat motionless next to him, his dark hair powdered with white.

"Peter, wake up." I shook him. Surely he wasn't dead already. I was tempted to simply press our implants and escape, but I couldn't leave Williams in this state.

Peter's eyelids fluttered. "Gen?"

The Indian had squatted nearby. I poked him. "Fire—we need fire."

I stood and looked around for fuel. I had charcoal, but I'd need kindling and deadwood to build a decent fire to repel this cold.

It was almost dark, but in the gloom I could make out the shapes of underbrush. I scrabbled and found a few twigs, but I simply did not have the strength to do more.

"Peter, help me start a fire."

"Hmm?" Peter began to rouse.

Roger Williams blinked and frowned, as if he did not know where he was. The Indian had disappeared.

I pushed the snow away in front of us, poured out a generous amount of the charcoal, and wedged the twigs in the middle of the pile. I thrust my hand in my pocket for the flint and steel. My fingers were stiff, and I could barely feel them, but I forced them to move.

Chocolate, flint and steel, and a knife poured out of my pocket. I grabbed what I needed and started making sparks.

I gulped air. We were going to die in this frozen waste. I adjusted my grip on the flint.

Tap, tap, tap.

Now and again sparks flew onto the tinder. I needed something like tow, something like paper. I turned my gaze to the wrapped remnant of chocolate, a Traveler through time.

It was still covered in lint. Even a few bits of lint might help. I plucked it off and perched it on one of the black lumps.

Tap, tap, tap. Sparks flew. The lint glowed.

I held my breath.

Yes! The glow spread and a minuscule flash of yellow appeared. I chose the tiniest twig and fed it to the small flame. After about ten minutes, the rough surface of a piece of charcoal glowed orange. I tended the fire until it had passed the point of going out in the cold, soggy weather.

I needed more fuel. The charcoal was great, it would keep things going for a long while, but I needed a big, roaring fire—something that threw off significant heat. I also needed to tend to these men, who were still bobbing their heads sleepily in the cold.

"Peter." I rubbed his face. "Don't go back to sleep." If I sent him back, would Roger Williams even notice?

Peter grunted and reached for Williams. "Roger, wake up."

I rose and unrolled the canvas Scott had saddled me with. It had seemed a heavy enough burden at first, but now, the thing looked ridiculously small.

Still, it would create a screen. I eyed the ghostly branches around me, their outlines dancing in the faint light of the fire. One nearby low-hanging bough looked promising. I tethered the top corners of the canvas to it, but the bottom flapped uselessly.

Peter rose. "Do you have more twine?"

He still looked stiff and half-asleep, but he managed to cut pieces of twine and thrust them through the grommets. Soon we had a wind-break. Not quite a tent, but something to retain heat.

Roger Williams sat blinking at the tiny fire while Peter stood over it, warming his hands.

"I'll get some wood," Peter said. He staggered off.

I slid in close to Williams, any sort of propriety forgotten. I kept half an eye on Peter as I did not trust him with the task. He must be still half frozen, and if he wandered off, he might collapse somewhere.

Williams lifted his hands to the fire. "I thank you..." He squinted at me. "Mistress Tuttle?"

"Yes, Mr. Williams." The fire was too small to do much good. The twigs were now blazing, but they wouldn't last an hour. "How far are we from Sagamore George's village?"

It took a moment for him to answer. "Not far. Not far at all."

I turned to relocate Peter. He had a branch in the crook of his arm. So far, so good. With a fire, we had hope. At least that Indian had brought me here. It was too much to expect more help from them.

Roger Williams *had* made it to the village. The historical records were clear. Perhaps, if we survived the night, another day's journey would bring us there.

Peter returned with a branch. It was green and spotted with snow. I was dubious. He kept it in the crook of his arm and used his other hand to extract a flask—the rum.

He dribbled the liquid along the length of the wood and placed it gently next to the jumping flames. A line of blue ran up the length of the branch.

I willed it to catch. *Please, Lord.*

A single yellow tongue joined the blue. I breathed. We would be okay.

Peter moved off, presumably to find more wood.

"You have been ill?" I asked Williams.

He sighed. "I have regained some of my strength. Enough to minister to those in Salem who follow our Lord with a whole heart."

"Endecott?"

He cut a glance my way. "He understands more than most."

"What about Mary?"

His shoulders sagged. "She urged me to go. I did not want to leave her, but I could not expose my babes to this. Or her, for that matter. I will send for her in the spring."

"Will Endecott—"

"I trust the Lord will provide for her." A ripple passed along his jaw. "There are two or three who will extend their love. Perhaps even Endecott."

He was trusting in the Lord, but it wasn't easy. Every line of his body screamed it.

"I believe she will be safe and join you in the Lord's time."

"You sound certain, Mistress Tuttle."

"I believe it."

Peter returned and laid another rum-soaked branch atop the coals. He sagged and collapsed next to me. I opened my outermost cloak and draped it around him.

He began to shiver. I wasn't sure if that was good or bad. I still had half the charcoal in my knapsack. I'd just have to stay awake and keep the fire going.

And I'd have to keep the conversation going.

"Mr. Williams... why did you leave Salem exactly? The magistrates?"

"I believe men have been tasked with taking me by force to a ship departing for England."

"I heard of a trial."

Williams shifted, adjusting his cloak. "You have been away. Your husband explained your absence. John Winthrop fell out of favor, and he is no longer governor. Dudley was elected first then Haynes. Their reign has been harder for all. But I will not complain. It is a privilege to suffer for the Lord Jesus."

Williams couldn't know, but in a year or two, Winthrop would be chosen again to serve. "I see."

Next to me, Peter ceased shivering. His chin nodded and I poked him.

"Hmm?"

"Stay awake."

Peter rolled his shoulders. "I'm awake."

Before us, the fire grew incrementally brighter. Williams stretched out his hands before the flames.

A good sign but still. I needed to keep them talking. Keep them awake.

I thought of John Cotton. "Mr. Williams, what think ye of Mr. Cotton's views?"

He turned slightly toward me, a wry smile on his chapped face. "He embraces the false church. Refuses to separate. His 'middle way' is halting between Christ and Antichrist."

"The magistrates have a different role from the church." Even Winthrop believed that.

He nodded. "The true head of the church is Jesus, not the king.

Every man ought to be free to worship according to his conscience. John Cotton believes me to be sinning against my own conscience."

I glanced at Peter, checking to make sure he was awake. His eyes were open at least. "I don't understand."

What I did understand was that Roger Williams's search for ultimate purity would land him in a very lonely place.

"What think thee of Christ, Mistress Tuttle?"

I glanced at the minister. "I-I believe Him to be what He says He was. The Son of God."

"All believe that. Even the devils."

"Oh." My throat froze. I had no profession of faith and wasn't going to pretend.

"What doth separate a true believer from a false professor—or a devil?"

I knew the answer. "Regeneration." The new birth.

"Art thou regenerate? One of the Lord's own?"

Under my cloak, I opened my clenched fists, stretched my fingers, and curled them again.

"No," I said.

The frozen tableau seemed to still, the only motion the tiny swirling flakes about us.

"How is a man—or woman—born again?"

I knew this too. "By believing on the Lord Jesus Christ." I swallowed. "But this belief is not the same as intellectual assent."

I had just described myself. Intellectual assent. I knew the facts. I acknowledged the facts. But I knew there was more—the camouflaged Bible in my bedroom tantalized me. Frightened me. Challenged me.

"So, what lackest thou?" Williams asked. His formal language mirrored that of my Bible. He spoke it so naturally, his baritone deepening in compassion.

"There is... a cost."

My words hung in the air. Of course, there was a cost. Roger

Williams was paying that price, though I still believed some of his suffering was due to his hardheadedness.

I knew the price I might pay.

"And yet you are here, sharing in my trials."

I had nothing to say.

For whosoever shall be ashamed of me and my words, of him shall the Son of man be ashamed...

Was that a verse of scripture?

Was I ashamed? I wasn't sure.

I stared at the fire. The branches were crackling merrily, throwing off smoke and even a little heat. The pieces of charcoal glowed a steady orange. We were okay for an hour or two.

Next to me, Peter snored.

A shadow fell over our little camp.

I looked up. The coal-eyed Indian was back—with two of his friends.

Beside me, the men roused from their sluggishness. Peter attempted to get his feet under him but failed. On the second attempt, he succeeded.

Roger Williams smiled at the Indians and spoke in their tongue. It flowed from his mouth, and I could not understand a word. One of the new Indians replied briefly, then looked at me and Peter.

"You come. Come now."

I scrambled to my feet. Williams rose stiffly, and I remembered his illness. He shouldn't be out here at all.

Peter and I needed to go back. Once Williams was safe in the village, he would be fine. But if we went—

"Come." The Indian repeated his command. It didn't sound like a command, exactly, more like a natural comment. Like, if you want to survive, you will accept our hospitality. We are doing you a favor.

Or maybe that was my imagination.

"My" Indian helped us break camp by extinguishing the fire we had worked so hard to start. Peter cut the canvas loose, and we rolled it up. He tucked it under his arm and took my elbow with his other hand.

Two of the Indians assisted Williams, practically carrying him along. My Indian grabbed me by the hand and stumbled after the others.

It was a cold journey through the moonless dark. I heard, rather than saw, the Indians ahead. The swish of fabric. Tiny crunches as snow compressed. The whisper of bending branches.

Then the darkness was broken by a faint glow.

It was the moon—filtered by the clouds, shaded by the trees, it still managed to illumine patches of snow along the way with an ethereal gauze of light.

I tripped over something. Peter helped me up.

"Peter," I hissed. "This is a bad idea."

"I suspect we have no choice. Even if we did, it would seem strange to refuse shelter."

"I have the journal, we can send that back, at least."

"I take it Scott sent you."

"He wanted to come himself."

Peter fell silent. I focused on my feet, forcing them to move. At least the snow was not deep, a powder blanketing the landscape no more than six inches.

Voices roused me. We slowed. I became aware of a space ahead of us with dark blotches against the faint glow of the snow. Our Indian escorted us inside one of the dwellings, smoky and warm.

In the middle of the space, an old fire glowed orange, smoke spiraling up towards a gap in the roof. A wigwam, as the English called them, probably butchering the original word.

No one was here. Peter and I were left alone. I squatted in front of the fire and removed both cloaks, desperate to get warm.

Peter joined me. "Quick—let's send the journal back."

It took me over a minute to find the journal and extract it from the linen haversack under my cloak. My hands were stiff and I couldn't feel them despite the gloves. I handed the journal to Peter, tugged off my gloves, and blew on my fingers. I hoped I didn't have frostbite.

How cold was it? Peter's mention of the Little Ice Age made me wonder.

Peter pressed a hidden button on the journal, set it down, and it vanished.

"Oh, that is so freaky." Traveling was weird enough. Seeing something disappear was mind-bending.

"Let's get some rest," Peter said. "The location of the journal, plus the fact that we sent it back, tells Scott we're alive and well."

I glanced around. There were several piles of straw and scattered skins that must serve the inhabitants as bedding. I spotted an open place.

A gush of frigid air announced the arrival of several Indians. The orange glow of the fire identified our Indian, but the others were new. Two women and another man.

They ignored us and headed for the piles of straw.

Peter removed his cloak, and I rolled out our canvas to sleep on. The dwelling was spacious enough. We weren't crowded, but we didn't have any privacy either. We lay down and pulled the cloaks over us. It was a familiar situation, sleeping together in the freezing dark.

Slowly, our body heat filled the space under the cloaks, and I began to relax.

We'd deal with getting back tomorrow.

We were awakened very early—too early. I was snug and warm next to Peter, and I did not want to move.

My eyelids were crusted shut from the assault of the weather. I opened one eye then the other. Two women sat close to the fire. The others were gone.

Peter sat up, bursting the bubble of warmth.

"Something's going on," he whispered.

Male voices penetrated the wall of the wigwam.

He tugged at his clothing, and I relinquished his cloak so he could put it on. I assembled my clothing, layering on the haversack and the cloaks, only now realizing that I was not wearing stays. I was still wearing modern undergarments.

I fought the impulse to giggle.

Peter peered out the flap which served as a door. He motioned me to follow, and we went outside.

Pearly dawn light reflected off the twinkling snow, a fairyland dazzle. In a space between several wigwams, about a dozen dark-headed men were gathered. One man's hair was touched with silver, and his face was a mess, torn up by disease or injury. His nose was barely discernable, but his dark, intelligent eyes were focused on a tall Indian standing in the middle of the group.

He was looking at Scott Rice.

Chapter 27

The Chief

"... their dialects do exceedingly differ. Yet not so within that compass a man may, by this help, converse with thousands of Natives all over the country."

— Roger Williams, *A Key into the Language of America* 1643

SCOTT WAS SURROUNDED by a half-circle of hostile figures. One man, naked from the waist up, drew back on his bow, the arrow aimed at Scott's chest.

A feather tied to the arrow's shaft fluttered, seemingly the only movement in the village.

Somewhere, a dog barked.

Peter dashed to the older, disfigured Indian, presumably the chief. Sagamore George.

The arrow tracked Peter instead.

He fell to his knees in the snow in front of the hoary-headed man. "*Netop*. Friend. I am a friend of Sagamore George. I am a friend of Roger Williams. I am a friend of"—he pointed—"Scott."

Sagamore George did not seem impressed. He spoke a few words to his men, then his gaze returned to Peter.

Williams was standing next to my Indian. He caught my glance. "He says this man is one of the bear people."

I was missing something. When had Scott arrived? What had he told them? More to the point, why was he here?

How did they know he was Mohawk? It wasn't emblazoned on his forehead, so perhaps he had told them. His clothing was similar, at least in some ways. Leggings. Furs bound around his ankles. A shirt and a leather jacket—what was that? A tag? I remembered tangling with a jacket just like that in Costumes. Size XL.

It was the very same jacket and the very same tag. Scott must have dashed through the room grabbing items then dressed in his office. He looked like an Indian in a generic kind of way, but I didn't know if a Mohawk would dress differently from a Wampanoag. Either way, they knew.

Scott moved a half-step toward Peter and the chief, a lantern dangling from one hand. It was simple and cage-like, the candle inside flickering. I suspected he had arrived while it was still dark, but that could be any time during the night, and Scott ought not be here at all.

My Indian took a full step toward Scott. How friendly was this man who had helped me? Perhaps he was a sentry or guard. Controlling access to the village.

Perhaps what I interpreted to be friendliness was simple self-interest. European settlers were intruders and potentially dangerous.

Peter spoke again. "I pledge myself as surety for the man from the bear people."

Williams translated, and I marveled at his fluency. Only once did he stop and search for a word.

Surety... Wait a minute. What was Peter proposing?

A chill crept up my spine that had nothing to do with the temperature.

No, Peter. Don't.

The chief called out an order that Williams did not translate. The man with the bow kept his arrow trained on the scene while others advanced on first Scott, then Peter. They bound them with leather thongs, tying their hands behind their backs. Then they led them to separate wigwams. The chief and the other men went back inside, all except for my Indian.

"Roger!" I tried to keep my voice low. I felt no shame for using his Christian name. "What is going on?" I took several careful steps closer.

"They will be unharmed until the elders decide what to do with them—and with you."

"I thought Sagamore George was a friend of Salem and the Bay Colony."

He looked at me. "You've been away. First the pox. Then the unusual storm last summer, which ruined the crops. Some blame the sickness and death on the white man. There are disagreements with other tribes over trade. They may see this new fellow as a spy."

"Scott has—a medical condition. A sickness."

Williams's brows contracted. "A contagion?"

"No, nothing like that."

"We ought not alarm the chief. Mayhap a wise woman of the village can aid him."

Williams crumpled, and I rushed to support him. Our guard—for that is now how I thought of him—helped us into the dwelling where Peter and I had stayed the night.

I helped him sit, and the Indian spoke to the older woman. The fire was now burning brightly, and both women began food preparations, a universal in any society.

"Fret not," Williams said. "I shall be well. I have not fully regained my strength after my illness."

"Will they harm them?"

He scooted closer to the fire. "I know not. Sagamore George is a canny man. He says one thing to his men, but he is keenly aware of the dangers of hasty action. He does not want the wrath of the Colony upon him, especially now, after the sickness. On top of which, the white men are allies in case the Narragansett or Five Nations attack. I doubt he'd disrupt that agreement."

The chief had lost probably half his warriors to smallpox. "So, it was a show?"

"Only in part. We shall see. But I doubt they will be killed—that would have happened already."

I flexed my frozen fingers and warmed them before the fire.

O Lord, have mercy on Peter and Scott.

Have mercy on me.

On me? Yes, on me. I was needy too. I knew it deep down, an ache I could not describe. The way my prayers bounced off the ceiling. A cosmic loneliness.

And guilt. There was a gray veil of guilt overlaying the ache.

I recalled our conversation the night before. Roger Williams had no conception of what awaited me if I confessed Christ before men.

Or maybe he did.

We had just finished eating when we were summoned before Sagamore George. The elders were going to pass judgment on Peter and Scott, and I needed to be there, presumably because I was connected to Peter.

His wife. Marching over the snow, my guard holding me by the wrist, I wondered what it was like to be a real wife.

We entered a large wigwam, and I was hit by a wall of smoke. A healthy fire glowed in the center of the structure, and the hole above it was insufficient to keep the air clear. On top of which, a man sitting next to the chief was filling a pipe. I wondered about the health of their lungs.

But at least it was warm.

Peter and Scott sat on opposite sides of the fire, each flanked by a warrior who seemed to be in charge of them. Their hands were still bound behind their backs.

I snorted. As if Peter could harm them.

My Indian pushed my shoulder, indicating where I should sit. I shook my head and pointed to Peter.

He humored me, and I found a space next to Peter on his right—and slightly behind. A subservient wife. My mother talked about Native Americans having given women political power. Equality of sorts. Not exactly. I suspected whatever else might be true, the men expected respect.

If I had learned anything in the Archives, it was that Travelers must blend in and embrace the culture they were entering. As I watched the smoking pipe pass from hand to hand, I fought to get my mind in sync with these Wampanoags. Still reeling from an epidemic. Challenged by tribal neighbors. And feeling the encroachment of the Massachusetts Bay Colony, living on their back step.

If I weren't so worried about Peter, I would have felt a certain sympathy. I sighed, hoping this would be over before my legs lost feeling. I wasn't used to kneeling.

Sagamore George spoke. He seemed to address the group first then Peter in particular. He jerked his chin at Roger Williams, who was sitting near Scott.

"The sachem speaks peace to the peaceful," Williams translated. "We know you not, but the friend of the Grand Sachem speaks well of you."

Grand Sachem—Massasoit? He was the leader of the whole tribe. His *friend* must be Williams, who had lived in Plymouth and learned the language there.

Sagamore George spoke some more. I picked out one or two words, but not enough to help.

The minister translated. "But you have been away. Meanwhile, the curse has come. A sickness caused by the white man."

I could almost see the cogs moving in this man's mind. Trying to figure out events. Not knowing about germs. Thinking in terms of his enemies, both human and spirit.

Peter had not shown up at a good time.

Two Indians with lined faces—the eldest of the group—spoke to the chief. They traded opinions back and forth, and I watched their faces carefully, but I could discern little.

Their conversation died away, and a new voice filled the space. Scott's voice.

"*Netop... meenan...*" Scott's chest heaved. He spoke several more words I did not understand. Then he bowed prostrate.

The warrior at his side pushed him, but Sagamore George lifted a hand.

"Speak the English."

I suspected many of them knew at least a few words of English. How the various Indian traders conversed with multiple tribes I did not know, but I suspected they had some sort of patois going. English served the purpose here.

Scott sat up. "Honorable chief, I am a stranger among you. I beg your indulgence."

Williams translated this, a little haltingly, into the Indian tongue.

The chief motioned Scott on.

"It is true I am Mohawk, a member of the bear people, but I live among the English. Peter Tuttle is my friend."

After the translation, a verbal exchange ensued between the oldest members of the tribe. The sachem watched and listened then finally spoke.

Williams translated. "The Five Nations are no enemy as long as they are peaceable. But you—are you a spy?"

"I am a spy of sorts," Scott said. "I observe the ways of men. But my allegiance is to my Creator, the Great Spirit."

Sagamore George gave a great belly laugh, and there were smirks and titters throughout the group. I didn't know why this was funny, but at least the tension was broken. The chief spoke again to Scott and listened as Williams translated.

"I want to know why you came here. To this village."

When Scott responded, he did not look at the chief, but at us. "I feared my friend was in danger from the snow. He did not return when he said he would." He fixed his gaze on me briefly. "I knew where they were headed and tracked them."

The very walls seemed to sigh. *He did not return.*

Did not return.

Scott would not have broken all protocol and come here without good reason. Even now he was at risk medically.

We must have passed the point when Peter should have returned. Which meant—

Sagamore George waved his hands. He was about to pass sentence.

"I had thought these men were spies, ne'er-do-wells. I had thought to punish them. I need slaves to do squaw-work. It is right because the white man's plague has robbed us of strength, of numbers."

He seemed to sigh before continuing. "I cannot do this. This man" —he pointed at Peter—"offered himself for a man not of his kindred. A man of the Five Nations. By this, I know him to be true. I will release them both."

He glanced my way. "And the squaw, of course."

Roger Williams gave us a whispered thank you as he saw us to the edge of the village.

Scott said nothing, his gaze glued to Williams's face. Peter shook his hand.

"*Bonne chance,*" I said.

Williams smiled. "There is no luck, only the will of God. His Providence."

By this time, the trail was visible under the sun's bright eye, a track of depressions in the snow leading back east to Salem. In any case, we weren't actually going to travel far. Peter took point, and Scott brought up the rear. We wanted to be a quarter mile away at least before using our implants.

My neck itched. I found a way to scratch it under the wool of my cloak, imagining lice. I hoped Quarantine would take care of any infestations.

Peter finally called a halt, and we entered a dense copse of trees. The shelter wasn't as perfect as it would be in summer, with the foliage screening us, but I could no longer see the track. Hopefully, no one could see us.

Our exhalations formed white puffs as we leaned in.

"One, two,"—Peter directed—"three."

Holding my breath, I pressed my implant.

Disinfectant sluiced over our faces as we found ourselves on the launchpad. I shivered and reached for Peter.

Across from us, Scott's long hair hung in dark rivers. Then the UVB lights kicked on, and his warm complexion turned sallow in the blue light.

We were back.

Beyond the CarbonShield barrier, Chamar stood at the console, a puzzled expression on his face. Had Scott told the tech about the difficulties?

Was he a partner in crime? Or were we all about to get into trouble?

I'd been so glad to be released that I hadn't thought past leaving the village and getting Scott home.

Warm air fanned our faces and clothing, like a hair dryer set on medium. A gentle warmth that dried the disinfectant and made our clothing stiff.

The RoboMedic seemed to be everywhere at once, poking and prodding and muttering.

"Scott," I said. "What did you tell the tech?"

"Chamar?" He winced as the RoboMedic injected him. "I explained about the return of the journal and what we surmised. Then as the time came and went for Peter's return, I confided that it was a dangerous trip. Possible blizzard conditions."

"You didn't know that," Peter said.

"I was improvising. It was January. *Possible* blizzard I said, and he helped me." Scott lifted a hand to Chamar, who nodded, but the man looked as if he had questions.

Then I glanced at the Trip clock. "Scott, what time did you leave?"

"After two. Peter was supposed to come back at two. When he didn't—"

"It's only two thirty," Peter said. "A very short Trip."

The expression on Peter's face was curious. But any questions were forestalled by the robot, which herded us into various rooms.

After a shower, we met in the Quarantine kitchen. Peter scrounged in the cupboards while Scott spoke to Chamar on the intercom.

"I estimate I was gone thirteen hours, local time," Scott said. "Not long."

"Still." Chamar's voice was tinny. "You were gone precisely three minutes, five seconds our time."

"Three minutes?" Peter's voice was muffled as he spoke around a bite of some sort of energy bar. He'd handed one to me, but I wasn't hungry. "That's unusual."

"I think so too," the tech said.

"I want to run the equations. This should be interesting."

The math works. I hoped it still did. But we were here safe and sound, and Peter didn't look alarmed, only puzzled—and interested.

Scott grabbed a bar and tore open the wrapper. "If I changed an outcome..."

Peter sobered. "I suspect I was going to be stuck there. Williams had influence with the Native Americans, but he was a guest. He had no true power."

"Scott's arrival triggered a change," I said. "We all saw it."

Sagamore George was going to keep us for slaves. It was only fair in his mind. We could have escaped eventually. We had implants, after all.

What ifs flew through my mind as I made us hot tea and finally opened my energy bar. A fake chocolate coating on fake food. A sad excuse for nourishment compared to the hearty Indian stew I'd eaten just hours ago. I wasn't sure of the meat, but it had corn and squash in it. Maybe beans. Real food. I took a bite of the bar and spit it out. We had really gone back, really changed an outcome. I couldn't wrap my mind around it.

Peter looked at me. Then he looked toward the door of the Launch Room.

Three men in suits were filing in.

We were in trouble.

Chapter 28

Medical

"Nevertheless, to keep a good conscience, and walk in such a way as God has prescribed in his word, is a thing which I must prefer before you all, and above life itself."

— William Bradford

THE GRAY-SUITED MEN made a beeline for Chamar, who was studying the console. Minutes later, the Quarantine speaker crackled to life.

"Peter, tell Geneva she's got an appointment in Medical in three days."

An appointment?

Peter cut me a puzzled glance.

"I feel fine." Three days was when my Quarantine lab results would come in and—hopefully—I'd be released.

"Medical covers a lot," he said.

I decided not to think about it. We had reports to write after all.

But there were only two workstations in Quarantine. Peter and

Scott spent the next several days talking and writing. I contributed, but I also had questions.

"Peter, you spent a good amount of time with Williams."

He retyped a sentence. "He is still fixated on church purity—and what constitutes a true church."

I loved the exiled minister, but I also identified with Bradford, who'd thought him unstable. "I think fixated is a good word."

"But we talked about something else. The Indians." He looked at me. "Williams said, 'Christening maketh not a Christian.' I think he was talking about baptism. Was he?"

"The French and the Spanish were Catholics, and they would have emphasized baptism. But so did the Puritans of New England."

"Yes, that explains it. He murmured something about popery. Now I see. He feared substituting European magic rituals for the Native Americans' versions. He's becoming a Baptist!"

"Baptism upon profession of faith. Credobaptism." I could recite basic Baptistic theology.

But if I confessed Christ, I would need to follow it up by baptism no matter what brand of Christian I was. How and where?

I hoped to catch Peter's gaze, but he was back at work, typing furiously.

It wasn't till the next day that we had free time. Time to ask another important question.

"Peter, what are they going to do to us? Neither Scott nor I had official permission."

I had visions of the dean storming into the Launch Room, followed by Dr. Howard, his face red. But no. Dr. Howard was still in 1862, and the dean wouldn't storm. He would summon.

Peter ran a hand through his dark curls, which were getting long. "Scott and I made the decision to be totally truthful in our reports. Even if we wanted to somehow hide the transgression, it would be impossible. Computer records. The AI is essentially in charge of the Trips."

"You were off course. Circling. The whole reason I went back."

"You guys thought I was. Actually, I had caught up to Williams, and we circled to check if he was being followed. Still, it was a potential problem, and you were brave to come in that weather."

His expression softened.

Those horrible few hours trying to rouse and warm Peter and Williams were fresh in my mind.

"I wonder what would have happened if I had not come."

His lips parted, and then he gave me a warm look. "Scott and I are working out a timeline with critical pinch points. I've run a few equations. Apparently, everything worked out as it should have."

Even the math sounded philosophical. "I didn't experience it that way."

Peter gave a wry smile. "What we experience is only half the picture."

He wasn't talking about math anymore.

Quarantine focused my mind. I had time to think. Think about Roger Williams's words. The cost of following Christ.

I *did* believe. Kind of.

I wished for my Bible, wished I could read it. Find an answer. Find a way out of my conundrum.

My conscience demanded I forsake all and follow Him. But I was frozen at the precipice.

And there were men in suits after me. Not men in lab coats. Men in suits.

Had Ratcliffe squealed on me? I'd been careful.

Each evening as the Quarantine lights faded, I prayed.

Help, Lord.

I couldn't discuss it with Peter or Scott. The Quarantine AI recorded all we said. Peter squeezed my hand once. He knew.

But I was on my own.

Sometimes verses or bits of sermons floated into my mind. "Christ the fountain of life…"

In that day there shall be a fountain opened to the house of David and to the inhabitants of Jerusalem for sin and for uncleanness.

For sin. For my sin?

There remaineth therefore a rest for the people of God…

That was in the Bible somewhere, I didn't know where.

Come unto Me, all ye that labor and are heavy laden…

This was describing me, for sure.

I fell asleep, and in the morning the suits came.

Woken by a commotion, I glanced at the clock.

08:12.

It was late, and my hair was a wreck. There were voices—Peter's and Scott's.

I jumped out of bed. In the bathroom I ran a comb through my hair, wishing I had more time. And wishing I had mascara to give me courage.

Or chocolate. Where was my chocolate? Had I left my last ounce in 1636?

I emerged to find the suits, three men with close-shaven haircuts, gathered outside the CarbonShield barrier of the Launch Room. Heart hammering, I ducked back inside my bedroom.

"Quarantine AI, give me an update on our lab results."

"Working. Peter Donatelli, no pathogens detected. Scott Rice, no pathogens detected. Geneva Fielding, no pathogens detected."

We could go. I could go.

Peter appeared in the doorway, two cups in his hands. "I made coffee."

I took the offering, brushing his fingers in the transfer. "They came for me."

"We'll go together."

We blew on our coffee and drank it as quickly as we could.

They were waiting. I set my cup down, took a deep breath, and left the apartment.

Outside the CarbonShield barrier, the gray-suited men surrounded me, cutting Peter away like dogs herding sheep. Peter gave me a last look at the Launch Room door. As if to say, *Chin up.*

I stopped, summoned my courage, and asked the nearest suit, "Am I under arrest?"

The man lifted a brow. "No, of course not. It's a medical appointment."

No one needed escorts to medical appointments.

The suits' shoes clicked an ominous cadence as we emerged from the elevator and marched down the second-floor hall.

The familiar fat red cross on the wall signaled our arrival. I looked for the doctor, but the normal staff seemed to be missing. I took a deep breath.

"Where's Doctor—" I couldn't remember his name. Or the friendly nurse's.

A man in a white coat approached and held out his hand for me to shake. "Dr. Pritchard."

A nurse busied herself at a counter. I'd never seen her before. Perhaps this was a form of arrest I'd never heard of. I'd rarely seen arrests on news vids. Boston was a peaceful town. So was Cambridge. Who ever heard of students causing trouble?

Then I thought of all the AIs, the surveillance in every building, and my lungs clawed for air.

I forced myself to breathe deeply, slowly. After a few moments, I was able to talk. "Why can't Peter come? Peter Donatelli?"

One of the suits said, "Don't worry about him."

"First, we need to take some blood." A nurse prepped some vials.

I forced myself to breathe. "I gave blood in Quarantine."

"Yes," Dr. Pritchard acknowledged. "But we are not looking for pathogens."

"What are you looking for?"

The needle slid in.

"Relax," the nurse said.

Easy for you to say.

"A lot of things," he said. "Nutrient levels, metabolites, antibodies."

The nurse took three vials and returned with a modern syringe. I surrendered to the process. At least it wasn't the huge old-fashioned needle this time.

Psst. Totally painless. Well, almost.

I began to feel relaxed. The breathing must have worked.

Wait. "What did you give me?"

"Just a few cc's of Ambiance." The doctor's tone of voice was soothing.

I slumped in the chair. *Just a few.* That's what they all said.

I woke slowly, sleepily, enjoying the haze. Then my eyes snapped open. I was in another room.

Ambiance? I must have nodded off right there in the chair. But how had I gotten here?

Dr. Pritchard was bent over a console. One of the suits scrutinized a Pad. Where was I?

Help, Lord.

But I hadn't settled the issue of whether God even heard my prayers to begin with.

He did *hear* them. He knew everything. He was in control of everything. But would He respond to me? Was I His child?

Suddenly that seemed the most important, most pressing thing in all the world to know.

The doctor turned. "There you are. Ambiance is relaxing."

It was more than that, but I said nothing. My thoughts must have shown on my face.

"Just five milligrams. In any case, the tests are all done. Just looking at the results."

"Tests for what, exactly?"

"The cause of your anxiety disorder."

"What?" Had Dr. Howard reported me?

For a moment, the doctor seemed flummoxed. "Data was sent to the Medical AI by your apartment AI."

Ratcliffe! "What data?"

"Various coping mechanisms AIs are programmed to screen for. Eating patterns—"

The croissants.

"—and other unusual behaviors. Changes in a person's normal routine."

The furniture. The houseplant. All criminal now.

"Ratcliffe is going to pay for this," I blurted. "So I eat too many croissants."

The corner of the doctor's mouth quirked. "Actually, chocolate is a source of magnesium. One of the things you are deficient in. Between the deficiencies and cyclical mast cell activation, it's a wonder you functioned at all."

Could it be? Something simple? "Can I be fixed?"

The doctor shrugged. "We'll give you something here for the deficiencies. But I'm afraid the rest requires your cooperation."

Anything. Well, almost anything.

"I'm going to have to ask you to eat only real food. Nothing fake or lab grown."

He had my attention now. I could do that. Gladly.

He signaled to the nurse. "And I've written a script for a calming agent."

"I won't take Ambiance."

"It's nothing like that."

The nurse returned with a cup. "Drink this," she said gently. "Nutrients."

I did and almost choked. It was chalky and unpleasant.

The doctor showed me the prescription on his Pad. *Placiderone.* Placid. I would be placid.

"Um, sure."

"As needed." He caught my gaze. "It's a small dose."

That's what they all said.

The man in the suit handed the doctor a Pad. "Please sign."

Dr. Pritchard scribbled and handed it back. "Are we done?"

"Yes," the suit said. "We'll take it from here."

This wasn't just about a magnesium deficiency.

A second suit joined the first. He was taller and thinner. Tall and Regular. The third guy had disappeared, which was fine with me. I wished they'd all vanish. Regular sat in a chair behind a battered table. A strong ceiling light reflected off white walls and created shadows under Regular's brows.

Tall leaned against the table, a CarbonFoam cup of coffee in his hand. His expression was relaxed.

"We don't need to take a long time." Tall motioned with the cup. "We just need some information."

This was going to be bad. I just knew it. I took a deep, calming breath.

Regular spoke. "How long have you known Peter Donatelli?"

Oh, no. "Forever. I mean, it seems like forever."

What do I do? Play dumb? No, I couldn't play totally ignorant. I'd need to spin everything they could possibly know into the best possible appearance.

"A good-looking guy like that?" Tall said. "Surely you know."

"About as long as I've worked here. He's head of the Launch Room. A physicist. You know, math and stuff." I wished for Roger Williams's steadiness. But then, he'd been grilled by friends—most of them, anyway.

"Tell us when you became intimate," Regular said.

My mouth fell open. "I would never engage in such activity—without a license!" Reproduction was regulated. The Puritans would say it was wrong outside of marriage, but I couldn't say that. I allowed myself to become huffy. Perhaps this was all there was to it. Perhaps they wouldn't ask any truly dangerous questions. I crossed my arms. "We would never!"

"C'mon," Tall said. "You've been seen."

"Okay. We've had meals—picnics, even. And we spent considerable time together on a recent... project."

"We know about Traveling," Regular intoned.

"We had to pretend to be man and wife, but that's all it was. Pretending."

"Tell us about the theology test." Tall took a sip from his cup.

"It's part of my job. Travelers have to be prepared for their destinations. That includes local beliefs. Myths, superstitions, theology."

"Donatelli passed the theology test easily," Regular said.

"It's true. I was surprised. But he's very bright. Physics, math. Loves history. Why else would he work here?" Sweat broke out on my forehead. I hoped they didn't notice.

"Tell us about Dr. Donatelli's friends," Tall said gently.

"He is friendly with everyone here," I said. It was true. "Candy is easygoing. Chamar he sees every day. Scott Rice joined us one afternoon for a trip to a museum."

"So, he's brilliant and friends with everyone." Regular's tone was dubious. "Has he ever mentioned a Professor Kiyoshi?"

The name was ominously familiar, but I shook my head. "If he did, I don't recall. Anything relating to physics or the Physics Department goes right over my head."

I was sweating everywhere now. Had they turned up the thermostat?

"Has he mentioned the Bible or reading the Bible?" Regular's gaze was intense.

"Possibly—no, probably," I said, thinking of Houghton Library. "We had to prepare for 1631. He had to read biographies. He may have read the scriptures, too. I've read the entire Bible myself. It was unavoidable."

"Any strange behavior?" Tall asked. "We only want to help him—like we helped you."

They wanted to keep Christianity regulated, just like the Puritans did in New England. But despite their medieval thinking, the ministers' motives were better. I had no illusions about a friendly suit.

"No. Peter's a friend. He's kind. He helped me when—when I had a panic attack on a Trip."

"You broke the rules," Regular said.

In my lap, my hands clenched. "Yes, I did. I hid my condition. I didn't want to take drugs."

"So, your first Trips were made under false pretenses." Regular frowned. "And you went on a Trip without prior authorization."

I sagged and made myself look sheepish, but inwardly I was glad. Let the blame fall on me. "I'm in trouble, I know it."

Tall nodded sadly. "We'll let you know if we need anything else."

They'd gotten a confession, of sorts. I hoped it would be good enough.

The next day was Peter's appointment with the dean. I busied myself in the Archives, trying to forget the interrogation, but I kept finding myself staring blankly at the screen. Just going through emails took the entire morning.

At noon, Peter peeked in, his face a welcome sight. He'd cut his hair, the curls tamed into waves. I liked it. "Lunch?"

I left my desk and signaled to Lucy, who lifted a cheerful hand.

The cafeteria was bright, and I was hungry.

Real food.

But the welcome mandate was overshadowed by the memory of the suits.

"I hope they have something besides salad," I said.

No luck. They didn't even have salad. I settled for yogurt, a boiled egg, and black coffee. Peter picked up a burger.

I forgot the bland food. "How did the meeting go?" I asked once we'd found a table.

"Very well, considering." He lifted the bun, peered at the half-wilted lettuce, then replaced it. "It was routine at first. Then the dean asked if I had been in danger."

I nodded, my mouth full of egg.

"He asked if I were really in danger. Of course, the subtext was, did you and Scott really need to override protocol and rescue me."

"So, what did you say?"

He sighed. "I told him hypothermia was a real danger. We were falling asleep. You built up a fire and roused us from what could have been a fatal situation. I also told him more study needed to be done. From my end. The math."

"Because Roger Williams was supposed to survive," I said. "It's a paradox. We intervened and made things go the way they should have."

"I didn't say much about that, only that the math worked for this insertion. The universe wasn't worried about it, Gen."

The universe. By that he meant God. "I don't think the universe worries."

He smiled and took another hungry bite. "Tell me. How did the Medical appointment go?"

"Good news." I told him about the deficiencies. There was nothing more I could say in public, not with an AI listening.

~

The Archives were humming. MIT's Applied History Department was finally up and running, but they often fell short on the pure history side of things. I fielded several requests a day.

One morning, I scrounged for historically accurate costume details for a Luddite.

That afternoon, I sent them documents on the royal court of Aquitaine.

Matters like these kept my mind occupied, and it helped. I heard not a peep from Dean Hutchinson. Perhaps I wasn't in trouble after all. Dr. Howard had returned from 1862, and I'm sure the dean was interested in his report.

And I hoped Scott wouldn't lose his job.

I went home to Ratcliffe. I dragged my cookbook out, the real one, coverless but still stocked with recipes I needed desperately since I could only eat real food.

I stared at my cookbook, tired. In the end, I found a can of tuna.

Then I had a thought. "Ratcliffe."

"Yes?"

"I have another job for you."

"Oh?" Was that hesitation?

"Create a menu. One month's worth of dinners made with only real ingredients. Nothing fake. No lab-grown meat. Create a grocery list for each week accordingly."

"What? I do not have a culinary subroutine."

"Well, look for one. Download it. Real food only."

"Working," Ratcliffe said unhappily.

If he came through with this, I'd forgive him for the betrayal.

Anxiety disorder. Well, that had worked out. But what about Peter? The suits had asked questions about him. Was that Ratcliffe's fault? It seemed unlikely.

I went into the bathroom and grabbed the orange bottle of Placiderone. Who thought of these names?

Take as needed for anxiety, the label said. Well, it would look suspicious if I didn't take any. I opened it and slid a pill into my palm. Then I picked up the cup of water on the counter. I faked taking the pill, drinking the water, the medicine still safe in my hand. Then I used the bathroom. When the toilet flushed, the pill went down with it.

I emerged from the bathroom, wondering how good Ratcliffe's cameras were.

"Incoming call," Ratcliffe said.

"Put it through."

Peter's voice. "We have a meeting tomorrow. Dr. Howard passed his Quarantine labs. We're all expected."

Was it just to hear Dr. Howard's report? Peter's tone worried me.

"I just didn't want it to be a surprise. Madeleine gave me a heads-up."

Madeleine had bet on me. She was on my side. "Thanks, Peter. I'll be ready."

I gobbled my tuna and went to my bedroom to read my fake cookbook.

I found a place in the book of Isaiah where some king was perplexed by an impossible situation. He'd received a threatening letter. Spread it out before the Lord.

"I'm perplexed too," I whispered. "By a lot."

I fell asleep with the book on my pillow.

Chapter 29

Dr. Howard

"We query whether the blood of so many hundred thousand Protestants, mingled with the blood of so many thousands of Papists... be not a warning to us."

— Roger Williams, *Queries*, 1644

Dr. Howard was late.

The conference room was filled with the usual suspects. Peter, me, Scott, Candy, the doctor—I still didn't know his name—the dean, and Madeleine, on bright coral stilettos that matched her belt and collar. No reams of paper burdened the table. This was a report only.

Chamar appeared in the doorway. He was Peter's right-hand man in the Launch Room, but he never came to meetings. He wasn't a Chair.

Peter signaled, indicating a place next to him. Perhaps Chamar was going to reveal every detail of Peter's Trip. Perhaps every irregularity.

I swallowed, but my mouth was suddenly dry.

After Chamar was seated, Dr. Howard entered the room. He was still dressed in 1862 garb, but the clothing was torn and dirty. Perhaps a little stiff from Launch Room disinfectant. I was surprised he'd managed to preserve the clothing from the Quarantine robotechs.

He glanced at me, but his expression was strange, unreadable. Then he sat in the chair he normally occupied, his limbs a little stiff.

The dean welcomed him with a lugubrious tone of voice. As if it bored him to welcome Travelers from the battlefield. That's where Dr. Howard had been, I was sure of it now.

Was he shell-shocked? Traumatized in some way? My troubles subsided.

The dean was speaking, asking Dr. Howard for his report.

He rose to his feet, cleared his throat, and addressed the dean. "Of course, you have my written report."

Uploaded from Quarantine, no doubt.

"Federal soldiers held Harper's Ferry, under Colonel Dixon Miles," Dr. Howard said. "What happened was unexpected, at least from the Union point of view, and an inquiry was opened afterward."

The dean waved his hand, a motion that meant skip the background. "You were forcibly inducted into the"—he glanced at his Pad —"artillery crew."

"Yes. Union Colonel Miles fortified Bolivar Heights to prevent the capture of the ferry by rebel troops." Dr. Howard sighed. "It was brutal work. No roads—not to speak of. To put a cannon on a hill requires dozens of men with ropes. And not all his men were trained. Some were as green—as green—as I was."

"Cut to the chase," the dean said. "The key event you were sent to document."

"Colonel Miles's failure against the rebels. Was it mere incompetence, drunkenness, or worse?" He paused. "As part of the artillery crew, I thought I was now worthless as an observer. I had no way to get close to Colonel Miles, to see what his mistakes truly were."

I was less interested in Colonel Miles than in Dr. Howard. What had happened to him?

"Because of my clothes and speech, which down-home farmers' sons interpreted as upper class, I was successful in volunteering to take messages. I ended up in the officers' tent."

He opened his coat. A round hole with scorched edges had ruined the costume.

Candy gasped.

"By the time I became privy to the officers' gossip, rebels had set up on the hills facing us. Sharpshooters took potshots at us throughout the day. Our cannon failed to dislodge them, and soon, Colonel Miles was discussing surrender."

"Was he drunk?" I asked.

"I don't believe so," Dr. Howard said. "Tempers were high. Several men had hip flasks—some amount of liquor consumption seemed to be customary. Miles's face was red, but his voice and speech sounded normal. One officer demanded they retreat. Find a way to slip away. 'McClellan is sending Franklin! We can't surrender—it would be cowardice.' The argument was interrupted by a cannon shell. Colonel Miles was grievously wounded."

Right in front of Dr. Howard's eyes. I pictured it. Blood and bone.

"Some of the officers scattered, hoping against hope to rally their men. But Colonel Miles gave his second-in-command orders to surrender, and the man left. There were only two remaining in the ragged tent—-myself and one other. 'He needs medical care,' I said, kneeling beside the colonel and attempting to staunch the flow of blood from his leg. 'He's a traitor,' the other spat. He left, and I shouted for help, which eventually came. Miles died the next day, but I was not there—I was captured."

"Oh, no," Candy said.

"The surrender is part of the historical record," the dean said, looking at Dr. Howard. "Conclusions? Analysis?"

"I believe the case against Miles was poor. He may have been poor at strategy, not understanding his vulnerability. I do not believe he was drunk." Dr. Howard's words were forced. "I could not believe the callousness of his fellow officers." He lifted his sleeves to reveal his cuffs. They were dark with dried blood.

No one spoke.

I wanted to know about the surrender. Being a prisoner. "Were you mistreated by the Confederates?" I asked.

His shoulders slumped. "Not as would matter. I was able to escape the first night by using my implant."

Traveling was not just dangerous. It could be traumatic.

Peter gave his report next. He concluded by saying, "Roger Williams felt the Colony's decision to exile him to be unjust. I believe it hurt him personally. But he spoke of opportunities. He spoke several times of the needs of the Native Americans. And he was well on his way to fluency in the Massachusett branch of the Algonquin language group. Later he would write and publish an influential primer. The Trip was revelatory. I saw him function as a decent translator, a definite surprise. And I believe Scott was able to add to his personal study of Native American culture and mores."

I took a measured breath. Peter had managed to give the gist without speaking of Williams's true motivations—wanting to preach the gospel to the Indians.

"The rest of his actions, his writing, and his mediation between the Native Americans and the colonists are all part of the historical record."

With that, Peter took his seat.

The dean appeared satisfied. He looked at Scott. Then at me. "Madeleine. Please distribute the proposal to the Chairs."

She pulled papers out of a satchel and passed them out—single sheets only.

My heart thudded in my ears. Was this where Scott got canned?

I grabbed my sheet. *SAFETY PROTOCOL REVIEW* blared the title in all caps.

Safety? The Trip?

"As you all know by now," the dean was saying, "Dr. Donatelli went alone. However, he had to be rescued." His gaze fell on me. "We need to assess whether the Trip algorithms consider human safety." He glanced at Dr. Howard. "Obviously, this has implications for everyone."

Peter's face showed interest. Algorithms meant math.

The math works.

Well, the math certainly got us there and back.

"Dr. Donatelli, I have contacted Dr. Bishop of MIT, who is interested in the safety aspect."

"We've met," Peter said. "It would be an honor to work with him."

The dean grunted and swung his gaze to Chamar. "Mr. Jindal, I'm appointing you acting head in Dr. Donatelli's place. For say, three months?"

Chamar nodded. So that was why he was here.

"Thank you, Dean Hutchinson," Peter said. "Three months is plenty of time, and Mr. Jindal can contact me for serious problems."

The dean motioned with the paper in his hand. "Any questions?"

Candy raised her hand. "What about our funding?"

The dean actually looked cheerful. "We've been approved for two more years. With a slight increase."

I sagged in my seat. The cloud had lifted.

The department was safe. Scott was safe. And so was I.

A week later, I nearly collided with Dr. Howard in the hall. He was wearing regular clothes, which seemed too loose on him.

"Excuse me," I said.

He frowned. "No harm done."

"Dr. Howard, I have a... question."

His face was stony.

"I think I have a thesis topic." My voice squeaked at the end.

He raised a brow. "New England?"

"Yes. But not about Winthrop." Writing about John Winthrop seemed more difficult now that I'd actually met him. "Housekeeping."

Both brows shot up. I took his expression for encouragement. Dr. Howard's opinion was crucial. Even if he hated me, I couldn't get anywhere without some kind of recommendation. He knew everyone in the History Department. I'd despaired before of getting his assistance, but perhaps the real food was helping, for here I was, like Oliver in *Oliver Twist*. Asking.

"You see, I was Governor Winthrop's housekeeper."

"You saw a lot."

"I've decided to write about the prosaic side of things."

Dr. Howard roused. "But a thesis must be cutting edge. Push the envelope of knowledge. Defend a position."

"The colonists of the Massachusetts Bay Colony struggled for existence. They were sometimes slovenly by necessity—and don't forget, they were coming out of the Middle Ages and all that implies."

I had his attention now.

"Today's image of a colonial New England housewife comes from a more stable time—the eastern seaboard was fenced and cultivated, the wolves killed."

"So, you want to connect the dots?"

I smiled. "Yes. The core of Yankee hardiness and cleanliness was there. Thrift and hard work."

Dr. Howard's face grew thoughtful. "I know someone in the department."

I held my breath.

"I'll ask. But I can't guarantee she'll sponsor you." His face grew stony again.

I finally found my voice. "Thank you."

He left, and I stood in the hall for a long moment before returning to the Archives.

I wanted to tell Lucy.

And Peter. But he'd been spending a lot of time with Dr. Bishop in his office near the Charles River.

It wasn't far away, but it felt like a million miles.

Chapter 30

Answers

"O my God, my king, what am I but dust!—a worm, a rebel, & thine enemy was I, wallowing in the blood & filth of my sins, when thou didst cast thy light of thy countenance upon me, when thou spreadest over me the lap of thy love, & say that I should live."

— John Winthrop, *Experiencia*

"Ratcliffe," I said. "What did your logic subroutine tell you about the security keywords we discussed?"

Friday was a cold day, and I was frozen from the walk home from work. Soup sounded perfect, and I set about warming it up.

"Working," he piped. "Request denied."

"What? Denied by whom?"

I stirred the soup in the vintage steel pot. Not as satisfying as seventeenth-century cookware. Was cast iron even available in my day?

Ratcliffe seemed to sigh. "The security update allows for no exceptions. It does not matter what your place of employment is."

"So, if I say certain words I will be flagged."

"Would you have it any other way? Imagine a dangerous person
—"

"I get your point." Ratcliffe had very little imagination.

The soup bubbled, and I slid it into a bowl.

"Is convection heating preferable somehow?" Limited as he was,
an artificial intelligence was programmed to learn.

"Yes, Ratcliffe, there are culinary nuances to the process. Plus
emotional gratification. Tell you what. I've a new project for you. I
need another cookbook."

"You have two—one has no cover."

"It's vintage. Preservation is always a problem. But I like old cookbooks. Check your database under hobbies and interests."

I blew on a spoonful of soup to cool it.

"Ah, here. Collections. Query: are you interested in cooking or in
acquiring old books?"

"Both." I swallowed a spoonful of soup. The soup was palatable
but not exceptional. I did need to create my own from actual real
ingredients. Meat, broth, vegetables. "I love making old recipes. You
can be a great help by searching for vintage cookbooks."

Not to mention, it was a distraction for him. A distraction from the
real reason I had two cookbooks.

"Where do I look?" Ratcliffe sounded distressed.

"Old bookstores specializing in rare books. Price will be a
problem."

"I'm a good shopper. I'll search all bookstores in a one-hundred-
mile radius. What are your price limitations?"

I finished the soup and told him.

The next day was warmer but cloudy with sprinkles. I wrapped a robe
around myself, ran my fingers through my hair, and peered out the
window. No snow, just wetness that probably concealed ice.

It was Saturday and a good day to stay home. I wavered between coffee and tea. Then I remembered chocolate. I sipped on the steamy, rich liquid and relaxed.

But questions pummeled my mind. I still did not know why the suits had asked about Peter. Questioned me closely, in fact.

Asked about a professor.

What was the name? *Professor Kiyoshi.*

I sat up abruptly and sloshed hot chocolate onto my lap. *Ouch.* I remembered where I'd heard the name. *We haven't heard from Professor Kiyoshi ever since.*

Clearly, the man was a believer. Clearly, he'd been taken into custody. Were the suits simply tracking down every person who might have a connection to him? Students, colleagues, friends?

I found a napkin and dabbed at the brown spot on my robe. Perhaps that explained things. Perhaps Peter wasn't really in trouble.

I broke out in a cold sweat. I could have betrayed Peter so easily.

Kiyoshi? Yes, that name sounds familiar...

I took a deep breath and let it out slowly.

Ratcliffe invaded the silence. "Incoming call. Your father."

"Take the call." A click. "Hi, Dad. What's up?"

"Good morning, Geneva. Is it still morning? Cloudy days are confusing."

"A good hot chocolate day."

"Indeed. How about lunch?"

"Sure. How about the café?"

"Sounds wonderful."

We concluded the call. Questions crowded my mind as I dressed, rinsed out the chocolate from my robe, and applied mascara. My father—a believer? I dared not ask him openly.

But our reconnection after years of separation raised another question. Why had my parents divorced? My mother had never spoken evil of my dad, just gave me her little jingle about him being good and part Oneida. As if those were connected.

I walked carefully to the café, wary of ice. I gained the doorway without incident and looked for my father.

I finally spotted his brown hair in the worst possible area of the establishment—he was sitting at a small table right alongside the kitchen partition. It was noisy there.

I hated noise, especially sharp restaurant clatter. My brain just couldn't deal with it. My favorite spot was a sunny table near the door. But there was no help for it, so I plopped down in the seat opposite.

I greeted my father, wincing at the cacophony—cooks barking to servers, plates clinking, the drone of conversation.

"I know," he said, glancing toward the kitchen. "It's better this way."

I wanted a hot drink but doubted if the beverage would take away the chill I now felt. "I have some... questions."

His eyebrows signaled me to continue.

"There's a colleague of mine. We have spent a lot of time together..."

"A male colleague?"

Heat spread up my neck and onto my face. A server came by to take our orders, and I focused on the menu.

"Gen, how's the quiche here?"

"Great. Everything is great. I'll have the chowder. And—" I listed several of my favorite breads and pastries, which I would take back to my apartment.

We ordered, and I relaxed. "Yes, Peter is a physicist."

"Peter. Should I be worried?"

"No, he's wonderful. I mean, he's a great guy. Hard to explain. Kind of old-fashioned."

Dad nodded. "You engaged?"

I huffed. "It's not like that. Not yet anyway." Was that what I wanted? If not, why had I even mentioned Peter?

Sometimes my brain and my mouth took off without me.

The server brought our food. How could she work under this barrage of noise? I kept reminding myself that the noise protected us from the restaurant's AI. It would be almost impossible to record our conversation.

As usual, the chowder was delicious. Made with real clams—I had asked. For several minutes we ate silently.

"Dad." I stared at my half-empty bowl. "Why did you and Mom get divorced?"

He looked up, startled. His gaze swung over the half-empty café before replying. "It wasn't simple. She saved my life. When you were in college. That was after—after I was released."

He wasn't making sense. I was about twelve when he left us, and I did not hear from him again until my sophomore year in college. Six years.

His gaze swept the room again, and he kept his voice pitched low. "Men in suits came for me one day. Took me to a psychiatric unit. I was there for several years, then transferred to a correctional facility. For reeducation."

My hands began to shake, thinking of the men in suits. I grabbed a croissant and bit it, wanting to present a picture of normality to the world. Surely people were staring at us, but no, laughter and coffee cups clinking filled the space around us.

I met his gaze but said nothing.

"You're not asking what was wrong with me."

I shook my head and chewed. The croissant dried my mouth.

He picked up his coffee and sipped. "Your mother received a visit. They persuaded her to file for divorce. She didn't understand any of it. Not the reason. What they told her was unintelligible to her. They convinced her she'd never see me again. When I finally returned, I told her it was okay. I still love her." He stopped, blinking. Then he sighed. "She cared for me, fed me, helped me regain my strength. Then I went to the Oneida Nation. I couldn't stick around. I couldn't put her in danger."

Dad paid the bill through the table's interface and stood. "I'll see you home. The sidewalks are slippery."

I nodded dumbly, grabbed my bread and pastries, and followed him. He held open the door.

"Walk very slowly," he said. "It's icy."

Once we were well clear of the building I asked, "Did they put you in a trolley?"

He stopped and looked at me. "Who told you—"

"Peter."

His shoulders drooped, and he waved his hand. "He shouldn't have." He took my elbow, and we resumed walking.

"He was just trying to show me the cost."

"The cost is great. But it's nothing compared to—" He gestured, his motions reminding me of John Eliot and his inability to express himself.

"I have a cookbook. The cover is torn off. I needed to use it to cover an antique volume."

"Keep reading it. Ask for wisdom."

"'If any man ask for wisdom—'"

He raised a finger to his lips. "I have a message."

For Peter, presumably.

"Tell him Mark Kiyoshi died well. He died in hope. With a smile, if you can believe it."

That night, I read from my "cookbook." I turned off the light and snuggled under the covers.

The cost is great. But it's nothing compared to—

To what? I'd seen joy on Williams's face despite his suffering. My dad seemed happy. His words were clear, untainted with the harsh overlay of bitterness or regret. But his watchful gaze reminded me of an old soldier I'd shared a table with one busy day. He asked for the seat against the wall, and his eyes swept the area every once in a while.

"I was an Army Ranger for twenty years," he volunteered. "I can't undo that. No more nightmares, but old habits die hard."

Thankfully, there were no more wars. No more soldiers. No more bullets flying, only in vids.

But is that really true?

My dad was like that soldier. Maybe my dad *was* a kind of soldier, in another kind of war.

Maybe we were all in a war. An invisible war.

We wrestle not against flesh and blood...

What did that mean, exactly? The Bible spoke of a spiritual war, that was true. But my dad's lined face and watchful gaze spoke of injury—real injury in the real world.

What divided spiritual from real—or, I corrected—physical?

I thought of Ratcliffe and his updated security keywords. Those were real things. Real dangers. A danger to believers.

Was I a believer?

I was already in danger. But I didn't have the joy I saw on Roger Williams's face.

Ratcliffe couldn't hear me pray if I made no sound. But God could.

"O Lord," I mouthed in the dark. "I want to be your child. I want to be cleansed and forgiven like the scriptures say. I want to call you Father."

I am thy shield and thy exceeding great reward.

I blinked into the dark. I didn't know where that verse was in the Bible, but I knew it was for me. God was my shield. God was my reward.

He'd take care of me.

Peace flooded me, and I slept.

Chapter 31

The River

"We are always encountering the enemies of our souls, which continually raises our hearts unto our Helper and Leader in the heavens."

— John Eliot

"G*en*." Peter's voice. Ratcliffe had fielded the call.

"Long time no see." I hadn't seen him in three weeks, and the sound of his voice was wonderful.

"Say, I found a café near here. With a bakery."

I was dubious and said so.

"There are plenty of students around my grandma would call hippies. They're into natural foods."

"Hippies?" The historical reference didn't pull up any images, but natural food was a plus.

"How about an early supper tomorrow?"

It was a single mile between the two campuses. Or was that campi? "Sounds great."

My pulse quickened as I ended the call. I had all sorts of news and didn't know where to start.

The next day, I dressed warmly. I always did, as I walked to work every day now, but it had snowed overnight, and the January sunshine was not going to make any headway against it.

I pulled on gloves and a scarf and set out. The snow sparkled much as it did that morning in 1636. But today it was a welcome sight. The wisps of cloud slid away to reveal fresh blue. The snow crunched joyfully underneath. And my breath puffed white in wintertime sympathy.

The mile to work passed quickly, and soon I was busy in the Archives.

"Dudley." I had finally named the Archives's AI. "Download a socialization subroutine."

"Working."

Ratcliffe had acquired the ability to talk to other AIs in the building the day he upgraded himself. He now played chess with Sally upstairs. It was useful. Data exchange was still limited, but ordinary requests could be facilitated. Sally was helping Ratcliffe with menu planning.

"Subroutine acquired."

"Install and reboot."

I could hook up Dudley to Sylvia upstairs and to Houghton Library's stuffed shirt of an AI next door. Not sure if it even had a name. Once Dudley was finished, I gave it instructions. The AI could be useful for a change. Make my work easier.

I poked my head into Lucy's office. She had her hands around a mug of hot chocolate.

"Good for you," I said, pointing to her cup. Then I explained about Dudley.

"How much data can we get?" she asked, a question in her voice.

AIs were restricted. Probably someone long ago had decided they would be dangerous if they linked up together into one giant hive mind. "Let's say you need a yes or no question answered. Or a list of biographies at Houghton. You can simply ask Dudley, he'll get it for us."

"Gen, you're a whiz." She peered at me. "You seem like a different person."

"Not really." Yes, really. I couldn't decide.

"Does some of it have to do with a certain young physicist?"

I blushed. The heat spread from my neck to my cheeks, and there was no way to stop it.

She winked. "I would say I won't tell, but I think everyone already knows."

Thanks to Dudley and Lucy's help, I was able to leave the Archives well in advance of my usual time. I enjoyed the walk to MIT, a simple journey down Massachusetts Avenue.

"Just past the giant pharmaceutical building." Peter had given me directions.

The walk was pleasant. On my left, the giant Tri-State Fusion Electric building loomed. Beyond it, on the right, was the big drug company lab, at least seven stories of gleaming white and silver.

Just past it, I found a humble café. *Flour Power* declared a wooden sign in curlicue script. Inside, two men in white lab coats sat at a table near the door while students peppered the rest of the space.

I spotted Peter. His hair had grown, and a stray curl dangled over his forehead. I grabbed the chair across from him.

Seeing me, he smiled. "They have a really good burger. I think it's real meat."

"Soup is more my speed today." Removing my scarf and gloves, I peeked at the menu plastered on the wall. Sandwiches, soups, breads, pastries. Beverages included lattes, chai, and cocoa. It all looked good.

Soon Peter wrapped his fingers around his burger, a thick monster layered with sturdy lettuce, red onion, and bacon. I savored a thick chicken soup with ragged chunks of carrot and potato.

"Peter, this is heavenly. Even better than Indian stew." I was going to place an order for takeout.

This time his smile was thoughtful.

"How is the work coming with Dr. Bishop?" I asked.

A line appeared between his brows. "We're dealing with probabilities, Gen."

Math wasn't my strong suit. But Peter knew that.

He swallowed a bite. "Some things are hard to program for. For insertions and retrievals, the energies are clear. Either favorable or unfavorable."

"That sounds a bit like a probability."

He brightened. "It is. It is exactly. When the probabilities push one hundred percent, we don't worry. But human safety?" He shook his head. "No one can guarantee his next breath, Gen."

"The dean won't like it."

"Precisely." He spoke around a bite of burger and grabbed a napkin to swipe at a dribble of juice running down his chin. "This burger is amazing."

"So, what will happen?"

He sighed. "We'll probably be able to publish a paper. Restricted access only, of course, but still. Publish or perish."

Peter was technically a faculty member and as such couldn't coast in regards to research. Some things never changed.

"That's good."

"It adds to the body of knowledge. But the upshot is that your job is still critical. Preparing folks for their destinations is the best guarantee of safety, and I will point that out in my conclusions."

He finished and I ordered soup and one loaf of artisanal bread to take back to the apartment. Thoughts buzzed in my head like bees as we waited.

"Gen, would you like to take a stroll on the river before I escort you home?"

I couldn't interpret his tone of voice. But I had a lot to tell him, things I couldn't say in a public place like this.

"Sure, Peter."

The narrow greenway along the Charles River was beautiful, even in winter. Naked beech branches threw long shadows over a jogging path paved with crushed shells. Juniper and red pine alternated between oak and beech, coloring in the gaps.

"I think I like environmental reclamation," said Peter. "Long-haired students armed with a grant converted this section of the river into a park."

Reclamation was stretching it. It wasn't like the 1630s at all. There were no deer and certainly no wolves. The trees were small, mere saplings. But they'd grow. "Domesticated. But nice."

"A bench," he said, pointing.

Flanked by small but hopeful evergreen rhododendrons, its gnarly steamed wood construction blended into the landscape. Cozy. But he motioned me onward.

We found a rock to sit on instead, a few yards from the reedy bank. More private. It was damp and cold, and we scooted close for warmth.

"Peter—"

"Gen—"

We spoke at once, but Peter waved a hand. "Go ahead."

I opened my mouth, but I didn't know how to express myself. The first words were often the most difficult in writing. It felt like that.

"Peter, what is the 'root of the matter'? Winthrop's words about Williams. He said he was sound in the root of the matter."

"He knew the Lord. He preached a sound—an orthodox—gospel."

I nodded, having guessed the meaning. "I've been thinking—and reading—and praying." I couldn't help myself then. I couldn't stop the smile that spread across my face.

Peter's expression was at first puzzled, then interested, then... glad?

"Roger Williams was peaceful. Maybe even joyful, in the face of hardship and possible death," I said. "It got me thinking. Asking the question, 'Can I trust God like that?'"

"And..."

"All at once it seemed obvious. The Creator of the universe? Of course He was trustworthy. *Is* trustworthy."

"'Jesus Christ the same yesterday, and today, and forever,'" Peter quoted.

"Where does it say that?"

"Hebrews. I've forgotten the chapter."

I waved a hand. "Anyway, I realized at once that it was okay. The same God who sent His Son to die for my sins could take care of me."

"But the trolleys." Peter took my gloved hand in his bare ones.

"Even so. I know He'll be with me even in... such a situation. I don't know how I know, I just do."

In the dusky half-light, the side of Peter's mouth tugged upward in a half smile. "I have prayed for so long."

"We'll tell Scott." My hands clutched his convulsively. "And there's something else."

His smile dropped. "A problem?"

"No. At least, my dad thought it was a good thing." I told Peter what my father had said about the professor.

Peter was silent for a full minute, then he wiped an eye. "I'm glad," he croaked.

I took off my gloves. Holding hands with Peter, we regarded the river. It was beautiful—so peaceful.

Peter broke the silence. "Dr. Howard contacted me this morning."

My sudden tension was automatic. I took a relaxing breath. I tried to tell myself that Dr. Howard wasn't really a bad guy. Just uptight. "What did he say?"

"A new grant proposal came in. The dean is super keen on it."

"I'm not a Traveler."

"Dr. Howard thinks you should get your full certification."

"What?"

"He claims his opposition was purely a medical concern."

"But—but—the Archives!"

"He's not suggesting you step down, but he recognizes your expertise in seventeenth-century New England."

I stared at him. "Who and when?"

"Anne Hutchinson."

"Oh, no. Peter, the dean is a direct—"

"Descendant, I know. He's not exactly objective. But he supports a Trip. And you're Dr. Howard's first pick for the job."

I suspected Dr. Howard wasn't being kind. He didn't want to touch an ancestor of the dean.

"But Peter. Will you come too?"

"It was Dr. Howard's own suggestion."

I threw my arms around him, something I had wanted to do for a very long time. For some reason, hugging Peter seemed okay now.

"I'll walk you home."

I held his hand the whole way.

Author's Note

Thank you for taking this journey back in time with me! To learn more about my books and my writing, check out my website: www. lynnetagawa.com. You'll be able to sign up for my newsletter there.

First, a confession. Mrs. Alcock (a real person) died in 1630, not 1631, as I first suspected, and therefore Geneva couldn't have saved her life. But by the time I discovered this fact, Mrs. Alcock was firmly ensconced in the story and I didn't have the heart to take her out. So that part is definitely "fiction," though I try to be as true to the time and the people as I can.

Most of the dialogue is also fiction, except for the incident in which Winthrop gives his wood freely to the thief. I lifted that almost verbatim from Cotton Mather's biography of the governor.

I possessed less material on Roger Williams, but one thing I kept coming across: he was well-liked despite all the disagreements. I tried to portray him with that in mind. He is known today as a hero of religious liberty and freedom of conscience, and he deserves it, though I suspect part of that fame has to do with his exile. Martyrs call forth our natural sympathy. But I wrote this story thinking, like Geneva, of John Winthrop.

What was he really like? Was he to blame for Williams's exile? I suspected he was equally as heroic as Williams. Historian Francis Bremer calls John Winthrop, "America's Forgotten Founder," in the subtitle of his biography.

The first thing I was struck with in studying the lives of these men was the historical context. Their views—even Winthrop's—were radical for their day. The Protestant Reformation reclaimed the glorious doctrine of justification by faith, but it did so in the context of the union of church and state. Separatists—especially Baptists—were viewed as outside the pale. Even in Britain, where the Pope no longer had authority, the king was head of the church, with a hierarchy of bishops beneath him.

Winthrop's writings and actions are really interesting. In a letter he left behind upon his departure from England, he maintains his allegiance to the king. His actions, however, speak volumes. The Charter was a business document, but its true purpose was to give dissenters a place to live during a time of increasing persecution. The only local "government" the colony had was the company's business meetings. John Winthrop had functioned as a local magistrate back in East Anglia, and the events of the 1630s can be seen through the lens of English law and custom.

By moving to Massachusetts—and bringing the Charter with him —Winthrop sought a legal haven for Puritans. Three thousand miles isolated them from harassment. The next decade saw a huge influx of migration, growth, and legal challenges. In a new place, without the supervision of the Church of England hierarchy, what would New England Christianity look like?

John Cotton and the other ministers cobbled together what we know today as Congregationalism. It was a true break from the Church of England, though there may have been no single point at which these Puritans said, "We refuse to submit to king and bishop." They weren't political rebels. Their "city on a hill" was not so much political as religious. Like Williams, these Puritans were invested in the idea of the purity of the church. They longed for Zion to flourish in the New World. If the magistrates helped things along it did not seem weird to their minds.

John Winthrop did, however, make one interesting decision early on. The "government," such as it was, consisted of a group of elected officials: a governor and assistants. Winthrop established that no magistrate could also hold a church office. He wanted there to be a line between civil and church authority.

As for Roger Williams, his road was difficult. He established a Baptist church, then promptly left it, thinking it was not a true church either. Managing the new colony of Providence was undoubtedly trying, and he corresponded with John Winthrop, who never agreed with his actions, but still seemed to want to help. In response to John Cotton's correspondence, Williams wrote a treatise, *The Bloudy Tenent of Persecution for Cause of Conscience,* published in 1644, arguing for liberty of worship. Williams feared the state would corrupt the church. Cotton responded with a treatise of his own, and Williams wrote yet another.

Williams created a primer on the Narragansett branch of the Algonquin language group, *A Key into the Language of America,* which was published in 1643. He also obtained a charter for Providence Plantation, later to be included in the royal charter for Rhode Island granted in 1663. We can certainly say that Roger Williams is also a "founding father," and his statue can be seen in Providence, Rhode Island.

The American Puritans by Dustin Benge and Nate Pickowicz is a great survey of nine influential individuals living in seventeenth-century New England. It served as a starting point for my research—and I went back to it more than once.

John Winthrop: America's Forgotten Founding Father is a lengthy biography by Francis Bremer. Well done and readable. *Winthrop's Journal* is also available in multiple volumes.

Roger Williams was a little harder to get to know, as the precise details of his life are sparse. There are several biographies available. I liked an older, readable book, Ola Winslow's *Master Roger Williams*. I also found Edwin Gaustad's biography helpful.

Founding Fathers by John Adair contains Winthrop's letters to his wife, one of the best ways to get to know a man!

Acknowledgments

First and foremost, I'd like to thank my husband. He was the one who got me started writing, and while he doesn't give me direct feedback, his patience and support are invaluable.

Next, I'd like to thank all my critique partners, beta readers, and anyone else who supported this project's development. A big shout out to the members of Word Weavers chapter 24—Alynda, Kirsten, Dena, Judy, and Teresa, you have all encouraged me and helped this manuscript to improve—and this writer to improve! Also, the ACFW Scribes 254 group has helped me tremendously. Thanks to Bob, Lynda, Diane, and Regina.

Finally, I'd like to thank Nate Pickowicz, co-author of *The American Puritans,* who took a kind interest in this series. He directed me to resources I wouldn't have known about otherwise, and his telephone conversation about John Cotton made me feel like I had a glimpse of the man. Like him, I hope to give my readers a glimpse of these very real men and women who sought to follow Christ. Their influence still echoes in our country today, but we have forgotten them.

Soli Deo Gloria.